ALSO BY HILARY DARTT

The Intervention Series

The Dating Intervention

The Marriage Intervention

The Motherhood Intervention

The Garden Club Series

Jasmine's Pact

Studying Sequoia

The Seedling Homestead Series

The Order of Composition

The Architecture of Vision

The Structure of Perfection

ISBN: 978-1-950335-07-7

JUST HOLLY

BOOK THREE IN THE GARDEN CLUB SERIES

HILARY DARTT

CHAPTER ONE

At first, Holly Carr thought the flickering red and blue strobe lights dancing around the inside of her convertible were meant for someone else.

So when she saw them bouncing off her dashboard, she put on her turn signal to indicate she was getting out of the way, so the police could pursue the driver they were really after. It didn't even occur to her to be nervous until she realized the lights remained behind her ... even when she came to a complete stop.

Then she thought about the two double margaritas she'd downed with dinner, one with a side car of some sweet orange-flavored liqueur of which she couldn't even recall the name. She also thought about the way her insides felt warm and liquidy as she traipsed out of the restaurant, and the way her heels didn't seem quite steady on the parking lot pavement. She'd blamed the gravel. Cara, her drinking buddy for the night, had asked her several times whether she was okay to drive. The first time was when she twisted her ankle walking back to the table from the bathroom. The second was just before they ordered their final round of drinks. And Holly had said, "I'm fine! That's why I'm ordering a beer, to chase those margaritas down!"

Had she really said that? Yes. Yes, she had.

The third and final time Cara had asked her whether she was okay to drive was just before Holly got into her car … after accidentally locking the driver's door rather than unlocking it, and then trying to open it three times before she realized she'd turned the key the wrong way.

And again, she'd answered, "I'm fine!"

And truly, she felt fine. She'd consumed the margaritas and beer over the course of several hours. Things *were* a bit fuzzy around the edges, but Holly attributed this to the camaraderie she was sharing with Cara.

The two of them had gone out on this crisp November evening to celebrate being single in a sea of happily-paired-up women in their thirties. Sequoia, the oldest Carr sister, had (surprisingly) settled down with another cop, Elijah Sawyer. And Jasmine, Holly's middle sister, had pledged her undying love for Hudson Parker, photojournalist, just recently. Cara, a newcomer to the newspaper where both Jasmine and Hudson worked, had witnessed the budding romance firsthand.

Then, on a whim, they'd planned a shopping date for the following morning. Cara had declared she needed a makeover, and Holly, who loved nothing more than revolutionizing people's wardrobes, offered to act as her personal stylist.

But now, Holly was going to end up in jail. She waited for the policeman to approach her car, a horrible, cold feeling of foreboding taking root in the pit of her stomach. She should have taken a cab, like Cara had, just to be safe.

Holly put her forehead on the steering wheel. Going to jail wasn't the worst-case scenario. The cop who pulled her over could be her sister, Sequoia, rather than some random patrolman. "Oh, God," she said. "Please don't let it be Sequoia."

After what seemed like an interminable wait, she heard a tap on her driver side window. Holly jerked upright and, half-blinded by the flashlight that was now shining in her eyes, rolled the window down.

Although she could make out nothing other than a trim waist, she knew right away that it was a man, and therefore, not her sister.

She exhaled, then, with a tiny shred of hope that he'd pulled her over for something like not using a turn signal, she turned on her best mega-watt grin.

"How can I help you, officer?"

The flashlight clicked off, and Holly blinked to let her eyes adjust. The police officer put his hands on the bottom of her open window and bent down so they were eye-to-eye.

The first thing she noticed—well, the first thing she noticed after noticing this guy didn't look like a police officer at all with the tattoos lining his forearms—was that he didn't look charmed. Not one tiny bit.

I guess the Carr Sister Charm isn't going to work in this scenario. She toned down the smile.

"You wouldn't happen to be related to Sequoia Carr, would you?"

Uh oh. Holly's toned-down smile turned into a grimace. She did the weird, noncommittal nod-head-shake thing Sequoia always made fun of her for. *No, never met her. She's only been bossing me around for the past thirty years.* She couldn't deny it, though. The three Carr sisters shared a strong resemblance from their oversized teeth to their pointy noses.

"You're not going to tell her you pulled me over, are you?"

"You been drinking tonight?"

"You taking me to jail?"

Even in its state of panic, Holly's brain took an automatic profile: the cop had skin the color of coffee with cream, and thick, dark eyelashes that made her envious. His lips were full, and if they'd been in any other shape—something besides the thin line of disapproval—she would have thought them quite kissable. Her eyes skimmed over his name tag—Bravo—and landed on the very well-defined bicep just beyond that name tag?

He cleared his throat. "Ah—"

"You do lots of curls?" she said.

Shut up, Holly. Shut up. She hadn't felt drunk, but this must be some kind of delayed response to that final beer. Mr. Bravo flashed a smile at her, and his teeth were straight and so white they practically glowed. He spoke into the radio at his shoulder.

"You speaking code?" she said.

Shut up!

"Have you been drinking tonight, Ms. Carr?"

She nodded, then, her head moving up and down so quickly her vision blurred. "Just a couple of margaritas, really. You know."

Mr. Bravo cocked his head to the side as he listened to a tinny voice coming through his earpiece.

"There's three of you?" he said to Holly.

"No, but there are three of you," she said, and she couldn't stop herself from giggling. "Just kidding. Totally kidding."

"Your sister—Jasmine?—is coming to get you. Carr, well, Sequoia, I guess is what you call her, is working. As you probably know. She called Jasmine."

"Oh, thank *goodness*," Holly said. She could hear her heart beating in her ears and she could feel relief flooding her veins.

"What?" Mr. Bravo said. "You thought you were going to the drunk tank?"

"No," Holly said. "I thought Sequoia was coming to get me."

When Jasmine pulled up behind Holly's car, her headlights hit the rearview mirror. Holly winced, then watched as the Jeep's passenger door opened. Hudson appeared. He opened her door and offered a hand.

"I hope you know we just saved your ass," he said. "Sequoia's off in twenty minutes and said she'd come get you if we couldn't."

"I'd rather go to jail," Holly said. She tested her legs and found that her heels still felt very unsteady. *Must be the pavement.*

"I'll drive your car home," Hudson said. "But first I'm going to walk you back to Jasmine's Jeep."

Holding her under one elbow, Hudson navigated her right into the passenger seat and even pulled out her seatbelt and handed the buckle to Jasmine, who buckled it.

"See you in a minute," she said to Hudson. He nodded and closed the door.

"I miss your Golf," Holly said to Jasmine, who pulled onto the road only after Hudson had. "I wish you hadn't crashed it."

"Holly," Jasmine said.

Holly flinched. She hadn't expected *Jasmine* to lecture her. Sequoia played her role as the oldest sister by lecturing, and Jasmine played the role of the middle sister by keeping the peace.

"Well, I just wish you hadn't crashed it, that's all," she said.

"We both know I wasn't talking about the Golf."

"Oh. Yeah, I guess so. Thanks for coming to get me."

Jasmine sighed. The streetlights passing overhead made Holly dizzy. She closed her eyes, but then she saw a whole kaleidoscope of colors and had to open them again.

"Holly, what were you thinking?"

Holly shrugged. "I don't know. Cara and I had a few drinks and—"

"Oh, Cara, was it? You're blaming Cara for your debauchery?" Holly glanced at Jasmine and saw that her lips were twitching. In an undertone, she added, "Although, that girl has gotten me drunk on margaritas, too, I admit."

"It isn't—wasn't—debauchery! It was just a few drinks, okay? Honestly, we were there for hours. I didn't feel drunk."

"Imagine if this got leaked to the press, Holly," Jasmine said. "Seabreeze Police Department is still recovering from a public relations nightmare. Imagine the sister of a cop, thrown in jail for drunk driving."

"Do I have to remind you that you *are* the press, Jas?"

Hysteria hit, and Holly felt tears leaking out the corners of her eyes. They were tears of shame—who gets pulled over for drunk driving at the age of thirty?—and they were fat and juicy and rolled down her cheeks and plopped onto her jeans.

"The only reason I'm not lecturing you right now is because of the state you're in," Jasmine said. "But rest assured that you can look forward to a good talking-to."

"I mean," Holly said, her voice coming out as something between a squeal and a wail, "couldn't you just not report on that particular news item?"

She glanced over at Jasmine and saw that a slight smile had formed on her lips. In her role as the youngest sister, Holly had always been able to perform, to entertain her sisters.

"What would your headline be, anyway? Sister of Sequoia Carr riots at jail after being forced to wear state-owned underpants while sleeping off a bender?"

Jasmine's smile grew, just the tiniest bit, and she shook her head. "You interrupted a perfectly lovely movie night, you know."

"Did I? I'm sorry. You can get right back to it. When you and Hudson have been married for forty years, you can look back and remember this night as the night you had to save my life."

"Save your life? Save your ass, more like. I just saved you from a verbal lashing by Sequoia, is all I saved you from. We were in the middle of *City of Angels*."

They'd stopped at a red light, and Holly looked out over the ocean to her right. Nighttime lights from the harbor sparkled on the water's surface, which undulated peacefully.

"I'm sorry," she said. "Really, I am. I had just run into Cara at the store, and we were both lamenting the fact that we were buying Hungry Man frozen dinners to eat alone on a Saturday night, and wondering why they don't make Hungry Lady dinners, and we decided to go out to eat, instead. I drank too much, thought I was fine, and started driving home. And again, thank you. Seriously."

"Does it really bother you that you're single?" Jasmine asked. "I mean, tonight obviously went beyond dinner. You're sloshed. This borders on binge drinking as a pity party."

Holly shrugged. Her sister had a point.

"I admit, I was feeling kind of down," she said. "It's not so much being single. It's just that everyone else seems so settled, and I don't even know what I'm doing with myself, you know?"

Jasmine nodded and made a humming noise in the back of her throat. The discussion about what Holly was doing with herself was ongoing.

This would be a good time to tell Jasmine she'd been living a lie, Holly thought. For the past several months, she'd told her sisters that she was pursuing a personal training certification. And she had been. But a month ago, she'd dropped out of the program.

Personal training didn't feel like a calling or a passion, and she felt like she was old enough that whatever she did next *should* be. The problem: she wasn't sure what would feel like a calling or passion.

It certainly wasn't waitressing, which is what she'd been doing at the Broken Egg for years. She was good at it, for sure, but she didn't want to to it forever.

If she told Jasmine about dropping out of the personal training program now, she'd have to tell Sequoia later. She didn't look forward to telling either them, at all. It seemed even worse to have to tell it twice.

"What are you thinking?" Jasmine said. "You're doing that finger-tapping thing."

Holly pulled her finger in, making a fist.

"Did you see that cop who pulled me over?"

"I didn't get a good look at him, no," Jasmine said. "Why?"

"Just wondered," Holly said. Even to her own ears, her voice sounded unnaturally high.

Jasmine gave Holly an uncharacteristically caustic response: "I'm sure he thought you were hot, Holly, especially as he thought about taking you and your blue hair to jail."

Jasmine pulled the Jeep up to the curb in front of Holly's house, and Hudson pulled Holly's convertible into the driveway. Just as Holly swung her legs down onto the pavement, which, she noticed, was still wobbly, another set of headlights came around the corner. Sequoia. Holly and Jasmine realized who it was at the same instant, and emitted identical gasps of surprise and horror.

Holly heard Hudson bark out a laugh. She could have sworn he muttered, "This is getting good," but it may have been a figment of her drunken imagination.

"Well," Jasmine said. "I'm out of here. I can tell you right now this isn't going to be pretty."

Before she could get back into the Jeep, Sequoia's voice broke through the quiet evening air.

"Oh, no you don't," she said to Jasmine. "You're not leaving me alone with Holly."

Holly yelped. "You mean, she's not leaving *me* here alone with *you*."

The alcohol was wearing off, and Sequoia's appearance was siphoning the last of its warm, calming, soothing effects right out of Holly's bloodstream. In fact, this November nighttime air was chilly. Holly noticed that Sequoia was wearing a pair of running tights. She thought about how Sequoia's boyfriend, Elijah, had remarked more than once that a similar pair of pants played a role in his falling for Sequoia.

"Those pants look good on you," Holly said.

Jasmine snickered.

"Thanks," Sequoia said. "They do. What the—"

"Is Xena with you?" Holly said. Xena was Sequoia's K-9 partner at work. Although their relationship had gotten off to a rocky start, it had developed into a cute friendship.

"No," Sequoia said. "I didn't want her to witness this. What the hell were you thinking?"

Sequoia was now leaning against the spare tire on Jasmine's Jeep, her arms crossed. She pinned Holly with her stare, her bright green eyes intense and without even a hint of humor.

"It's cute that you're worried about Xena's sensibilities," Holly said, trying to keep the mood light. When Sequoia continued staring at Holly, Holly blanched.

"I don't know," she said. She leaned back against her passenger door so she didn't have to look Sequoia in the eyes any more. She mimicked her oldest sister's pose and glared out into the darkness. Jasmine, apparently convinced she wasn't leaving, sat down on the curb.

Hudson held up Holly's keys and shook them so they jingled. "Beer?"

"No, thanks," Holly said, at the same time as Sequoia said, "I think she's had enough."

"I meant for me," Hudson said.

"Oh," Holly said. "In the fridge. Help yourself."

A beat of silence passed. Jasmine picked at her shoelaces. Sequoia took a deep breath. "What's going on with you, Holly?"

"I don't know, honestly," Holly said.

She thought:

I'm single and lonely.

I'm keeping a huge secret from you.

I don't know what I want to be when I grow up.

I'm thirty years old and almost just got arrested for drunk driving.

I hate my life.

Where Sequoia would have waited her out, stood there in silence until Holly broke, Jasmine jumped in with questions. Two completely different interviewing techniques for two completely different professions.

"What do you mean, you don't know?" Jasmine said. "I mean, something must be going on. You look miserable."

Holly nodded. She felt her throat constricting, and bit her bottom lip to keep herself from crying. Her sisters had lived to tease her about being a crybaby.

"I'm not miserable in general," she managed in a strangled voice. "I'm just embarrassed, I guess. I should have shared a cab with Cara or something, but I didn't realize how drunk I was."

"You know, with all the hair dyeing you've been doing recently," Sequoia said, and Jasmine jumped in, "You think chemicals are seeping into her brain?"

"No," Sequoia said. Apparently she wasn't in the mood to joke around. "I think this might be a symptom of a bigger problem."

Jasmine looked away.

"Why do things always come down to my hair dyeing?" Holly said. "At first it was funny. But now you're saying it points to emotional problems. I just like changing my hair color. I mean, I could come up with a psychoanalysis based on your overuse of the French braid."

"I know I make fun of your hair all the time," Sequoia said. "I mean, most big sisters would, right? One day it's pink, one day it's leopard print, and one day it's banana sunset. But I sometimes think your failure to settle on a single color is indicative of a lack of direction in your whole life. I think you're having an identity crisis."

"Ohmygosh," Holly said. "I just like changing my hair color. The hair dye, the drunk driving, they're not symptoms of a bigger problem."

Now Jasmine stood up. "Holly, don't get irritated. She's just asking, okay? I'm not talking about the hair dye" (here she shot Sequoia a Look) "but I do think a drunk driving incident, at our age, is pretty serious stuff. Especially when you're on the cusp of a new career and everything."

Why did Jasmine have to bring up the new career issue? There *was* no new career. Holly was a tiny boat, a dinghy without a rudder, bobbing on the surface of the ocean, following the tide wherever it took her. A tiny, rudderless boat with a hole in it. Maybe this would be a good time to tell them. She could just blurt it out. She could say, "About that. I'm not actually getting a new career. Did you know I'm still waitressing at the Broken Egg. It *is* a career, actually. Want to hear the breakfast special?"

Or she could say, "Actually, I've decided to become a gypsy. I'll change my residence as often as I change my hair color."

But she didn't. Instead, she said, "I know. It was a one-time deal, okay? I promise. You guys don't have to worry about me. I've got it all together. Thank you both, so much, for showing up tonight. Now get home and get some rest. *City of Angels* is waiting, Jas. And Sequoia, I'm really sorry for getting pulled over."

ALONE IN HER quiet living room, a blanket draped over her lap and a cup of too-hot tea in her hands, Holly tried to find some mindless distraction to watch on TV. But every show she put on seemed to mirror her life. Not a regular mirror, but one of those bendy ones that shows a grotesque version of reality.

First, there was a soap opera where a woman woke up from a coma and didn't recognize her life, at all. She didn't recognize her friends or family members or the people at her job. Holly felt as if she'd just woken from a coma and was realizing she didn't recognize any of the choices she'd made.

Then, she found a based-on-real-life movie where the hero got his arm caught between two rocks, and he had to saw it off to get free. She wondered if that was the predicament she'd gotten herself into. One where changing the course of her career—after spending an arm and a leg on a certification she didn't plan to use—meant the metaphorical sawing-off of a limb.

She came across a show where contestants ran an obstacle course that tried to knock them off kilter. She turned off the TV when she saw a mechanical arm extend, the boxing glove on its end punching a woman off a narrow, raised walkway and into a pit of mud.

With nothing to distract her from thinking about tonight, Holly sighed. She took a sip of her tea and felt her face twist into an involuntary grimace. She didn't even like tea. She was drinking it now only because Jasmine had made it for her before leaving.

Holly stood up, marched to the kitchen, dumped the tea in the sink, and set the empty mug down on the counter. Then she went to bed.

CHAPTER TWO

THE NEXT MORNING—THE DAY AFTER WHAT HOLLY WAS NOW CALLING the Drunk Driving Incident—Cara picked Holly up for their shopping date.

"I think you need coffee, first," Cara said, and they didn't speak until they were seated at a little table at The Grind, the coffee shop overlooking the ocean.

"When you texted me last night," Cara said, "I thought you were joking."

Holly, having just filled Cara in on all the details, just shook her head.

"I wish. That was the most humiliating event of my life."

"Was Sequoia mad?" Cara wanted to know.

"She seemed worried, more than anything," Holly said. "Surprisingly. She thinks the hair dye and the drunk driving are indicative of a deeper problem."

"I have to ask," Cara said. "Are they?"

Holly shrugged. "I mean, I've never thought about it that way, but now that I am, maybe they *are*. I'd never admit it to Sequoia. She's always so sure of herself and I think it frustrates her that I'm not."

It felt good to say the words out loud.

"Have you tried to talk to her about it?"

Holly shook her head, which only made it pound more severely. Sequoia's home remedy of two glasses of water and three aspirin wasn't quite kicking the hangover. Holly watched through the window as a couple strolled by on the sidewalk, pushing a baby in a stroller.

Cara took a sip of her coffee and a bite of her muffin before speaking again: "I hate to say this, but—"

Holly groaned. This sounded like something Jasmine would say. Cara held up a hand. "Just hear me out, okay? I know we were talking dating strategy last night. And I know you want to fall in love, start a family, and go for walks on cool fall mornings. But I think maybe you should just take some time to, you know, find yourself. That's what I'm doing."

Even as Holly said, "What does that even mean?" she drew the parallel between Cara's words this morning and her own thoughts the previous night.

"Okay, don't kill me," Cara said. "But you know I'm a straight shooter. It just seems like you're so unsure of yourself all the time. You struggle to make decisions on your own about even the simplest things."

Holly felt herself sitting up straighter. Her mouth dropped open.

"Don't get indignant," Cara said, misreading Holly's reaction. Her blue eyes, framed by thick black eyeliner, twinkled with humor. "Just listen. Take, for example, this morning. Just like every time we have coffee or lunch or drinks, you made me choose the spot. And then you had me order first. And then you ordered the same thing as me. You haven't even touched your muffin. You don't even like blueberry muffins, I think you told me once. But when it was your turn to order, you said, 'I'll just have what she's having.' And it's not just this morning. You do it all the time. I mean, you drive a convertible."

Okay, so the muffin thing was true. But the convertible? "What does that have to do with anything?" Holly said.

"You can't decide whether you want a roof or not." Cara shrugged. "It's symbolic."

Arguing was Holly's natural inclination, but not after last night.

"You know," she said, "you might be on to something."

Cara tilted her head, waiting.

"I did a lot of thinking last night. Did you know I don't even like tea? That's what started it. Jasmine made me tea before she left, and I was just sitting there, drinking it."

"You have tons of tea in your cabinet," Cara said. "I never would have guessed you don't actually like it."

"Hate it," Holly said. "I'm no good on my own, Cara. I can't make plans or decisions or form an opinion."

"Ever?"

"Well, when I do, they flop. When Sequoia and Jasmine and I were little, we'd always make these little stands, and we'd sell cookies or lemonade or hot cocoa in our cul de sac. One weekend, the two of them both had birthday parties to go to, and I thought, 'I'll show them.' I set up the stand, and I went inside to make cookies. We always made the cookies together, you know? With one of us reading the recipe and one of us gathering ingredients and one of us measuring. Divide and conquer, you know?"

Cara nodded and sipped her coffee.

"Well, they weren't there that day, and I messed up those cookies. Badly. The ones I didn't burn to a crisp were flat and as hard as bricks. So I thought, 'I'll just make lemonade. Scoop and stir. What can go wrong?' But believe me, a lot can go wrong. At first, I under-scooped and ended up with lemonade that tasted like water. And then I overcompensated. As I was pouring the powder into the pitcher, my elbow slipped and all the powder went in. It tasted horrible. I went outside to clean up our little stand, and the whole thing had crumpled to the ground. I'd forgotten to latch the legs of the table, so when a gust of wind blew by, they folded in."

Once Holly started talking, she couldn't stop. She'd never verbalized any of this before, and Cara was such a good listener (probably thanks to the years she'd spent as a journalist).

"And then there was this talent show. The three of us had done a little performance every year in elementary school, when we were all there together. Sequoia aged out first, of course, and then Jasmine didn't want to do it without her. But I did. I wanted to do a little dance. Alone. Big mistake. It was *Singin' in the Rain*. And what did I do? I practiced and practiced at home, torturing the entire family to no end with my singing and dancing and humming. And then I got up on stage and ruined the entire thing. Can you believe I forgot my umbrella? And I know it's because they weren't there with me."

Holly told Cara about how going solo—and failing at it—became a pattern in her life.

At Sequoia's urging, she'd joined the track team her freshman year. She quit halfway through the season because she didn't have either of her sisters to cheer her on (Jasmine was playing chess or something and Sequoia was in college by then).

When it came time for Holly to choose a college major, she chose English. But midway through her second year, Jasmine made an offhand comment about how Holly should find a career that would make a positive difference in the world. Holly, with both sisters at different colleges and no one there to give her direction, suffered an identity crisis. She took a wide variety of classes but never earned her degree.

Meanwhile, she started working at the Broken Egg, and in her free time she became what Sequoia called a "gym bunny," making best friends with free weights and elliptical machines.

"You spend so much time there, you should just become a personal trainer," Sequoia had said at one point.

Holly, like a hunting dog who spots a fox, had looked up, ears pointed and eyes sharp, and grasped onto the idea as if it were her own.

Only, it wasn't.

"And now," she told Cara, who'd listened, rapt, to the long list of Holly's failures, "here I am. Rock bottom. I've quit the personal training program and all signs point to me being a lifelong waitress at a mid-scale diner. Which isn't bad, but it's not what I'd say if you asked me about big dreams I have for for my life."

"What would you say?" Cara said.

"I have no idea," Holly said. "That's the problem, isn't it?"

"Let's shop," Cara said. "A little retail therapy never hurt anybody."

It was true: as soon as they stepped into the air-conditioned sanctuary of the mall, Holly felt her entire body relax.

"I love it here," she said.

Cara snickered. "I'm glad you do. It gives me anxiety. Which I'm pretty sure is the reason I started wearing all black."

"I think it's time we did something about that," Holly said. "This way."

Since the moment they met, Holly had envisioned a different wardrobe for Cara, one that showed off her curves and brought out her eyes. Of course, she hadn't proposed a shopping spree until they'd become closer, but when Cara said, "Yes," Holly had leapt out of her chair and given Cara a big hug.

"Here?" Cara said. Her forehead wrinkled as she looked up at the entrance to Flair, a women's boutique where mannequins dressed in multi-colored outfits lined the walkways, and sweaters in reds, oranges and greens sat on tables. "Holly, I don't see a single black sweater on that table."

"You'll be fine," Holly said. "Trust me."

While Holly's stride became longe and more confident, Cara lagged behind. But only for a few seconds, because Holly started piling her arms with sweaters, pairs of jeans, and shirts.

"You're going to run my bank account dry, woman," Cara said, her voice muffled from behind an infinity scarf Holly had added to the pile.

"You're not going to buy all of it," Holly said. "Just try stuff on. Okay?"

"Okay," Cara said, drawing the word out. "If you say so."

The sales girl raised an eyebrow when Holly asked for a dressing room.

"I'll wait out here," Holly said. "But you have to promise to show me everything."

"Everything?"

"Everything."

"There's so much. I don't even know where to start. And I can't guarantee I'll wear any of it. You're going to make me look like a lollipop," Cara said.

"Better than looking like the angel of death," Holly said.

Cara set the clothes down on the dressing room bench, and Holly began separating them into outfits: jeans and a sweater, a sweater and a scarf, a blouse and a pair of corduroy pants.

"Hit it, sister," she said, gently pushing Cara into the dressing room. "You can do this."

When Cara emerged, wearing the first outfit, she had a shy smile on her face.

"I'm not sure about the color of this sweater," she said, "but I'm digging it."

Holly sat on her stool, stunned, her mouth hanging open.

"You look so…"

"Terrible?" Cara said.

"No!" Holly said. "You look great, Cara. Amazing. That sweater brings out the color of your eyes, and the fit is so good on you. Turn around."

Cara obeyed, but her posture suggested she was still nervous.

"Your ass looks so good in those jeans," Holly said. "You know, I don't think I've ever seen your ass."

"Funny," Cara said, her voice flat. But by the time she'd finished her revolution, her smile looked more confident.

"Okay," Holly said. "I've given that one a score. Try the next one."

Cara's self-assurance increased with each showing, and by the time she'd tried on the final pairing—a pencil skirt with a floral blouse—she was glowing.

"This is the prettiest I've felt in years," she said. Then she clapped a hand over her mouth. "And I never thought I'd say that."

"You look great," Holly said. "I mean, you always look pretty— you are pretty—but I feel like you hide behind all those dark colors. These brighter colors, they make you shine."

Cara grabbed Holly's hands and pulled her to standing, then gave her a big hug. "Thank you so much, Holly. This means so much to me. You have no idea."

Hours passed. They conquered several more stores, adding shoes, accessories, and makeup to Cara's bounty. When they were done,

Cara said, "You ran my bank account dry and I'm starving. Take me out to lunch."

They opted for the sushi place across the street, and when the hostess seated them, Cara slid into her side of the booth with a sigh.

"I don't think I've ever been more exhausted in my life," she said.

Holly leaned forward. "So, tell me. Which outfit are you going to wear to work on Monday?"

Cara smiled, but didn't answer.

"Don't tell me these clothes are going to sit in your closet," Holly said. "You wouldn't."

"No," Cara said. "But I'll admit, I'm scared. I've worn all black for the past five or six years. That olive-green skirt? Totally foreign. But I'll do it."

"If you wear it on Monday, with that blouse, I'll buy you a present."

"Wait. Are you bribing me? Like a little kid?"

"Totally," Holly said. "Wear it Monday."

"You know," Cara said, her tone of voice and her expression turning serious, "you're totally in your element right now. Remember earlier, when I was saying how you never form your own opinion?"

"I do remember," Holly said. "And you're right."

"But not when it comes to this. You were on fire today. I mean, I've never seen you like this. You turned into some kind of wardrobe drill sergeant. It was amazing."

"Ha," Holly said. "Too bad I can't spend all my time shopping. Unless you want to pay me some kind of stylist fee."

"I can't," Cara said, deadpan. "Like I said, you ran my account dry."

The bell above the restaurant's door tinkled, and both Holly and Cara turned to see who'd entered.

Of all the people in Seabreeze, it had to be Mr. Bravo. In this setting, he looked even less like a police officer and more like a surfer getting ready to head to the beach.

Holly wished she could slide down in the booth and hide under the table. She had the insane thought that maybe if she closed her eyes, he wouldn't see her.

Still, as she turned her head away from the door he'd come through, she noticed the way his light blue t-shirt showed off his muscular, tattooed arms. And those jeans! She'd never seen a guy look absolutely edible in jeans before.

She licked one corner of her mouth and looked down at her menu.

Holly had seen Sequoia scan a room upon entering, and she was positive Officer Bravo was doing the same thing. She could practically feel the moment his eyes skimmed over her, and almost involuntarily, she made eye contact with him—and saw the recognition dawn on his face.

His expression went completely blank, and he gave her a curt nod. After giving him what she hoped was a polite smile in return, she spent a full second wondering what his blank expression meant. Probably that he found her reprehensible after last night's Incident. When she realized her own face probably looked like a Botox nightmare, she turned her attention back to Cara, who was leaning forward, her eyes boring into Holly's.

"Hey, do you know that guy?"

"Huh?" Holly said. "What guy?"

Cara rolled her eyes. "That guy, with all the tattoos. The one that just turned your brain to mush."

Fortunately, or unfortunately, Mr. Bravo didn't seem prepared to stay long. He took his order in a to-go bag, and walked toward the door. Holly took another long look at his tapered waist and his toned back muscles and sighed before she could stop herself.

"Nope," she said. "Don't know him at all."

Cara leapt into questioning mode. Since Jasmine had become a real reporter (Sequoia's words, not hers) after meeting Hudson, Holly was used to it.

"What are you thinking right now? You don't know him, but you'd like to, wouldn't you? You've met him before, haven't you? Wait—wait. Don't tell me. You had a one-night stand with him and never called him again."

Holly shook her head.

"Okay," Cara said. "Let me think. He's the one who got away, like in high school or something."

"Nope," Holly said.

Then, Holly could practically see the realization dawning in Cara's eyes, a lightbulb on a dimmer switch, gradually brightening.

"He's the cop who pulled you over last night, isn't he? His face—your face—it's all making sense."

When all Holly could manage was a nod, Cara said, "You know, Holly? I'm surprised. He doesn't seem like your type."

Holly shrugged, and Cara said, "What *is* your type, anyway?"

"You know, Cara," Holly said. "I don't actually know."

ALTHOUGH SHOPPING and lunch with Cara had bolstered Holly's mood temporarily, she found herself sinking back into low spirits when Cara dropped her off at home. The whole afternoon and evening loomed ahead of her, as empty as a two-lane highway running through the desert. If she were still pursuing a new career, she'd have plenty to do. But she wasn't. So the truth was, she would probably end up sitting on the couch, binge watching reality TV shows.

No, she couldn't waste even another hour watching women make fools of themselves vying for a man's proposal. She would be productive. She would vacuum. And dust. This place could use a good deep cleaning. She got the vacuum out of the closet and plugged it in, letting her thoughts wander as she picked up discarded shoes and socks to clear the carpet.

Maybe she should get a dog. Jasmine had Ruby and Sequoia had Xena. Those relationships seemed to be working out well. Holly turned on the vacuum. The thought of Sequoia and Xena made her smile. As a police officer on graveyards, Sequoia had always relished her alone time. She'd never cared for dogs, in their hairy, slobbery existence. So when her boss assigned her to the K-9 unit, and she was suddenly stuck with a four-legged companion, twenty-four-seven, they all thought she'd lose her mind and resign. Grudgingly, though, she grew to like Xena, and surprised Holly and Jasmine with how quickly she adapted to having a dog in the house (and, to hear her tell it, in her bed). Holly wasn't sure whether it was Xena or Elijah who had helped transform Sequoia's personality from brusque to … well, to a gentler brusque.

Sequoia paired up with Elijah after Xena came along. And just before that, Jasmine had met and fallen for Hudson while working with him at the paper.

Both of her sisters seemed so happy, so calm and centered and sure of their places in this universe. It wasn't just about finding a man, Holly thought. It was about knowing who you *were*. Of course, finding a man would be wonderful. But how could she find a man when she didn't even know herself?

At this rate, she'd be alone, lonely, and rudderless indefinitely. Was this night representative of her future? Pathetic and alone every weekend, vacuuming the carpet, debating between dishes and TV, while thinking about getting a dog for company?

She was looking forward to a pretty sad existence. She decided to wash the windows after all. If she was going to live a sad existence, at least it would be in a clean house. Was it possible that she was just meant to be alone?

"Maybe I should get a cat."

How many cats would it take to earn her official Cat Lady status?

Three? A dozen? She began assigning them favorite spots. One could sit there, in the picture window overlooking the street in front of the house. She could buy it one of those hammocks that hang on the windowsill. Another—two more, actually—could sit on the back of the couch. Some cats liked sleeping in house plants, so she'd have to get a new house plant, too, one she could keep alive. Maybe if there was a cat living in it, she'd remember to water it.

Sequoia would just die. If there was one thing worse than dogs, it was cats, with their long, shedding fur and their sharp, scratching claws.

At that very moment, Holly's phone dinged, signaling a text message from Sequoia: *What are you doing?*

Holly shook her head, and replied with a lie: *Studying.*

Why couldn't she just be honest? Why couldn't she just tell her sisters she'd decided not to pursue personal training? Holly set her phone down. Then, when she realized it was strange for Sequoia to text her with that kind of unimportant question, she picked it back up and added, *Why?*

Sequoia responded immediately: *Just wanted to make sure you're safely at home.*

Holly wrote: *Where else would I be?*

She fully expected her sister to write some snarky response related to the Drunk Driving Incident, but instead, she wrote, *Are you sure everything's ok?*

Holly wished for the confidence to tell her sister everything. But confidence doesn't develop overnight. *Everything's fine. Promise.*

Okay, Sequoia wrote. *If you promise.*

Cleaning gave her too much time to think, Holly decided. She'd cleaned the entry window, and that was good enough. Watching TV would stop this madness. And she'd watch something stimulating, like the news. She threw away the wad of paper towels, sat down on the couch, and turned on the TV. She picked up her phone and opened the Blackbook app to see what her friends had been up to.

Then she got a sign. From a Blackbook advertisement. It was a video: the camera panned the beach in Seabreeze. Holly could tell from the watercolor sky and smooth-as-glass ocean that it was sunrise. The dawn of a new day. Text started scrolling over the image: *Are you at a crossroads in your life? Are you searching for purpose and meaning?*

Holly sat up straight, nodding. "Yes," she said quietly, and then more loudly, as a seagull flew through the frame, "Yes!"

The camera had finished panning the beach, and now there was a view of the forest.

If you want to discover your true life's purpose, the scrolling text read as the sun rose over the horizon and shone through the branches of the redwoods, *then you are in the right place, right now. Introducing … Compass Coaching with Tristan Compass.*

A photo came up into the frame—a photo of a very, *very* good-looking guy. *Award-Winning Life Coach Tristan Compass.*

Tristan Compass could be Holly Carr's compass any time. Yes, he was wearing a tank top in the photo, which her sisters would say proved he had a big ego, but he deserved to, didn't he? With that physique?

We're scheduling complimentary Find Your Way consultations right now to help you determine whether Tristan is a good match for you … whether he can guide you towards a life filled with purpose, meaning, and true joy, starting in the New Year.

The text directed Holly to a link where she could sign up for a consultation. Holly realized she was literally sitting on the edge of her seat. She tapped the link, and the web browser opened. There it was, the web page for Compass Coaching … and the form to sign up for a consult.

Yes, this was a sign. It had to be.

THE NEXT EVENING, Holly, Jasmine, and Sequoia met at Jasmine's house for the weekly meeting of The Garden Club—the term they'd coined as kids when they realized their parents had named them all after flora.

Things were a little quiet as they settled in around the table, and Holly blamed the Drunk Driving Incident. Jasmine's dog, Ruby, who sat in her customary spot at Holly's feet, yipped, probably anxious for a piece of carrot or bell pepper. Holly tapped her fingers on the edge of the table. She had been looking forward to tonight, but now that they were all together, she was afraid to tell her sisters about Tristan Compass.

"You're tapping," Sequoia said.

"Sorry." Holly curled her hands into fists. "How are you?" she asked.

Sequoia shrugged. "I'm good."

Holly didn't press for further conversation. Instead, she said, "Should we dish up?"

She decided that this moment, while her sisters were distracted by serving themselves salad and meatloaf, she'd tell them.

She cleared her throat. "So," she said. "I've had a sign from the universe."

She went on to explain how she'd taken a break from cleaning on Saturday, and while scrolling through Blackbook, she'd seen the Compass Coaching advertisement and was considering signing up for a complimentary Find Your Way consultation.

Later, she would reflect on this moment and wonder how stupid she looked to both of her sisters, as she sat there bright-eyed at the table, accidentally revealing to them that she'd neglected, for months, to tell them she'd stopped pursuing her personal training certification. She was sure that in a few years' time they would all find the memory humorous: her expression changing from expectant, like she deserved a cookie, to surprised—when she remembered her sisters didn't even know she didn't have a life's purpose—to disappointed that she'd have to explain herself.

"Wait," Sequoia said, at the same time as Jasmine said, "A life coach?" and added air quotes.

They both said, "I thought you—"

Jasmine motioned for Sequoia to continue, and Sequoia said, "You said you were studying."

Jasmine held up a finger. "I thought you *had* a life's purpose. I thought personal training was, like, your thing. All those tofu burritos and everything."

"Look at that face," Sequoia said. "Deer in the headlights. What's going on, Holly?"

"Shit," Holly said. She scooped some more salad onto her plate.

"You weren't getting your personal training certification, were you?" Sequoia said.

"She wasn't," Jasmine said. "Her face just confirmed it."

Holly found herself slightly bent at the shoulders, looking at the lettuce like she was reading tea leaves. She had the urge to talk to Ruby, to bemoan the fact that her sisters were talking about her like she wasn't here, but she knew that would only make matters worse.

"I have so many questions right now," Sequoia said. "Like, why you didn't tell us you didn't want to be a personal trainer and what do you plan to do, instead? But what I really want to know is, a life coach? I mean, those people charge you thousands of dollars, Holly. Thousands. You're a waitress. A waitress! Are your tips really going to cover the expense of hiring some slick, hair-gelled prima donna to ask you deep, probing, thought-provoking questions that will ultimately lead to your life's purpose? Why not just ask yourself those questions?"

"This is exactly why I didn't want to tell you guys," Holly said. "And Tristan doesn't wear hair gel. At least, not in the photo they showed on the advertisement."

"Tristan?" Sequoia said. "I see why you didn't want to tell us. Because we'd think it's ridiculous. Especially with a guy named Tristan. Tristan!"

"You're right," Holly said. "It probably is ridiculous."

"Now, now, ladies," Jasmine said. "Let's keep it civil here, okay? Holly, I think Sequoia is just concerned that you're wasting your money."

Sequoia and Jasmine had no way of knowing Holly had built a serious savings account over the course of the past several years— one a bank teller told her she should be proud of.

"All I said was that I was thinking about signing up for the free session," Holly said. "It's free! You can't waste money on something that's free. I thought it would be good timing, with the New Year approaching and everything. I haven't even signed up yet! And I didn't sign up for the coaching."

"But you're going to," Sequoia said. "I can see that light in your eyes. You're excited about this in the same way you were excited about losing your virginity to Dylan Sanderson your sophomore year of college. You had already decided on it, before you even went on that date to the drive-in."

Holly sighed. It was true. She'd already decided she'd sign the life coaching contract. Just like she'd decided she'd sleep with Dylan Sanderson at the drive-in well before they were laying in the backseat, his pants around his thighs and her panties shoved off to one side.

"I can afford it."

"I still can't believe you lost your virginity at the drive-in," Jasmine said. "But that's not the point. Sequoia's right. You do get this light in your eyes."

"It's like the bright, shiny object thing," Sequoia said.

Jasmine must have stomped on Sequoia's foot under the table because she winced and pressed her lips together before Jasmine continued speaking, undoubtedly presenting the same idea Sequoia had planned on, only with nicer delivery. "You find something new to focus on, and you're all excited about it for, like, a minute, and then it loses its luster and you want to move on. Like the personal training thing."

If she was being honest with herself, Holly couldn't think of a single way to refute what they were saying. Even if she could, they'd just argue. She wasn't sure they were wrong.

Before she left that evening, Sequoia put a hand on Holly's arm and said, "Don't waste your time, Holly. You don't need a coach. You just need to decide what you want to do with your life."

As if it were that easy.

When she got home from Jasmine's, she walked through the house turning on lights—in the entryway, the clean living room, and the kitchen—to camouflage the fact that she was alone, again. On autopilot, she filled her teakettle (a gift from Jasmine) and put it on the stove. Then, abruptly, she turned off the burner, moved the kettle to the back of the stovetop, and marched over to the pantry. She pulled a couple of teabags out of each box to save for Jasmine, and threw the rest of the tea in the garbage. And so what if she felt a little thrill when the lid slammed shut?

Then she poured herself a generous glass of wine and sat at the counter twirling the glass between her forefinger and her thumb. If she was, in fact, easily distracted, how would she find the focus and perseverance to stick with any particular project for a decent length of time?

Wasn't life coaching the answer? She took a sip of wine.

In her research about Compass Coaching, Holly had learned that coaches didn't focus on why you employed a certain behavior or fell into a certain pattern; rather, they identified action steps for creating positive change from wherever you were.

Isn't that exactly what she needed to do?

The wine hit her bloodstream. She felt warm, her limbs heavy and pliable.

True, she hadn't been able to find a price tag for coaching programs with Tristan Compass, and that probably meant he cost a lot, like jewelry on display at Tiffany & Co. But maybe what it said on the web page was *also* true—she was investing in her own happiness, her own future.

Right?

Right, she told herself, draining her glass. She felt emboldened, and wasn't sure whether that was due to the wine or to the possibility of a new path to purpose.

She slid her phone across the counter and opened up the web browser again. Tristan Compass's face popped up, his blue eyes staring intensely at her from the screen.

She'd just sign up for the free consultation. It was free, and the website promised she'd walk away with at least one action step she could take to move closer to her biggest goal. Besides, she reminded herself, the end of the year was approaching, which meant that she'd start off the New Year with momentum and enthusiasm. And action.

What did she have to lose? Nothing but an hour of her time—or a complete lack of purpose and direction, she thought wildly as she typed in her name and email address and tapped on *Schedule My Session!*

CHAPTER THREE

As waitressing at the Broken Egg became a long-term endeavor, Holly developed a community of regulars. Two of them, Jaclyn and Phil Connelly, walked in now, and Holly waved and went to retrieve the coffee pot. When she walked back into the dining room, Holly's feet froze to the floor. In all the years she'd worked here, she'd seen Jaclyn and Phil every week. But she'd never seen Mr. Bravo at the Broken Egg … until today. Not only was he at the Broken Egg, but he'd also seated himself in her section, two tables down from the Connellys. Apparently he'd missed the *Please Wait to be Seated* sign.

As soon as she saw him, all freshly showered and shaved, she felt a tingly, fluttery sensation in her stomach. She couldn't tell whether it was humiliation or attraction. Or a strange combination of both. He made eye contact with her, and, automatically, she began guessing what he'd order. She had a knack for it, and was almost always right on. This was the single skill that could impress her sisters, her customers, and her co-workers.

"It's not about their body language or what they're wearing," she always said. "It's more about the vibe they're putting off."

Mr. Bravo was putting off a vibe Holly didn't like. It implied that he wouldn't want her touching his food, much less breathing the same air he was. He would probably order dry toast and choke on it.

He couldn't have known she worked here, and he definitely couldn't have known he'd seated himself in her section. She'd just play it cool. She was a professional.

She put on her most cheerful smile as she approached his table. "Good morning! Can I get you a drink?"

"Good morning," he said. "And yes, please. I'll take a coffee."

"Creamer?"

"Nope." His tone sounded irritated. "Just coffee."

She should have known. Black coffee: straight up.

Holly turned his mug over so it was upright, and as she poured his coffee, she noticed that his menu lay unopened on the table.

"Do you know what you want?"

His dark eyes glinted at her. She couldn't blame him for disliking her. As a drunk driver, she was a danger, a menace to society.

"Can you make any recommendations?"

His expression still looked surly. Maybe it was lack of coffee. She tapped her pen against her lips, twice, and then stopped. It was a nervous habit. He was a cop. He could pick out nervous habits like a carnival worker picking out people desperate to win a goldfish in a tiny bowl.

He definitely wasn't the pancake type. In fact, he probably cooked fancy meals at home. Frittatas with hummus or something.

"I like the egg-white omelette with veggies," she said. "I add feta cheese. Comes with breakfast potatoes, which are excellent, but I usually substitute a bowl of fruit."

The way he watched her when she spoke was unnerving. Did he want to light her on fire with his eyes, or was he just really serious about his breakfast? Maybe he was one of those people who felt grumpy before eating. Like Sequoia. Or maybe he was just testing her to see whether she actually had a recommendation. Or maybe—

"I'll get that," he said. He nodded curtly, as if signaling for her to take his menu and her coffee pot and beat it. She did.

She couldn't say why she found him intriguing. She stood in the kitchen and watched the way he ate, cutting one bite at a time into a perfect square that almost exactly matched the shape of his finger-nails. She refilled his coffee more often than necessary, each time trying to catch a whiff of his cologne. And then, when he set cash on the table, which meant she couldn't get his first name off his credit card, she felt a little disappointed.

He left her a tip of exactly fifteen percent (two dollars and fifty-eight cents) and she spent the rest of her shift brainstorming about what his first name could be.

Driving home from the Broken Egg, Holly pondered the answer to the very important question, What did one wear to one's first life coaching session? She assumed she wouldn't be meeting with Tristan, himself—he was too important to wade through prospective clients—but still.

She knew she'd be talking to whomever it was online, which meant she could put up a photo of herself rather than streaming a video from the web cam. But she was afraid that would make her come across as vain, no matter what she did.

If she posted a selfie, Tristan or one of his coaches would read into her expression and concoct some kind of story about her based on the tilt of her smile or the lift of her left eyebrow or the amount of mascara she put on. If she posted a photo one of her sisters had taken, it would probably seem like a glamour shot.

If she did decide on video chat, she would have to wear a shirt that was neither too revealing nor too frumpy, one that brought out her eyes and made her skin look healthy and radiant. Maybe she was putting too much thought into this, but she felt like it was the first decision she was making as she pursued her new life.

She imagined herself back at the Broken Egg, with Mr. Bravo sitting in her section. What would he think of her options? In her mind's eye, she held up the front-runners, a bright green tank top that accentuated her eye color, and a plain black tunic that made her waist look slim and her chest look curvy.

Which one would he choose? What would her sisters say?

It was possible she was overthinking this.

Cara's words came floating back to her: *It just seems like you're so unsure of yourself all the time. You struggle to make decisions on your own about even the simplest things. Take, for example, this morning. Just like every time we have coffee or lunch or drinks, you made me choose the spot.*

And then you had me order first. And then you ordered the same thing as me. You haven't even touched your muffin. You don't even like blueberry muffins, I think you told me once. But when it was your turn to order, you said, 'I'll just have what she's having.' And it's not just this morning. You do it all the time. I mean, you drive a convertible.

As Holly stood in front of the full-length mirror in her closet, indecision paralyzed her, just as it had throughout her life. She was cursed with it.

Once, at her elementary school's field day, she missed out on snow cones because she couldn't decide between red and blue. Maybe, she thought now, it was because neither of her sisters were there to make a suggestion. When she got to the front of the line, she stood there looking from one side of the table, where the red cones sat, to the other, where the blue cones sat. The adults selling the snow cones looked expectantly at her—for at least three minutes.

The kids behind her started to get restless: "C'mon, Holly! Hurry up. Just choose one! Ask for a mix!"

When she still couldn't decide, one of the adults signaled for the boy behind her to choose his. As easily as if he were deciding whether to wear socks to school that day, he chose red, calling out the color as he pushed roughly past her, jostling her with his big, beefy shoulder.

This continued, child after child, until the bell rang to signal it was time to go back to class. Still, Holly stood there staring at the few remaining snow cones, unable to make a decision on her own.

Sometimes her sisters saved her. When it was her turn to choose which TV show they'd watch on a particular evening, Sequoia or Jasmine would "highly recommend" one they wanted to watch, which spared her the agony of having to choose, herself.

She'd lost her place in lines at fast food restaurants because she couldn't choose between crispy or grilled chicken sandwiches. She'd walked out of coffee shops empty-handed because she couldn't choose between a mocha and a latte. Even if she asked someone for a recommendation, she often had trouble taking it. What if this cashier liked sweet stuff more than she did? What if this guy wasn't as health conscious as she was?

And now, at the age of thirty, she was going to be late for her first life coaching appointment because she couldn't choose between black and green.

"This is so *stupid*," she said to her reflection.

Finally, one minute before the meeting time (and she still had to turn on her computer and load the video chat), she pulled the black tunic roughly over her head and smoothed her hair. Black was perfect. It said, "I'm sensible."

Or maybe it said, "I'm morbid."

She took it off and put on the green tank top. Then she realized it showed off her cleavage and if she leaned forward just the tiniest bit it was possible that Tristan Compass could see her bra. With an impatient growl, she pulled the black tunic on over the green tank top.

Then, to reassure herself she'd made a good decision, she nodded. And as she marched into the kitchen, she resolved to start making decisions more quickly.

SO SHE *WAS* MEETING with Tristan Compass, himself.

For just a second, she saw her face in the video chat window: eyebrows furrowed, mouth pursed, concentration evident. It took a conscious effort to smooth her features, and she was pretty sure she looked like she'd had one too many facelifts.

Then Tristan greeted her. He said, "Hello, there," and paused to consult his notes. When he looked up, staring straight into his web cam so it felt like he was right there in the room with her, and said, "Holly Carr," she felt a goofy grin spreading across her face.

Yes, she thought. *This is exactly the right choice. Tristan Compass will help me find my way.*

She caught herself nodding with a bit too much enthusiasm. She realized she'd never responded to Tristan's greeting, so she smiled and said, "Hello, Tristan Compass."

He cut right to the chase: "What made you sign up for a consultation?"

Oh, my. Holly had not realized she'd be put on the spot like this. She had expected Tristan Compass to do all the talking in his soothing voice.

"Well," she said.

On screen, she saw herself tuck her hair behind her ear, which was another of her stupid nervous habits. Watching herself during video chat was definitely going to be a distraction. She sighed and leaned forward with her forearms on the counter. Tristan blinked and waited.

"My sisters tell me I lack purpose."

"Do *you* think you lack purpose?"

No one had ever asked her that before, and she was unsure of how to respond. Tristan shifted forward, so his face was close to the webcam. He raised an eyebrow.

"Well," she said. "I've worked as a waitress for half a decade because I don't know what else to do with my life. What do you think?"

"This isn't about what I think," Tristan said. "It's about what you think."

His voice was gentle. Sequoia would say it was feminine, but Holly liked it. Jasmine would want to get a good look at his hands. Tristan was holding a pen, poised above his notebook. His fingers were long and thin. Jasmine would say that was feminine, too.

Tristan cleared his throat. "What do you think, Holly? Do you think you lack purpose?"

"Oh," Holly said. "I suppose I do. Which is why I'm here. I, um, don't want to work at a diner forever, you know?"

Tristan nodded. "Okay. Let's dig deeper. We're approaching the end of the year, right? So let me ask you a question: if you had a magic wand, and you could wave it and create your ideal life over the course of the next year, what would it look like?"

"See?" Holly said. "That's the problem. I don't know."

"Okay," Tristan said again. "Let's shift gears. You said you've been working at a diner for half a decade, correct?"

When Holly nodded, he said, "What is it that appeals to you about it?"

"About working at a diner? I don't know. I guess I like chatting with my customers, getting them what they need, all that stuff. I'm good at it, which makes it enjoyable."

"What do you dislike about it?"

"Well, my sisters say you can't make a career out of waiting tables at a diner. Somewhere fancy, maybe, but not at the Broken Egg."

She thought of the "fancy" places Sequoia had listed, places with white linen tablecloths and fifty-dollar steaks and real candles on the tables.

"What do *you* say?" Tristan said.

Holly made that weird, nervous laughing-sighing sound. "I say I want to really help people, you know? I thought about being a personal trainer but as I started to go through the certification process, I realized it didn't, you know, light me up."

Tristan nodded. "Okay, now we're getting somewhere. What appealed to you about being a personal trainer?"

Holly shrugged. She was tempted to say she didn't know, again, but she was realizing how stupid it sounded that she didn't know anything about her own life.

"I liked the idea of helping people get healthy, so they could feel good and enjoy life more."

"Why didn't personal training light you up?"

"Now, that's a good question," Holly said. Tristan smiled, and she continued, surprising herself by verbalizing the epiphany she'd had just a couple of days ago: "The personal training thing wasn't even my idea. My sister, Sequoia, suggested it when I went on a health-food kick a while back. I latched onto it because I couldn't think of anything that sounded better. And I mean, personal trainers help people, right? More than waitresses do? But once I got knee-deep in it, I realized it doesn't sound as fun as I originally imagined. It doesn't suit my personality like I thought it did."

Tristan nodded, and Holly felt like he truly understood her.

She kept talking. "Then I realized that every time I would go to study, or research my next step, something else would come up."

Tristan nodded. "Like what?"

"Like, I would have to get my car washed, or I would need to do dishes. Or run errands. You know, day to day stuff. As much as introspection isn't my strong suit, the procrastination was an obvious red flag."

Tristan nodded again.

"Holly," he said.

She felt her face flushing and wondered if he could see it.

"Yes?"

"Was it really that personal training didn't light you up, or was it that you were afraid to finish?"

She did it.

Holly Carr made a quick decision. She took control of her life. Finally.

She signed on to work with Tristan Compass for six weeks. Yes, it would cost her a small fortune—at least a year's worth of the tips she'd been saving. But it was worth it. As the Blackbook commercial had promised, she would find her way.

When she told Tristan to send the contract over, he said, "Congratulations. When we work together, you'll gain clarity about your own direction, develop a plan for pursuing your new vision, and maintain the relentless focus to put that plan into action."

It sounded great. Focus. She could do this. Her first assignment: to create what Tristan called a "Direction Board."

He forbade her from procrastinating on this project. "Don't use this assignment as an excuse to go shopping for crafting supplies. That's a loss of focus."

"Are you a mind reader, too?" she said. "Do you know how much I love shopping?"

"I'll make note of that for the session when we discuss your hobbies," he said. "And no, I'm not a mind reader. But I've seen it before. Anyway, for now, skip the shopping. Just use what you have at home. Cut pictures out of magazines, or use those coupon books you get in the mail, whatever. But I want to see it in two days."

"Two days?"

Now, he smiled. "Yes. Two days. Let's schedule our meeting for noon, okay? That gives you forty-eight hours. Remember, choose pictures that represent your vision for your ideal life. If you could wave a magic wand and make some changes now, what would your life look like? Don't worry about the *how*, for now. Let go of that and think about what you want."

They disconnected and Holly downloaded the instruction sheet from her new Client Portal before she closed her laptop. For a moment, she felt a thrill, an exhilaration to which she was unaccustomed. The possibilities were endless, weren't they? She loved this question! If she could wave a magic wand, what would her life look like? The next thing she knew, she was sitting on the floor next to her coffee table, magazines stacked on one side and her Direction Board —blank, for now—on the other.

Here was an advertisement for a couples resort. A nicely tanned man and woman sat on the beach with a bottle of champagne in a bucket between them.

"I'd like that," she said out loud. "But how would you keep the champagne from getting sandy?"

At first, Holly nearly passed up the picture and flipped on to the next page, but then she remembered this was her magic-wand life. She didn't have to worry about the how, and she'd really love to sit on the beach with champagne and a sexy, tan man. Even if it meant sandy champagne.

"Officer Bravo," she said to herself, then. Officer Bravo had a nice tan, for sure. And she was positive he'd look beyond sexy without a shirt on. Out of nowhere, she saw an image of herself pouring cold champagne down the center of Mr. Bravo's bare six-pack, and then licking it off.

She shivered. Then she shook her head as she cut the couple out of the picture, careful not to cut off the champagne bucket.

"Geez, Holly," she said. "You're as boy-crazy as you were in junior high."

She glued them onto her Direction Board and returned to flipping magazine pages. A dog food advertisement showed the cutest little white puppy. It would be nice to come home to something other than half-dead houseplants.

She cut out the puppy.

Perhaps a pattern will emerge, providing you with a new direction for all aspects of your life.

She continued flipping, cutting, and gluing, choosing photos of beautiful locations she'd visit and beautiful accessories she'd use to adorn her house. At one point, her stomach growled, and she got up to grab a yogurt out of the fridge. The clock on the oven read 4:00 p.m.

Wow, focus makes time pass quickly.

"Where did the day go?"

Of course, no one answered, and the resounding silence was like a tiny pinprick in the balloon of hope and excitement she'd inflated throughout the day. Not to be deterred, she went back to her Direction Board. By the time she had it filled up, puppies and gorgeous flowers overlapping one another, framing that tanned couple with the champagne, the early evening light slanted through the sliding glass door.

Exhausted and energized all at once, she stood up and stretched. Then, she picked up her Direction Board.

"Hmm," she said. "It looks like I'll end up on the beach somewhere with Mr. Bravo and the champagne. And then come home to a fluffy puppy, flowers, a stack of new books, and a garden gnome."

Unsure of what to make of this, Holly popped herself a bag of popcorn and turned on the TV.

CHAPTER FOUR

"I HAVE AN ANNOUNCEMENT TO MAKE."

Jasmine and Sequoia sat on Holly's couch. She stood opposite them, on the other side of the coffee table. They looked at each other, wearing matching "Oh, geez, what now?" expressions. So Holly looked at Cara, who wore her new jeans and sweater and sat on a stool at the bar, her legs crossed, and her feet clad in ballet flats rather than big black boots. Because Cara hadn't been privy to Holly's many announcements and big ideas, she looked expectant, maybe even excited.

Bolstered, Holly clapped her hands together. "Ready?"

"It looks like you're going to break out in a cheer," Sequoia said. "I wish I had some pompons."

Jasmine elbowed her, and Holly nodded, too enthusiastically, she knew.

"Well?" Jasmine and Cara said.

"Right," Holly said. "So. I've decided to work with Tristan. That life coach. I signed up this morning."

Neither of her sisters answered. Cara opened her mouth as if she wanted to say something, but she closed it again after a glance at Sequoia and Jasmine. Holly could practically hear a clock ticking. Or crickets chirping. Immediately, she began to question her decision.

But then she remembered that she was working on standing more confidently in her choices.

"Say something," she said. Overcome by the need to fill the silence, she added, "I know what you're thinking. It's expensive. And I could figure this out on my own. But the truth is, I'm thirty years old and I haven't figured it out, yet. I need help. I can't work at the Broken Egg forever, can I? You guys don't want me waiting tables forever, do you?"

Sequoia cleared her throat. Jasmine looked at Sequoia. Cara looked at Sequoia.

Why is everyone looking at Sequoia?

"Plus," Holly said, "I had an epiphany. I realized you guys were totally right about the bright, shiny object thing. It's a lack of focus. And I think working with a coach will help me get clear on what I want, and then stay focused until I get from point A to point B."

Then Sequoia took Holly by complete surprise.

"Yes, Holly. I think this is great. You're right. You can't wait tables forever. Not at the Broken Egg, anyway. And maybe having an objective third party to ask you those deeper questions will help."

Now, Jasmine cleared her throat. "Um, yeah. What Sequoia said. This sounds fantastic. So have you had an appointment yet? How does this work? Give us the details."

For a moment, Holly felt surprise slowing her momentum. She couldn't believe her sisters thought this was a good idea, and she'd been in full battle mode, ready to defend herself.

"Oh. Um, okay," she said. "So I meet with him—Tristan—every week for the next six weeks. He already gave me my first assignment."

"Wait," Sequoia said. "Is Tristan Compass his real name? I thought you were joking when you said that before."

Jasmine elbowed Sequoia again.

"Um, I don't actually know," Holly said.

"It does sound like a fake name," Cara said. "But, I mean, who cares? Maybe it's like a pen name. We don't disregard authors who use pen names, do we?"

"It doesn't matter," Jasmine said, and Cara said, "So. Tell us about the assignment. How did your first session go?"

Holly explained the Direction Board assignment, leaving out the part about the beach couple she'd put at the center of her vision. And the part where she'd stayed up until midnight working on it.

Sequoia's mouth twitched.

"What's so funny?" Holly asked.

"What? Nothing."

"Your mouth is twitching," Holly said.

"What? No, it's not."

"Yes it is," Jasmine and Cara said in unison.

"Holly," Sequoia said. "This is great. I'm excited for you. You'll have to keep us updated on your progress. When's your next meeting?"

"Well, we have a quick check-in at noon tomorrow, so he can see the Direction Board I created. Then, Monday." Her head bobbed involuntarily, and for some reason, she felt the need to further justify her decision. "I saw this advertisement about him on Blackbook, and it sounds like he's really good at what he does. There were testimonials! From his clients! They said his work was life-changing!"

"I'm sure it was," Jasmine said.

While ninety-nine percent of Holly's brain power was focused on the conversation, the other one percent realized how strange Sequoia's reaction was. Her support had to be some kind of trap.

"Just wait," Holly said. "This isn't a bright shiny object. This is a life-changer. It's different this time."

She wasn't sure whether she was trying to convince her sisters or herself.

THE NEXT MORNING, Holly squared her shoulders as she walked into work. She'd made a conscious decision to look forward, to her new life, and it started right now. Yes, her track record left something to be desired. But the new, focused Holly was about to experience a metamorphosis.

The smells of bacon cooking and coffee brewing (which she'd

come to love) greeted her as she entered through the kitchen and put on her apron, taking care to smooth it out. She nodded a brief hello to the cooks, grabbed her order pad and a pen, and walked into the dining room.

At that very moment, the diner's front door swung open. Head still high, shoulders still set back, Holly stopped short when she saw who was making his way towards her section.

Mr. Bravo.

Mr. Bravo with the finely tuned machine for a body and the smooth, dark skin, and the neat and tidy fingernails.

Mr. Bravo, who had had the audacity to seat himself in her section. Again.

Mr. Bravo, who was a distraction.

Why was he here? The fact that he set her insides simmering was beyond awkward. He could never be interested in her. The confidence she'd mustered up just a moment ago began to dissipate as she approached his table.

"Coffee?" Without waiting for him to answer, she said, "Um, didn't you see the sign? You're supposed to wait to be seated."

He flashed her a grin, which threw her completely off kilter.

"I must have missed it. Yes, I'll have coffee, please, to start. Black."

He just sat there, making the kind of eye contact that incinerated her panties (although she was positive that was not his intention).

"Okay. Coffee. I'll be right back."

He was still smiling when she returned to his table with the coffee pot. He *was* good-looking. If there wasn't the matter of him pulling her over for drunk driving, and if she hadn't just resigned herself to starting over with laser focus, she would probably flirt with him. But, those two matters were fresh in her mind. She'd have to most past the humiliation of the other night—in the bigger picture, it didn't matter what he thought of her, did it?—and remain strictly professional.

She turned over Mr. Bravo's mug and poured his coffee. When she finished, she returned his smile with one of her own. There was something freeing about this new approach.

"What can I get you?"

"I'll have the meat lovers' omelet. And a side of bacon."

"Wait." The soothing music that had been playing on a record in Holly's mind screeched to a halt. "That's a heart attack waiting to happen. I can't let you order that."

Mr. Bravo closed his menu and set it down at the empty spot across from him.

"It's man food. Protein."

Holly couldn't help but feel amused. "It's heart attack food. Grease."

"I'll be fine," he said. "I'm in good shape."

Well, that was true. He was in good shape. *Really* good shape. Maybe even great shape.

Focus, Holly!

Holly shrugged one shoulder, wrote his order on her pad, and said, "Okay. One clogged artery with a side of heart disease coming right up."

She walked away, mumbling, "Man food. Protein," and she could have sworn she heard him mumbling, "Clogged artery. Heart disease."

If she were interested in men right now, she would find this flirtation quite promising. She entered his order on the computer and greeted Jaclyn and Phil.

By the time his order was up, her section was full, and she didn't have a spare moment for flirtations of any kind. She could feel Mr. Bravo watching her work, and refused to give into her typical inclination to tilt her head just so, or walk with that special sway to her hips.

For once, she was not Man-Hunting Holly. She was just Holly. That had a nice ring to it. Just Holly. Instead of thinking about how her butt looked in her jeans—and how it would look to Mr. Bravo— she thought about how strangely Sequoia had acted the night before.

Typically, Sequoia would have come up with something scathing to say about Holly's decision to hire a life coach. Her relative quiet was setting off alarm bells in Holly's mind. Maybe she'd ask her about it. The old Sequoia would get defensive. But the new Sequoia, the one who'd found a warm and fuzzy kind of love with Elijah Sawyer, might just give her a real answer.

Holly nodded to herself as she carried two stacks of buttermilk pancakes to the kids in the corner booth. She'd just ask. It couldn't hurt.

Mr. Bravo left without saying good-bye. Again, he tipped her exactly fifteen percent.

Yes, she was too focused on her transformation to go on the prowl for men. But this new interaction with Mr. Bravo would keep things interesting, at least.

Just as she finished up her shift at the Broken Egg, Holly received a text from Jasmine: *Emergency Garden Club meeting, ASAP?*

She'd included Sequoia in the group text, and Sequoia responded immediately: *Are you ok?*

Jasmine wrote back: *Of course. I'm great. Meet at Pâtisserie for drinks?*

It was barely past noon.

Drinks at noon? Holly wrote.

Jasmine sent back a winking emoji.

Pâtisserie was a tiny, trendy boutique restaurant in the heart of downtown Seabreeze. The menu featured items like finger sandwiches and tropical fruit tarts, all with foreign-sounding names. Holly usually just pointed at the items she wanted to order, rather than attempting to pronounce their names. And Sequoia always, always commented about the terrible value of the food. Most importantly, the eatery offered a special selection of handcrafted cocktails with prices in the double digits. Jasmine's choice of location seemed pretty celebratory.

Because she felt underdressed in her uniform of jeans and a black t-shirt, Holly applied fresh coats of lip gloss and mascara, and put her hair in a messy bun before getting out of the car. Sequoia, of course, was already waiting.

"Early is on time," was one of Sequoia's favorite sayings.

Sequoia had chosen a corner table and was facing the door, her black linen napkin already draped across her lap. She actually smiled when Holly came in, which made Holly stop in her tracks.

It's not that her oldest sister was unfriendly. She was just a bit cool, aloof, hard to crack. Maybe Elijah was helping Sequoia evolve. Romance could do that to a person. Holly unfroze herself and pulled out a chair. She pointed at the pink peonies in a small vase at the center of the table, and the crystal water glasses at each place.

"Fancy," she said. "How's it going?"

Sequoia raised an eyebrow, and said, "Fancy, all right. So what do you think this emergency meeting is about?"

"Well, if I had to guess, Jasmine's either knocked up or she got a new job. Probably the latter, since she wouldn't suggest drinks if she were pregnant."

Sequoia snorted. "Okay. Good deductive reasoning."

"What do you think?"

"I think you may be right about the job. A promotion, maybe? To editor or something? Or maybe she's—"

Just then, Holly heard the door open. She could tell from Sequoia's quick wave that Jasmine had arrived, and she pulled out the chair next to her.

When Jasmine sat down, Holly could sense her excitement. Her voice sounded breathy when she said, "Hello," and her eyes were shining. Her skin even had a bit of a sheen, which Holly would have thought was just sweat if the fall weather wasn't turning quickly to winter.

Sequoia cut right to the chase: "So, what's the agenda for our emergency meeting? What's this about?"

Jasmine gave them a cat-that-ate-the-canary smile, and Holly noticed her hand shook as she tucked her hair behind her ear.

"Did you get a promotion? Are congratulations in order?" Holly said.

Instead of answering, Jasmine signaled the waitress and ordered a water and a Famous Peach Bellini. Sequoia tapped her fingertips on the tabletop and Holly gripped her thighs to keep from fidgeting.

Sequoia ordered a Bloody Mary with an extra shot and Holly ordered "what she's having," which earned a disapproving look from her sisters.

When the server walked away, Sequoia inhaled like she was

going to say something, and Jasmine held up a hand. "Just wait for our drinks. You're going to want to toast me."

Holly giggled, Sequoia rolled her eyes, and they spent the next few minutes talking about the weather.

"Seriously, the weather," Holly said. "I can't believe we're talking about the weather."

"Well, it has been cold," Jasmine said.

"It's November," Sequoia said. "Of course it has."

This reminded Holly that Christmas was just around the corner. It would probably be different this year, since both of her sisters had significant others and she didn't. Would they still celebrate together? Or would Holly be home, alone?

The server returned, and Holly was grateful, as it halted that train of thought. After she deposited their drinks on the table and walked away, Jasmine held up her glass.

"So, I did get a promotion."

Holly made eye contact with Sequoia, who actually winked at her before they both looked back at Jasmine.

"But it's not what you think," Jasmine said.

Now Sequoia gave Holly a comically quizzical look, and Holly giggled.

"I'm being promoted …" Jasmine said, her voice trailing off. She took a sip of her Peach Bellini. Sequoia just stared at her. Holly giggled again.

"From girlfriend to wife!"

Sequoia clapped her hands together. Holly squealed and gave Jasmine a one-armed hug.

When Sequoia stood up to hug Jasmine, too, Holly took a long drink of her Bloody Mary. Probably too long, she thought as she realized the glass was more than half empty. She was happy for Jasmine. Elated, even. Hudson was a great guy, and her sister was in love. They would have a long life of nuptial bliss.

"It's wonderful news," Holly said.

But even so, a tiny part of her wondered why she couldn't be so lucky. And she hated herself for thinking that way. This was Jasmine's moment, and she wouldn't ruin it. Fortunately, Jasmine was so busy producing a jewelry box from her purse and sliding a huge diamond ring onto her finger, and Sequoia was so busy admiring it, that they didn't seem to notice the tiny lapse in Holly's good cheer. So quickly, Holly pulled herself together. "That's beautiful, Jas," she said. "It's all beautiful. So when's the big date?"

Both of her sisters—a police officer and a news reporter—were self-proclaimed purveyors of human behavior, and Holly thought Sequoia shot her a quick look before releasing Jasmine's left hand. But she didn't say anything, and Jasmine responded, "You guys are going to laugh. This is so funny. We're getting married in a month."

After Jasmine answered all the relevant questions about how Hudson proposed, whether she had any idea it was coming, and where they planned to tied the knot, the conversation veered wildly off-course.

"So, Holly," Sequoia said. "What's going on with your love life? I mean, you're going to need a date for this wedding."

Holly groaned, and Jasmine laid a hand on hers, offering a sympathetic smile.

"Let's not ruin Jasmine's big moment with talk about my nonexistent love life," Holly said. "It's like watching a romance movie that suddenly turns into a horror show. Where the main interest turns out to be a crazed axe murderer or something. Anyway, as you know, since I hired Tristan, I'll be focusing on myself. I don't need a man right now. And I'm perfectly happy to attend a wedding stag."

Where she would have expected Sequoia to agree wholeheartedly, her sister shook her head and said, "I disagree. Wholeheartedly."

Jasmine's mouth dropped open, and Holly felt her face burning. Jasmine recovered quickly to offer, "You could bring Cara."

"Shh," Sequoia said. "She cannot bring Cara."

"Did you really just shush me?" Jasmine said.

"Yeah," Sequoia said. "I did."

There was a pause in the conversation, and Holly wondered how Sequoia could turn on her now. This was as unexpected as her friendly smile when Holly came through the door at Pâtisserie.

"I should expect you, of all people, to understand me wanting to focus on myself," Holly said to Sequoia.

Something flashed in Sequoia's eyes, but Holly couldn't quite put her finger on what it was.

"You're right," Jasmine said, and when it seemed like she was going to keep talking, Sequoia cut her off.

"I just thought you wanted to settle down, Holly," Sequoia said. "I mean, you're thirty. Right? The clock's ticking."

"Never mind the fact that you just now settled down," Holly said. "And you're what? Forty?"

"Yes," Sequoia said, without batting an eye. "But it was a surprise settle. You, on the other hand, have always loved romance. Remember when you used to have posters of all of Disney's royal couples on your bedroom wall? Cinderella and the prince, Snow White and the other prince, Jasmine and Aladdin. Who else was there?"

"Ariel and that other prince," Jasmine said, nodding her head.

"Very helpful," Holly said. "Ariel's husband was named Eric, by the way."

"I've been waiting years for you to enjoy your own romantic story," Sequoia said.

"Lies! You have not," Holly said. "You're always telling me I'm too boy crazy."

Their voices were rising in volume, and Jasmine shushed them, scooting their almost-empty glasses toward the edge of the table.

"Too boy crazy, yes," Sequoia said. "But that's because you need to settle down with just one boy. Man. Whatever."

Finally, Jasmine stepped in to rescue Holly. "Right now you need to focus on me and my big day," she said. "I'm surprised no one said anything about how quickly we're getting married."

"Yeah," Sequoia said. "Why are you sprinting down the aisle?"

Holly half-expected Jasmine to announce a surprise pregnancy, but she just went all gooey and said, "Because we're so in love."

Sequoia snorted. "Seriously?"

Jasmine shrugged, then nodded. "Yeah. I mean, we know we want to get married, so why wait? We want a simple wedding, and I have the most Type-A wedding planner in Seabreeze—that's you,

Sequoia—along with the best fashion designer in the West—Holly—
so putting it together will seriously be no problem."

"Sounds reasonable," Holly said. "When do we go dress
shopping?"

While Sequoia and Jasmine started hammering out the details of
the upcoming wedding, Holly devoted most of her brain power to
thinking about Sequoia's new attitude when it came to her love life.
Why was she suddenly so interested, and why did she want Holly to
settle down? Something strange was going on here, and Holly had a
feeling it was more than just the fact that Sequoia was in love,
herself. She'd get to the bottom of this mystery, but first, she had a
Direction Board to finalize before tomorrow's meeting with Tristan.

The three sisters walked out to their cars together, and Sequoia
actually hugged and congratulated Jasmine, whose eyes were wet
with emotion as she got into her car. After she drove away, Sequoia
said to Holly, "Want to come with me to a party tomorrow night?"

"A party?" Holly said. "You go to parties?"

This was very suspicious. If Holly had suspected something
weird was going on before, she knew it now. "What about Elijah?
Why isn't he going with you?"

"He's working," Sequoia said. But even as she spoke, her eyes
darted to the left. "Okay, he's not working. He's going, too. I just
wanted you to tag along."

"Oh, great. I can be the third wheel. Sounds fun. What is this
party?"

"It's a retirement party for a guy I work with," Sequoia said,
apparently oblivious to (or ignoring) Holly's sarcasm.

"You socialize with people from work?"

"Holly. Do you want to come, or not? There's food, an open bar,
probably dancing. It's at that billiards place, what's it called? Sticks
and Balls? Anyway, come. It'll be fun. Better than prom."

"We both know that's not saying much. You never went to prom
because you thought it was stupid."

"And you," Sequoia said, pointing a finger at Holly's chest, "had
a disastrous time because your date made out with someone else
next to the girls' bathroom."

Holly rolled her eyes. "Fine. I'll come. What are you wearing?"

"Uh, that's a weird question."

"Fine, I'll rephrase. What should I wear?"

"I don't know, Holly," Sequoia said, some of her familiar impatience showing through. "Jeans or something. It'll be dark in there. No one will even notice what you're wearing."

Again, her eyes darted to the left.

"Fine," Holly said. "I'll wear jeans."

"Stop saying, 'Fine,'" Sequoia said. "I'm driving. I'll pick you up at seven. Oh. And I'm thirty-four. Not forty."

AS HOLLY REVIEWED her Direction Board in preparation for her meeting with Tristan, second thoughts—mainly around what Tristan would think of her work—haunted her.

Then she had second thoughts about her second thoughts. Why did she care about Tristan's opinion? It was his job to guide her, not to judge her.

Her doorbell rang, and she went to let Cara in. On a whim, Holly had invited her over to get feedback on her Direction Board. Come to think of it, Holly thought, why did she always seek approval? This was something to ponder another time. For now, she offered Cara a glass of water and with a flourish, displayed her project on the kitchen bar. She ran through what the images meant to her, and when Cara didn't respond right away, Holly said, "I mean, maybe I should add something more substantive. Like a Dream Job of some kind. But I don't even know what my Dream Job is."

She remembered a tip the instructions had offered: *Even if you don't know exactly what your Dream Job is, consider adding images that represent what that Dream Job would mean for you. For example, would it mean helping people? Time freedom? Traveling?*

What would Holly's Dream Job mean for her?

It would mean home ownership. But was that important enough to add to her Direction Board? Not really. Would it mean travel?

Sure, travel would be nice. But was she passionate enough about travel to strive for it? No. What was she passionate about?

She was passionate about shopping, but that hardly counted.

Of all the images she'd incorporated, she was most enthusiastic about the fluffy puppy. It would be nice to have someone to come home to. But did that count?

Tristan Compass would probably find this Direction Board amusing, and not in a good way.

"Holly," Cara said, bringing her runaway thoughts to a halt. "I'm just not sure if these are the things you're really supposed to put on your Direction Board."

After a beat of silence, Cara said, "I mean, I get it. You want a man. And he's a nice-looking man, too. You want to sit on the beach with someone. But I don't think that's going to fulfill what you want, like, for yourself. You know?"

Actually, Holly *didn't* know what she wanted for herself.

"I think you need to dial in on that before you get a man and go to the beach."

Part of her wanted to be annoyed with Cara for saying something similar to what Jasmine or Sequoia might say. But a bigger part of her knew Cara was right. Frustrated and a bit discouraged, Holly put her Direction Board face down on the counter.

Then she busied herself popping a bag of popcorn and turning on the TV. She and Cara sat down on the couch to watch recorded episodes of *The Miami Chronicles*, the soap opera Holly had been hooked on since she was a teenager.

"So how was your day drinking date with Jasmine today?" Cara said. "Pretty exciting news, right?"

Holly nodded. "Sure is."

The cheesy theme music ended and the complicated love stories started to play out onscreen. Cara's question caused Holly's thoughts to drift back to Sequoia and her strange behavior. Although she was kind of dreading this party, maybe it would provide her with a good opportunity to figure out what her sister was up to. If nothing else, it would give her an evening to relax, to take her mind off everything else.

CHAPTER FIVE

HOLLY STARED AT THE TOP OF TRISTAN COMPASS'S HEAD AS HE LOOKED at her Direction Board. She'd emailed a photo to him just this morning, and he viewed it on his tablet while his webcam showed Holly the tiniest hint of a bald spot forming.

She forgot all about that bald spot when he looked directly into his webcam and his startling blue eyes met hers. He did not look impressed. Maybe a little bit amused, but not impressed. Butterflies fluttered in her stomach as she waited for him to speak.

"So this is your Direction Board," he said.

Holly nodded. "Yep. What do you think?"

"Honestly?"

His mouth looked like it wanted to smile, but there was something else in his eyes … and it didn't look friendly. The butterflies in Holly's stomach went crazy.

"Yeah, honestly."

"Holly, this is …"

She waited while he searched for the word.

"It's shallow, Holly. That's pretty much all I can say about it."

Holly felt her face fall and Tristan shifted in his chair so that he was leaning towards his screen, his elbows on the table.

"Is this what you want for your life? A sexy man and a fluffy puppy? These are the aspirations you have for yourself?"

"Well, when you put it that way ..."

She paused, waiting for him to say something. He didn't, and she was forced to continue. "It's not that all I want is a man and a puppy. Or whatever. It's just that I want what those things represent."

Tristan nodded, but not as if he believed her. "And what do those things represent to you?" he said.

"You know. Like, having someone to come home to."

Tristan nodded. "So that's it for you, then? You hired a life coach so you could find a romantic partner and get a puppy?"

"Well, when you put it that way," Holly said again.

"Why did you really hire me? I mean, deep down, what inspired you, or motivated you to make that first call, to set up the session with me?"

This was uncomfortable.

"Well, because I—I need help with deciding what I want?"

"Is that a question, or your answer to my question?"

Suddenly, Holly wasn't feeling all that warm and fuzzy about this Tristan Compass.

"Um. I don't know. It's my answer? I need guidance in deciding what I want out of life."

"And is what you want out of life a slightly sandy, tan and muscular man and a small, fluffy white dog?"

Before she could answer, he said, "Holly. If I could wave a magic wand right now and give you a sandy, tan man and a white fluffy dog, would you feel completely fulfilled? Would you have every-thing you want in life?"

"No," Holly said. "But it would be a good start."

Tristan nodded, and pressed his lips together. Then he said, "I want you to recreate your Direction Board. I want you to think about the things that would make you truly fulfilled."

Holly felt like crying.

"I don't even know what those things are," she said, surprised at the force behind her voice. "That's why I hired you."

"Ah," Tristan said. "Now we're getting somewhere."

The rest of the session left Holly emotionally exhausted. So although it would have been reasonable to work on her new Direction Board, she worked on her outfit for the retirement party Sequoia was dragging her to, instead.

She went shopping. At her favorite shop, Ruffles Boutique, she compared skinny jeans to leggings, and boots to heels, all the while thinking about what had been plaguing her.

First of all, why did she always crave feedback?

As the youngest of the three Carr sisters, she'd always followed someone's lead. When Jasmine said she didn't like potatoes, Holly decided she didn't, either. When Sequoia said she loved Dr. Suess books, Holly decided she did, too. She always wore her sisters' hand-me-downs, so she never had to decide on outfits. Rarely did she have to come up with ideas; her sisters did that for her, and when they didn't, she didn't feel complete unless they offered a stamp of approval.

Now, here they were: adults. When her sisters built their own careers in professions that weren't especially appealing to Holly, Holly ended up just drifting along, by default.

Which brought her to the second thought that had been plaguing her: How the heck was she going to figure out what she really wanted?

Professionally, she wanted to help people. She wanted to make a difference in the world. That's why she'd always been drawn to personal training. But what exactly was it about personal training that had stopped her from completing her certification?

She pulled a turquoise tunic over her head. It contrasted with the cotton candy blue of her hair.

"Unacceptable," she said.

The white tunic looked much better with her hair, and paired nicely with the tribal print leggings she liked.

What would her sisters say about what she wanted out of life? She put that thought process on pause while she selected her shoes, ditching the boots and heels in favor of some ballet flats that felt like tennis shoes. She left it paused while she changed back into her clothes, paid, and drove home to change again. She didn't want to think about what her sisters would say, and besides, it didn't matter, did it? It mattered what *she* said. The only opinion that mattered was her own.

The doorbell rang, and Holly decided she'd come back to her life's purpose later. For now, she would just go out and have fun with the new, easygoing Sequoia.

"You look nice," her sister said when she answered the door. "You're always so good at picking outfits. You look sexy but comfortable. And strangely, your outfit actually looks good with your ridiculous hair color."

"Um, that's a weird thing for you to say," Holly said.

"About the hair color?"

"No. It's weird of you to give me a compliment."

Sequoia rolled her eyes. When Holly followed her to the car, Elijah gave her a long, low whistle through the driver's window. "Good looks run in this family. And good legs, too."

Holly smiled at him and got into the car.

"Did you tell her?" Elijah said to Sequoia.

Sequoia gave him a sharp look and Holly went on alert.

"Did she tell me what?" she said. When Sequoia didn't answer right away, Holly said, "Did you tell me what, Sequoia?"

"I don't know what he's talking about," Sequoia said. She turned up the music and sat back in her seat, but not without issuing one more disapproving look at Elijah, who grinned back apologetically. Holly didn't press Sequoia, but she decided she would corner Elijah at some point and interrogate him. For now, she sat back in her own seat and listened to the music.

Despite its vulgar name, Sticks and Balls was pretty swanky, for a pool hall. Black leather couches and chairs were grouped in dimly lit corners, and a half-dozen pool tables stood to one side, opposite a wooden dance floor. The long bar that ran along one entire side of the room was so shiny it mirrored the colored lights set into the ceiling. Holly perused the lineup of beverages behind the bar, impressed with the selection but sticking with a Shirley Temple. As she waited for the bartender to mix it, someone came up right behind her.

"I have to say, that outfit does way more for you than your waitress getup does."

She could feel his breath on her ear, and the deep, rumbly quality of his voice gave her the shivers. She turned around, already smiling, and felt her pulse quicken when her eyes confirmed what her body already knew: it was Mr. Bravo.

Sequoia, who stood on Holly's other side, waiting for her own drink—a club soda with lime—smiled and said, "Ah, the man of the hour. Holly, this is Mack, the guest of honor. Mack, this is my sister, Holly."

Holly found that she couldn't quite answer. Her body was thrumming from the feel of his breath on her ear. She could feel a strange expression taking shape on her face, something between a smile and the mask of a crazed maniac.

"We've met," Mr. Bravo said, his eyes boring into Holly's so intensely she thought she could hear her lady parts screaming in anticipation.

Holly tore her gaze away to look at Sequoia, whose eyes twinkled with amusement. Something strange was going on here, and Holly raised a questioning eyebrow at her sister. Of course, Sequoia shrugged a shoulder, gave her an uncharacteristic grin, and took a sip of the club soda the bartender had set down.

Mr. Bravo—or maybe she should start thinking of him as Mack—ordered a beer and Holly couldn't help but notice the way his arm muscles rippled when he reached over to take it. Then he faced Holly and put an elbow on the bar, like he meant to stay awhile.

"So," he said. "You do have a life outside the Broken Egg."

"I do," she said. "But only because my sister forced me to come out."

"You heard it was my retirement party and she had to force you to come out for it?"

Holly smiled. "Ha. Um, no. That's not what I meant. She said it was a retirement party for a co-worker but I didn't think it was you. I mean, she didn't say specifically who it was."

"You'd rather be home in your fuzzy bunny slippers, watching a movie and eating popcorn?"

"I don't even have bunny slippers," Holly said. "But yes."

Still staring at her, Mr. Bravo took a sip of his beer. "I'd like to see you in bunny slippers."

She looked down at her feet, and he said, "So if you'd known it was my retirement party, would Carr—I mean, Sequoia—have had to force you to come?"

"I wouldn't have come," Holly said. "I would be home in my bunny slippers eating popcorn, drinking wine, and watching soap operas."

"Why?"

Obviously, she wasn't going to tell him about the focus thing. But she could give him half the truth.

"Oh, I don't know. Probably because being around you is humiliating. I mean, how many classy women, at the age of thirty, get pulled over for DUI? It's mortifying. And I'm certain you wouldn't want any such woman at your retirement party. I see your face, and I'm embarrassed. You see my face, and you think I'm an idiot."

"Yeah, that *is* embarrassing," he said. Typically, Holly would say something sarcastic, or even playfully punch him on the arm, but she refrained, feeling uncertain of herself. At the moment, she couldn't think of anything to say. She shifted away from Mr. Bravo, hoping to bring Sequoia into the conversation, but her sister had disappeared.

"If I'm reading your body language correctly, and I think I am," Mack said, "you're looking for your sister to bail you out of this conversation. And now you're realizing she ditched us. I'm sorry to tell you, you're alone with me."

He had brought his hands up in front of him and was tapping his fingers together like he was the scheming villain in a horror film.

"Funny," Holly said. It took a conscious effort not to scan the pool hall for Sequoia, or at least for an escape route.

"Look," he said. "I don't think you're an idiot."

"That's not what your face says when you're sitting in my section at the Broken Egg."

"What?" Now he threw his head back and laughed. "You think my face says you're an idiot?"

"Yes! What else would it say?"

Mack took a deep breath. "It says I think you're beautiful and I'm terrified I'm going to make a fool of myself by getting egg on my chin or something."

Huh.

"Huh," she said. "Not what I thought you were thinking. Anyway. So, you're retiring?"

Mack sat down on a barstool and gestured for Holly to do the same. She did, and kept herself busy by examining the contents of her glass.

"I'm retiring," he said. "Off to new adventures and all that."

"Are you even old enough to retire?"

"I'm definitely not mature enough to retire, if that's what you mean," he said.

Holly took a moment to answer. It seemed strange that this guy, who couldn't be much older than she, was retiring from a full-length career, when she hadn't even started one, yet. Not a real one, anyway.

"That's not what I meant. I'm not even mature enough to start my first career."

"So the Broken Egg isn't your lifelong aspiration?"

Holly took a sip of her Shirley Temple. "No."

"What is?" he said.

Because she didn't want to admit that she had no idea, she tried the tactic she often used with her sisters: changing the subject.

"So what are you going to do with yourself now?" she asked.

He drained his beer and stepped off the stool. He extended his hand, palm up, to her.

"I'm going to dance with a beautiful woman."

Between relief that she'd worn the flats and anxiety about dancing with this intimidating, good-looking, law-enforcing man, Holly barely even noticed that a slow song was playing. But now that they were here, on the almost-empty dance floor, with a disco ball reflecting colored lights around them, she panicked.

Then Mack pulled her body against his, one hand on her lower back and the other taking her hand, and she stopped thinking of anything but the feel of his body against hers and the fresh pine scent of his skin as they swayed to the music. He'd called her beautiful, and now he was dancing with her like they were alone in a … in a *bedroom*, for goodness' sake! She fully expected him to strip off her clothes to the beat of this music. Suddenly, she found the situation amusing, which made her feel a bit less intimidated.

Sequoia and Elijah joined them on the dance floor, and she watched as Elijah whispered something in Sequoia's ear, and Sequoia smiled broadly before giving him a long, deep kiss.

"Never thought you'd see that, did you?" Mack said.

"Nope," Holly said. "And aren't you the mind reader? Sequoia, she's always been so …"

"So aloof?"

"Yes! How'd you know?"

"It was the word on the street," Mack said. "The word in the office, you know? But I always knew she had a good heart."

"She really does," Holly said. "Stony exterior, warm and squishy heart."

"I knew it the moment we started training with Xena."

"Oh, so you're the guy who helped her so much when she started in K-9 unit."

"She actually said that?" Mack said.

"Yeah, believe it or not," Holly said. "Actually, she said that you first humiliated her by making that damn dog follow her around the office. And then when you gave her a list of commands, she thought you'd made up some of them to make her look stupid. Wasn't one of them, like, 'Fooey,' or something?"

"Yeah," he said, his voice filled with merriment. "It is. Why would she think I'd make it up?"

"We asked her that—our other sister, Jasmine, and I," Holly said. She went into her best Sequoia impression: "Because. He got such a huge kick out of embarrassing me before. Why wouldn't he do it again?"

"Wow," Mack said. "I never would have guessed."

"She hates being a spectacle," Holly said.

They watched Elijah spin Sequoia under his arm, and then lay her back in a dip, and Holly shook her head.

"I admit, I thought I'd see her as a K-9 police officer even less than I thought I'd see her in love. But the transformation has been really cool to watch."

The slow song ended and something with a heavy beat and lots of electric guitar filled the room. Holly was surprised to notice that she felt a little disappointed that the dance was over. She wasn't surprised, however, to notice that she also felt awkward about what to do next.

"I'm guessing you don't want to headbang with me," Mack said.

"Not in front of all these people, anyway," Holly said. "Maybe sometime when we're alone. We can crank it up and rock out."

She realized too late that she'd just implied they'd be alone together in the near future, and had to resist the urge to slap a hand over her mouth.

Fortunately, Mack didn't seem to notice. "Want to grab another drink?" he said.

He led her off the dance floor toward the bar.

"Actually," Holly said, "I could use some water. I rarely drink soda. All that sugar makes me thirsty."

"Oh, you're probably taking it easy on the alcohol, right? After the other night?"

Holly froze. Why did he have to remind her about The Incident? And what was she thinking, dancing with this guy and enjoying his company? He'd never be able to see past the drunk driver he'd first met. His eyes twinkled with humor, even as a hollow feeling took shape in her chest.

They were now standing at one end of the bar, where a self-serve water station sat on a table. Before Holly could respond, Mack turned away and busied himself filling her a small plastic cup. He winked when he handed it to her, and she managed a small smile.

"Let's walk," he said.

She followed him around the dance floor, which was now mostly empty again, to a low black couch in the corner. He gestured for her to sit, and she did, despite the fact that she now wanted to go home and spend the evening alone. She really needed to get that fluffy puppy.

Mack sat next to her. She sipped her water and pretended to be very interested in the pattern on the dance floor.

"What just happened?" he said.

She feigned ignorance, raising her eyebrows. "What do you mean?"

"I mean, you just shut down. I can see it as clearly as I can see how you're pretending to be fascinated by the floor. It was the drinking comment, wasn't it?"

Holly sighed. Why was she so readable? Or, perhaps the better question was, why was he so good at reading her? Maybe it was what Sequoia always said about herself, after years of working as a police officer: "Observer of human behavior, and all that."

"I don't know what happened," Holly lied.

"It was the drinking comment." Mack leaned forward and put his drink on the table and his elbows on his knees. He looked at her, his expression serious now. "It was a joke, Holly. A bad one, maybe, but a joke. I promise, I'm not going to judge you on that one incident. I mean, I've seen way worse."

Now Holly set her water cup on the table, and was preparing to stand when Mack laid a hand on her arm.

"Oh, boy. I'm just digging myself even deeper, aren't I?"

Exasperated now, both with herself and with Mack, but also amused, Holly felt the first stirrings of a smile. "Yeah. That didn't actually make me feel better."

He shook his head. "Can we start over at the part where I was dancing with a beautiful woman?"

Maybe a trip to the bathroom would act like a reset button. Holly excused herself, and Sequoia must have been watching her, because she followed Holly into the restroom and right into the stall, where she leaned against the door just like she had when they were kids.

"Is there no privacy now, even though we're in our thirties?" Holly said.

Sequoia, glowing with the radiance only new love can produce, just smiled. "How's it going with Mack?"

Holly rolled her eyes. "Fine. How's it going with Elijah? Things are looking pretty cozy there."

"Oh, things are really cozy," Sequoia said. "Look, we're getting ready to go. Want a ride home? Or do you think you might, you know, catch a ride with someone else?"

She wiggled her eyebrows in a move that was so uncharacteristic, Holly had no choice but to laugh.

Keeping it light, she said to her sister, "Sure, let's go. I can drive if you want. I can tell you're, um, eager to get back. I'll drop you guys off at Elijah's and drive myself home. You can pick up your car tomorrow."

"Wow, you've been having so much fun that you're sober enough to drive, huh?" Sequoia said. "We have problems, my sister."

When Holly squeezed past Sequoia to wash her hands, Sequoia followed her to the sink and propped one hip on the counter.

"Holly, you can stay if you want," she said. "It seems like the party's just getting started."

Holly could stay. She could catch a cab home. But spending more time with Mack would only intensify the heartbreak when he never spoke to her again.

"Nah. Let's go."

She tossed her paper towels in the trash can and together, the girls walked back into the pool hall. Mack was sitting at the bar again, surrounded by a bunch of chanting guys with shot glasses raised. He held his own shot glass up, and as Holly walked past, she could have sworn he lifted it just the tiniest bit as he made eye contact, almost like he was toasting her.

Sequoia saw it, too, because she elbowed Holly in the side, hard enough to make her yelp, and whisper-yelled, "You should stay."

Holly shook her head, raised one eyebrow at Mack, and watched him toss the shot back before his friends enveloped him in cheers and back slaps and calls for another round.

As she'd promised she would, she drove Sequoia and Elijah to Elijah's house, then drove back to her own empty house, where she poured herself some sparkling water, changed into sweatpants, and sat on the couch in her silent living room, dancing with Mack in her imagination. She'd allow herself this one night of thinking about him, and then she'd erase him and his delicious smell from her consciousness.

CHAPTER SIX

ALL THAT DANCING BROKE HOLLY'S FOCUS.

Every time the door opened at the Broken Egg the next morning, she looked up, hoping Mack was walking through it. But he wasn't. Every time her mind had a spare moment to think—between taking orders, pouring coffee, and delivering plates of whole wheat pancakes and scrambled eggs to customers—she wondered why he wasn't there.

After last night, half of her had expected him to at least make an appearance. The other half figured she'd probably never see him again. Last night, after having a real, actual conversation with her, he'd probably decided she wasn't for him. He'd spent the evening with her only out of pity.

How else could she explain why he hadn't shown up at the restaurant this morning, even for a hot black coffee, after having been here for every one of Holly's recent shifts? Holly's memory kept replaying the night before: Mack's arm wrapped around her waist as they swayed to that slow song, his hand on her arm after he'd made a joke, his eyes meeting hers as they laughed.

"Who are you waiting for?" Jaclyn Connelly asked, her voice bringing Holly back to the Broken Egg's dining room. "Wait. Don't tell me. It's that dapper young man who's been stalking you like a tiger watches its prey."

"Aw, Jackie," Phil said. "Give the kid a break. She's just waiting for her next customer. Right, Holly?"

Holly winked at Phil and said to Jaclyn, "Yeah. He's been here every shift. He's becoming almost as much a fixture as you two. I keep expecting him to walk in."

"He will, honey," Jaclyn said. "He has the hots for you."

"Well, since we're still talking about this," Phil said, "I'll just say I agree with my wife's assessment. That young man definitely has an interest."

Phil wiggled his eyebrows up and down (much like Sequoia had the night before), and Jaclyn slapped him on the arm.

It was time for her break, so after refilling the Connellys' coffees, Holly poured herself a mug and carried it through the kitchen and into the alley behind the restaurant.

The fact that Mack's absence was having such a profound effect on her was proof that she couldn't get involved with him, she thought as she inhaled the cool, fresh air. She'd thought more about him in the past couple of hours than she'd thought about herself and what she wanted.

Just as she sat down on the concrete bench that looked directly into the storage room of the flower shop next door, her phone quacked, signaling a text from Sequoia. She'd searched for a ringtone that sounded like a chicken squawking, since Sequoia was such a mother hen, but hadn't been able to find one. A quack was the next best thing.

The message read: *So, how did the rest of your night go?*

This made Holly suspicious. Why was Sequoia asking about her night? Sequoia never asked about her night.

Holly responded: *Fine. Why?*

Sequoia's answer came in right away: *Just wondered. Anything happen?*

Holly decided to leave her hanging. No, nothing had happened … nothing noteworthy, anyway. Holly had spent her evening with a handsome, funny guy with whom nothing else could or would ever happen. What was there to say about it? She dropped her phone into her apron pocket and went back inside, cutting her break short.

Jaclyn and Phil had left her a twenty-dollar bill, with a note, in Jaclyn's handwriting, on the receipt: *Take your admirer out for a drink on us.*

Holly smiled and made the rounds, refilling coffees and clearing dishes. The remainder of her shift ticked slowly by, and Holly continued to half-expect Mack to walk in. When it became clear that the prospect of seeing him had decreased to nil, Holly resigned herself to settling for that one good night with him, and to the fact that she felt disappointment creeping in. She hung up her apron and went out to her car.

Just as she buckled her seatbelt, she received another text from Sequoia.

You never answered me. How was the rest of your evening?

Holly responded: *Sorry. Just got off work. I went home after I dropped you off, like I said.*

Sequoia responded, again, way more quickly than usual: *I thought you might do something else. You know. With someone else.*

Holly texted: *This is weird.*

Sequoia didn't answer; at least, not right away, and Holly pulled away from the curb, ready to face another evening alone. Just then, her phone rang. She expected it to be Sequoia, calling to interrogate her about last night. But when she looked at the screen, she saw a number she didn't recognize.

She did, however, recognize the very sultry, extra-gritty voice that responded when she answered. It said, "Holly. So nice to hear your voice," and it most definitely belonged to Mack.

Her first reaction would have been to blurt out, "I thought you'd come in today!" or "Where were you?" but instead, she managed to stammer, "M-Mack! Oh, um, hi."

She pulled her car away from the curb. Had she given him her number? She didn't think so, but maybe she had. Maybe, twitter-pated and overcome by girlish feelings of excitement after spending the evening with a sexy man, she'd written her number on a bar napkin and tucked it into his pants pocket as if she were still in her twenties. She had been known to do that on occasion. And so what if, on occasion, she'd changed her name spelling to Holli so she could dot the i with a heart?

Asking how Mack had gotten her phone number would be rude. And it would also reveal that she didn't remember, which would only make her come across as a ditz as well as a drunk driver.

The traffic signal at the corner of Beach Street and Pacific Avenue turned red. Holly stopped, and watched a thin, fashionable young woman cross the street with a short, fat pug. The juxtaposition was humorous, and Holly wondered whether she, too, should get a pug, or maybe a bulldog.

"Hi," Mack said, suddenly sounding uncertain of himself. He cleared his throat. "Sorry. I'm not good at these romantic shenanigans."

Was Mack calling their interactions, "romantic shenanigans"? Were *these* romantic shenanigans? The girl and the pug had stopped just after crossing the street. It looked like they were waiting to meet someone: the girl kept glancing down Pacific Avenue and then trying to look nonchalant. She was wearing a knee-length skirt and a tank top, and big silver earrings. Her hair was up in a messy bun, which had likely taken her a long time to master. It was a first date outfit, right down to the light shade of lipstick. First date outfits made Holly think about first dates. More specifically, about how first dates were always so awkward. What to wear, whether to hug, whether to kiss, whether to say something lame like, "We should do this again." There was no way she was going on a first date with Mack.

"It's okay," Holly said. The light turned green. "How are you?"

Holly took her foot off the brake pedal, keeping an eye on the girl with the pug so she could see her greet whoever she was waiting for. But he didn't show up, even as Holly watched in her rearview mirror. The girl stood there anxiously, smoothing her skirt, adjusting the wisps of hair hanging down around her face, and stooping every so often to pet the pug. Would Holly bring her fluffy white puppy on a date? Probably not.

"I'm fine, thank you," Mack said. "How are you?"

Instead of asking why he hadn't come into the Broken Egg, she said, "I'm fine. Just got off work."

"I guess you noticed I didn't come in today."

She thought, *I sure did*, but she shrugged, hoping to show some apathy. Then she remembered that he couldn't see her shrugging. "It was busy," she said.

"So you didn't notice," he said.

She could hear the humor in his voice, and she wasn't sure how to take it. If he was anything like Sequoia, he was reading more into her answers than she was putting out there.

"I'm a bit under the weather today," he said. "Actually, that's a euphemism. I'm completely, totally hungover. Last night was fun, but this morning is brutal. The guys kept buying me shots, hollering for more rounds. I'm pretty sure they poured me into the backseat to get me home. I'm too old for this stuff."

"Speaking of that," Holly said, "You're barely old enough to retire!"

"Don't make me laugh! I've got a killer headache."

"I hope one of your so-called buddies is bringing you a hangover remedy."

"What is this magic you speak of?" he said.

"You know, hot coffee, something greasy, three aspirin."

"I sincerely doubt it. They're all hiding under the covers today, like I am."

Holly sighed. Even though she knew this thing between them shouldn't go anywhere, should never amount to anything other than their being acquaintances—*focus, Holly!*—she said, "Give me your address."

He did, and she recognized the street name as being on the rural side of Seabreeze. It was only a ten-minute drive, but it felt like a whole different world.

"I'll see you in fifteen minutes."

Just one street up, on Front Street, there were several fast food restaurants. She pulled into the drive-through of the nearest one, which had a "Breakfast served all day!" sign, and ordered a breakfast sandwich with hash browns and a coffee. She paid with the twenty-dollar bill Jaclyn had given her, figuring that buying Mack a hang-over remedy was even better than buying him a drink.

Then she drove to his house. She'd just drop off the food and leave. She'd already decided she wouldn't—couldn't—date him. Because she was ultra-focused on her own transformation. She was just doing this as a friend. An acquaintance.

His little cottage was much cuter than she'd expected. It was painted light blue with white trim, and colorful flowers bordered a tidy lawn in the front yard, which was ringed with a picket fence. There was even a wreath on the front door.

A fenced corral stood behind the house, and the yard opened into fields behind that. Horses grazed there, and one of them lifted its head briefly to look at her as she got out of the car.

Mack opened the door before she even knocked.

"Wow," she said. "You look terrible."

Even though he did look terrible—pale and puffy-faced like someone who had indulged far beyond reason within the past twenty-four hours—he was still so, so sexy. He wore a white t-shirt, which showed off the curves of his muscles, and thin gray pajama pants that showed off—this line of thought would never do. Holly thrust the bag of food and the coffee cup towards him, and he smiled.

"Thank you," he said. "For the compliment and the hangover remedy. Would you like to come in?"

"Oh, no," she said. She shook her head, and realized she was probably shaking it a bit too fast. "No, thank you. Anyway, thank my regular, Jaclyn. She gave me twenty bucks to take you for drinks. I used it to buy you a hangover remedy. Anyway. I just, you know, got off work. So I'm heading home to shower."

Something flashed in his eyes, but he shook his head as if to get rid of a thought, and said, "Okay. Don't say I didn't offer to share my breakfast with you."

"You know it's three in the afternoon, right?"

"Oh," he said. "Right. I guess I did know that."

She nodded and twisted her fingers together. "Well, I guess I'll see you around. Oh, and here's aspirin."

She handed it to him and turned to walk to her car.

"Wait," he said. "Why did Jaclyn want you to take me for drinks?"

"She thinks you like me." Holly turned to leave, again.

"Wait," Mack said, again. "I never got to tell you why I called earlier."

"Oh," Holly said. "I thought it was to tell me why you didn't come in this morning."

He looked down now, as if he'd lost his confidence.

"I wanted to see if you wanted to, you know, go out sometime. Officially. Maybe dinner?"

Was this really happening? Was he asking her out?

"Um," she said. She'd just decided she wasn't going to date him or anyone else. She thought of the girl with the pug and the messy bun and the first date outfit, and how all that anticipation often led to disappointment.

"I can't," she said. And then, because she felt like she had to give him a good reason for saying no, she added, "I'm seeing someone."

Then she turned around and marched to her car without looking back—until she turned the car around and put her foot on the gas. Then, she couldn't stop glancing in her rearview mirror. Wait, *what?* Why had she *said* that?

Her phone rang before she made it home. Holly jumped. She figured it was Mack, calling her bluff, and didn't bother looking at the screen. Instead, she set the phone on the passenger seat and kept driving. It rang again. She groaned and picked it up this time, and jumped again when she saw that it was Sequoia, not Mack.

"Great."

She answered with a, "Yes?" and Sequoia said, "Geez. Nice greeting for your loving sister who is trying to set you up with a very good-looking, very nice man. Which you are sabotaging, by the way. What do you *mean* you're seeing someone? You're not seeing someone at all."

"Wait. He called you? I left Mack's house five minutes ago and he already called you? This is weird."

"Don't get defensive," Sequoia said. "He'd just asked me, last night, if you were single. And I said yes. So now he feels foolish. Anyway, I'm the one who should be mad at you. Now I look like an idiot. Also, you're lying. You're not seeing anyone."

"How do *you* know, Sequoia?"

At this, Sequoia chuckled, the sound less amused than Holly would have liked.

"How do I *know*, Holly? Because I know. If you were seeing someone you would have said so when we were talking about your date for Jasmine's wedding. You would never have agreed to come to that party with me last night. And because if you were seeing someone you'd actually be seeing someone. Not sitting home alone every night watching TV."

"How you know I—never mind," Holly said.

She stopped at the same red light where she'd seen the first-date girl and her pug, and decided maybe she should get a dog. Like, today. She had a few days off, and she could spend those days training her new puppy.

"Anyway, first of all," Sequoia said. "I don't know why you're shying away from Mack. He's a perfectly nice guy. And second of all, I don't know why you're lying. That's so *weird*. I mean, couldn't you just tell him you're not interested in dating anyone right now? Or that you're interested in your new, ultra-feminine life coach, what was his name? Crystal?"

"Tristan," Holly said.

"Right. Why are you lying?"

Sequoia had always been honest to a fault. As a teenager, if she criticized one of her sisters, which happened frequently, she'd say, "I'm just being honest. Honesty's a virtue, okay?"

So it only made sense that Holly's little white lie was rubbing her the wrong way. But Holly wanted—no, *needed*—to give herself this space. And unless she created parameters even Sequoia couldn't argue with, she'd never get it. Sequoia could multi-task like a ninja. She'd never understand that Holly couldn't date and focus on herself simultaneously.

And on another note, Holly knew there was no way a cop—even a retired one—would be able to successfully date a woman he'd pulled over for drunk driving. But Sequoia would probably disagree. She'd say Holly's insecurity was taking over.

Holly knew she had to put an end to this, so she made another quick decision—one she thought could fix everything. Potentially. She lied to Sequoia, too.

"I'm not lying, okay, Sequoia? I *am* seeing someone. I just haven't had a chance to tell you about it—I mean, him—yet."

Sequoia shook her head. "Okay, Holly. You go ahead and tell yourself whatever you have to. But I know you're lying."

"I'm not," Holly said. "And I appreciate your interest. But I've got to go. Just got home."

"Fine," Sequoia said. "Bye."

Holly pulled into her driveway, and was surprised to find that her hands were shaking. She was already questioning her decision.

"Why?" she wailed into the empty car. "Why did I have to lie to her, too? Stupid, stupid, stupid."

CHAPTER SEVEN

IT HAD TO BE DONE. IT WAS TIME FOR HOLLY TO INVENT HER NEW boyfriend.

What should she fabricate first? A name seemed like a good place to start. This would be entertaining, actually. His name had to be common enough to seem realistic but unusual enough to sound as if she wasn't making him up. It couldn't be John or Mike or Dave, she thought as she locked the front door behind her and went to take a shower.

He should be Latin. Latin men had good manners and they were great in bed … at least, that was the word on the street. She took off her shoes.

Santiago was a nice Latin name. Or maybe Jaime. What about Alejo?

"Ooh," Holly said. "Alejo. Yes, that sounds very sexy. Alejo Castillo."

Name in place, she had to come up with a physical description. Body type? Muscular, obviously. Hair color? Dark. Very dark. Eyes? Dark, as well. He'd be tall. Taller than her, of course. Even when she wore heels.

Holly started the hot water.

So what if her fake boyfriend was starting to look a bit like Mack?

She'd never said she didn't find Mack attractive. Maybe even Very Attractive. And so what if she found herself fantasizing that Mack was here now, helping her out of her work jeans and the ugly bra she'd dug out of her hamper this morning?

"This will never do," she said, tossing the bra in the trash.

If she was getting a new boyfriend, even a fake one, she was going to have to go underwear shopping. Neither Alejo nor Mack would find her very sexy in these stretched-out granny panties.

She stepped into the shower and sighed as she imagined Mack stepping in behind her. Yes, she'd have to make do with Alejo for now. But a girl could fantasize about someone else, couldn't she? Alejo would never know she was imagining Mack's hands sliding up her bare torso as he pressed her against the shower wall, then gripping her hips and taking her from behind.

"It'll be our little secret, Mack," she whispered.

This was going to be fun. Or stupid. It could either give her the space she needed, or it could ruin her life.

***

HOLLY SHOULD NOT HAVE BEEN surprised when Mack showed up at the Broken Egg the next morning, bright-eyed and refreshed, probably thanks to the hangover remedy she'd brought him the day before.

She should be annoyed, she told herself as she poured his black coffee without waiting for him to order. Why would he show up here the day after she told him she was seeing someone? Was he stalking her, like a tiger stalks its prey, as Jaclyn had said? Was he a glutton for punishment? Or did he just like the meat lover's scramble?

Yes, she should be annoyed.

But she was delighted … and a little disappointed Jaclyn and Phil weren't here to see Mack's return.

Even so, she planned to remain strictly professional when it came to service and conversation. "The usual?" she said when she saw that his menu was folded and set to the side of his table.

"No," he said. "Not today. I think I'll try the banana nut pancakes. Have you had them?"

"Yeah, I've had them, but they're not very meaty."

Was that too much? Was it weird to say, "meaty" to a man with whom you'd danced? Who you fantasized about in the shower?

He gave her a grin that bordered on wicked, and she felt herself blushing. Her first inclination was to fan herself with her notepad, so she froze in place. His smug expression made it look almost like he knew what she was thinking. He said, "You're right. Let's go with meaty. I'll get the meat lover's scramble. Side of bacon."

"Heart attack waiting to happen," she said. She snapped her notebook closed, picked up his menu, and spun on her heel. When she sneaked a glance at him after putting in his order, she saw that he was watching her. And he was smiling.

When she topped off his coffee, he said, "So what's his name?"

At first, Holly glanced around the restaurant, looking for whoever Mack was talking about. Then she realized he was referring to the guy she was supposed to be dating. The one she'd fabricated. She jumped, then looked at Mack quickly to see if he'd noticed.

He had.

For the briefest of moments, she found herself casting around the recesses of her memory to find the name she'd given the poor, imaginary fellow she'd be dating for eternity. "Alejo." That was it.

"Alejo what?" Mack said, not missing a beat.

"Why do you want to know?" Holly said.

"Just curious, that's all," Mack said.

"I'd rather not say. I mean, I want to protect his privacy."

Mental forehead slap. "Protect his privacy"? Who says that?

"Huh."

Holly walked away. Then, when she delivered his scramble, he said, "What does he do?"

Well, he's great in bed. His oral sex skills are incredible.

Is that what Mack wanted to know?

"You mean, for a living?"

"Yeah," Mack said. "For a living. What is this *Alejo's* job?"

Holly didn't like this. It felt like Mack was testing her.

"I'd rather not say," Holly said, again.

"Why? Is he into drugs or something? Money laundering?"

Now Mack's eyes twinkled with mischief.

"He's in finance, okay?" she said, setting his ketchup down with a *thunk*. "I don't even know how to explain what he does. The whole field is kind of mysterious to me."

"Hmm. Sounds like a pretty dry profession," Mack said. "Boring."

Holly dug a stack of napkins out of her apron and set them on the table.

"Anything else I can get you?"

"Nah. That'll do it for now."

Normally, she checked on her customers frequently, but she left Mack alone, except to refill his coffee. At one point, though, he gave her a little wave when she glanced in his direction, and she was forced to return to his table.

"Can I get my check, please?" he said.

"Of course," she said, her voice and her smile syrupy sweet. "I'd be happy to get you and your interrogation skills out the door."

She pulled his check out of her notebook.

"Speaking of that," he said, just as she turned around.

Holly could have pretended not to hear him, but she thought that would be too obvious, so she stopped and made a half-turn so she wasn't quite facing him. He was holding his card out for her to take.

"Yes?" she said, taking the card.

"This Alejo," Mack said. "Is he as good-looking as I am?"

Holly couldn't help it. She kept remembering how she'd thought Alejo was turning out to look almost exactly like Mack. Walking back to the cash register to run his credit card, she found herself laughing.

IT WAS time for another coaching session with Tristan Compass. Holly's pride still stung from the last one, when he'd said her Direction Board lacked vision and depth. Actually, he'd said it was lame.

Yes, she'd revamped the thing, and now, alongside the picture of the couple on the beach, it included an image of a single woman—who Holly thought represented herself—striding through some kind of park, looking purposeful.

Holly imagined how she'd explain this image to Tristan: "I mean, doesn't she look purposeful? See, the thing is, I don't know exactly what my purpose is. But I know that it's my vision to have a purpose. At least I'm clear on that, right?"

In addition to the purposeful, striding woman, Holly had added an image of a woman running. She really did need to get more exercise. Also, she'd found a few appropriate words and phrases in magazines: "Happy," "Voyage to Discover," and "Create Memories." The sandy beach couple and the puppy were still there, too, but they didn't take up as much real estate as they had before. And of course, there was the central theme: *FOCUS*, in big white letters she'd drawn and cut out of printer paper.

While looking through magazines for this assignment, Holly realized that she hadn't really striven to be happy recently. It wasn't like she was *unhappy*, but she definitely had not made any effort to find or do things that truly filled her with joy. Again, she didn't know what those things were—she was sensing a disappointing theme, here—but she was certain she could discover them.

After a quick post-work shower and outfit change, Holly set up her computer at the kitchen bar. She double-checked her mascara in the computer screen just before Tristan's face came up. Her stomach fluttered and she realized it was because she was worried about what he'd think of her Direction Board.

"Hi there," he said. "Let's see your board."

So. He was cutting right to the chase. She lifted up the board and her stomach fluttered even more aggressively.

"Focus," Tristan read. "What does that mean to you, Holly?"

Holly shifted in her seat.

"Um," she said. She wasn't pausing because she didn't know. She was pausing because she felt self-conscious putting it into words. There was no one here whose words she could copy, and that felt weird.

Tristan raised his eyebrows.

"It means I wake up each day knowing exactly what I'm going to do to move towards my goal, and actually doing it. It means sticking to a plan of action, moving towards that goal, steadily. Consistently."

She nodded.

He nodded, too.

"And what does 'happy' mean to you?"

Relieved, because Tristan asking another question must mean her answer to the first one passed some kind of test, she said, "It means looking forward to each day." Then she decided that sounded stupid. She tried again: "It means I actually feel joy rather than just, you know, a baseline. I want to be excited. About work, about my personal life, about coming home to my house. Whatever."

As she continued to speak, she recognized the truth in what she was saying. More importantly, she recognized a tiny spark of that excitement, and she attributed it to the fact that maybe this introspection would pay off. Tristan had perked up. His gaze had sharpened, and he had stopped moving around in the little square on her screen.

Encouraged, she went on: "I mean, I feel like I'm just realizing this now, but I am bored. I'm bored silly. Working at the Broken Egg? It's fine. I'm good at it. But I don't love it. This house? It's fine. But I don't love it. This life? I'm glad to be alive, but I'm bored. I'm just so *bored*!"

Suddenly, her voice had become loud and intense. It had gone from timid to passionate, and on her computer screen, Tristan was nodding, looking quite satisfied. Holly stopped to catch her breath.

"This is truth, Holly," Tristan said. "This is your inner voice talking. This is your inner wisdom."

"My inner wisdom is telling me it's time for a change," she said. "But the problem is that I don't know what it is. That's why I put 'Voyage to Discover' on my Direction Board. I know I want to be excited. I know I want to be stimulated. I guess that's what 'happy' means to me. The problem is, I'm just not sure how to get there. What will make me excited? I don't know."

The glee she'd felt just a moment ago began to dissipate as quickly as it had built up.

"This is great," Tristan said from his spot atop her kitchen counter.

"It's not great," she said. "It would be great if I knew what would bring me that joy."

"You're right," he said. "But you know what is great? That you are ready to discover what will make you excited. *That* is great. I'm delighted, actually. It's great that you realize you're bored. You want to be stimulated. Now we just have to figure out what that looks like for you."

Unbidden, an image of Mack came to the forefront of her mind. And not just any image, but an image of him, naked, on top of her. That would be pretty stimulating. She bit her lip.

"Everything okay?" Tristan said.

"Great," Holly squeaked. "Everything's great."

Tristan spent the next forty-five minutes asking Holly so many questions her head started to spin. What did she enjoy doing? What came naturally to her? Did she usually make decisions on her own, or seek advice?

Then he brought up romance. Of course he did.

"What about your love life, Holly?" he said.

She shrugged. "Nonexistent, I guess."

Then she thought about Alejo, and decided not to mention him. He was nonexistent, wasn't he? Except as a figment of her imagination?

"Is it important to you?" Tristan asked. "I noticed it was the biggest image on your original Direction Board, and you didn't remove it when you revamped."

"It is," Holly said. "I mean, I want to enjoy a life partner. I want to meet my soulmate. I want to experience those big moments with someone else. So, yes, it's important to me."

Tristan nodded, his expression thoughtful. "Okay. That makes sense. So I think the first thing you need to do is identify what is going to make you happy. This is before you become romantically involved with someone. Or are you romantically involved? You didn't say, but I was deducing from your people-on-the-beach image that you are not involved with someone you consider a long-term partner, and that you'd like to be."

Holly nodded, but didn't speak.

"Well?" Tristan said.

"I—uh, no, I'm not involved with anyone."

"I've been doing this a long time," Tristan said, "and I can tell when someone isn't giving me the whole truth. What's going on here?"

Had he really been doing this a long time? He couldn't be much older than twenty-five. Unless he'd had some plastic surgery.

"I need one hundred percent honesty," Tristan said. "Not because I'm nosy but because that's the only way this is going to work. Consider me your second inner voice. If you don't tell me what's going on, then I can't ask you the most powerful possible questions. Because remember, Holly, this is all about finding your own answers. So what's going on here? I want you to ask yourself why you don't want to tell me."

Holly sighed.

Why didn't she want to tell Tristan she'd made up a fake boyfriend to avoid dating a man she found really, really attractive?

Because she'd sound like an idiot, that's why.

"The fact that you don't want to talk about it should be a tip-off," Tristan said. "It should make you aware that your behavior doesn't align with your values."

Still, Holly couldn't bring herself to tell him. She remained silent, staring into the webcam.

"It's okay," Tristan said. "We'll talk about this eventually. For now, though, I want you to think about all the questions I asked you today. Think about them, and listen for the answers. Listen to your inner voice and let it guide you. Okay?"

Holly nodded. "Okay. I can do that."

The hour was up, and Holly prepared to disconnect.

"Before we go," Tristan said, "I want to give you a new assignment. Like I said, think about the questions I asked you, and listen for the answers. In addition to that, I want you to go out on a date."

"A date?" Holly said. It seemed weird for Tristan, a life coach, to be making recommendations on her love life.

"Yeah, a date," he said. The ultra-casual tone of his voice seemed suspicious. "I want you to take yourself on a date."

"Take myself on a date?"

If her sisters were here, they'd be making fun of her right now, for repeating what Tristan said in question form.

"Yes," he said, drawing the word out slowly as if he were explaining a new concept to a toddler. "I want you to take yourself out to dinner, for sure. And maybe a movie."

"Can't I just cook for myself and watch a rental at home?"

"Um, no," Tristan said. "That's not the same thing."

Holly imagined herself out at a restaurant, somewhere like Clouds Downtown, sitting alone at a table for two. It seemed desperate and humiliating. She'd pull out her own chair, sit down in silence, and stare at the cleverly-folded cloth napkin on the place setting across from her.

Or maybe the hostess would take pity on her and remove the extra place setting.

Either way, this did not sound like fun. "What is the point of this, this *exercise*?"

"The point, Holly," Tristan said (and she thought she detected a hint of irritation in his voice), "is that you need to spend some time with yourself. Spend some time getting to know yourself as you would someone you're dating. Spend some time asking those get-to-know-you questions."

"Can't I do that at home?"

"Nope," he said, and his tone had morphed to gleeful, which Holly found annoying. "You can't. At home, you have all the distractions of chores, the same old environment, the same old routines. You've got to switch things up, my dear, to get different results."

"I'm terrified," she said.

"I know," Tristan said. "It sounds weird, doesn't it? But I have a feeling you'll enjoy it more than you think."

Before she could answer, he continued. "I want you to clear your schedule tomorrow evening. And I'm going to schedule a quick email check-in for tomorrow night, okay?" He was already typing something into his computer—probably an automated email. "I'll send you an email around seven, and I'll expect a response around, say, nine p.m.?"

"I have plans tomorrow," Holly lied.

"Do not," Tristan said. "Call and make a reservation."

CHAPTER EIGHT

What did a girl wear on a date with herself?

This called for an emergency shopping trip. If she wasn't careful, she was going to end up spending a month's worth of tips on new clothes.

Twenty-four hours after meeting with Tristan, Holly stood outside the mall, Cara beside her.

"I think you're just using this as an excuse to shop," Cara said.

Holly smiled. "You might be right. I mean, I'm pretty easy to impress, so it's not strictly necessary for me to dress up. But the thing is, I want an outfit that doesn't scream, 'Desperate Lunatic.'"

"Holly," Cara said. "I'm sure nothing you own fits that description."

"Who am I kidding?" Holly said. "Showing up to eat alone at a nice restaurant screams, 'Desperate Lunatic' no matter what you're wearing. I need new bras, anyway."

Cara slipped her arm through Holly's.

"Come on," she said. "Stop wallowing. Let's go buy you something nice. We can make this enjoyable."

Cara was right. Holly could—and should—enjoy this. How often did she get to go on a date without worrying about what someone else thought of her outfit?

The two of them stormed store after store, putting together outfit after outfit, exploring combinations of sweaters and jeans, skirts and blouses, leggings and dresses. Cara presented Holly with some heavy black boots, and Holly selected a pair of soft hunter boots, instead.

By the time they were done, Holly was energized—and surprisingly, looking forward to her date. Cara followed her home and when Holly emerged from the bedroom, dressed in a pair of fleece-lined black leggings and a creamsicle-orange tunic that perfectly complemented the shade of her hair, she turned in a slow circle. Cara clapped her hands together.

"Your date is going to think you look awesome," she said. "And I love how you added that big necklace. That's a really nice touch."

Just before leaving, Holly looked at her reflection in the mirror and nodded. She was pretty easy on the eyes, if she did say so, herself. Lifting her chin just a bit higher, she walked out the door to her car.

SEABREEZE CAFÉ WASN'T the swankiest joint in town, but it was among the top five, to be sure. With wide windows overlooking the Pacific Ocean, the restaurant featured a view to die for and an even better seafood spread. Despite the linen napkins and fresh flowers on the table, the atmosphere was relaxed enough that a lone diner wouldn't draw too much attention.

Still, the hostess gave Holly a once-over, from the top of her head to her new hunter boots, and said, "Just one?" when she gave her the name for the reservation.

"Yep!" Holly said, her voice overly bright.

The hostess raised one eyebrow, grabbed a menu, and led her to a table next to the window. Holly chose the seat facing away from the main dining room so she wouldn't have to watch anyone notice that she was alone.

"Great view!" she said. "This is beautiful. Fantastic."

She never said, "Fantastic."

Holly sighed, ordered a water and an iced tea, and sat there for a moment, looking past the extra place setting and out at the sun, which was sinking closer to the horizon. It really was beautiful. Everything was turning a soft shade of purplish-pink, and Holly felt an unusual sense of calm. She'd have to remember to tell Tristan that perhaps this whole dating solo thing was a good idea.

So. Maybe she should follow Tristan's advice and get to know herself.

"Hi, Holly," she said. "I'm Holly. Nice to meet you."

Tristan had recommended that she ask herself some of those get-to-know-you questions you'd ask a date.

"Ever been here before?" Holly asked herself, her voice barely audible.

"Yes, lots," she said.

"What do you usually order?"

"I always go for the fish tacos. But you know what, Holly?"

"What, Holly?"

"I'm going to change things up tonight."

This was absurd. Holly chuckled, and stifled it by wiping her mouth with her napkin. Maybe it would be better to have this conversation in her mind.

Tristan had asked her was why she wasn't being honest with him about her love life. The answer was simple: admitting to anyone, especially a stranger, that she'd made up a fake boyfriend was humiliating.

Which led to the next question: why had she done it? Why had she fabricated a boyfriend instead of standing proudly in her new commitment to focus on herself?

This was a disaster.

"What would you like?" The server cut off her thought process.

The Jaws of Life, Holly thought, *to remove my giant foot from my mouth*, but she said, "The seafood platter, please. With mashed potatoes."

"No one else is joining you tonight?"

"Nope," Holly said. "No one."

The server pursed her lips, something Holly told herself she'd never do to a customer who was eating alone. She cleared that extra place setting and walked away.

Holly returned to her introspection. Maybe she was being too hard on herself. Even when she'd said she wanted to focus on her own life, and remain single, Sequoia had tried to hook her up with Mack. Actually, she thought, fabricating a boyfriend seemed like a reasonable action to take. When she realized she had shrugged and was nodding to herself, she took a deep breath and a sip of water. Getting to know herself didn't mean she had to lose her grip on sanity.

But why did you bring Mack into this? She imagined Tristan telling her to dig deeper. *Why not simply tell him you're not interested in romance right now?*

The proverbial lightbulb blinked on.

Because she *was* interested in Mack.

If she told him she planned to remain single, indefinitely, he'd move on. But if she told him she was "seeing someone," which implied things weren't too serious, maybe he'd keep her in the back of his mind and resurface when she became available. When she laid it all out this way, Holly thought, it seemed pretty selfish.

So, if she was interested in Mack—and he was definitely interested in her—then why not give it a whirl rather than keeping him hooked, but at arm's length?

"Because in addition to the fact that I truly am focusing on myself right now, I'm afraid he'll never be able to take me seriously because his first impression of me is that I'm irresponsible," Holly mumbled to herself.

She glanced around to see if anyone had heard her mumbling. Even though no one was looking at her, there was one woman sitting suspiciously still, like she was pretending not to have noticed the eccentric single woman talking to herself.

Holly and Mack would be destined to fail. And because Mack and Sequoia were friends, that failure would break Holly's heart and disappoint Sequoia. *That's* why she couldn't give it a whirl with Mack.

Holly nodded to herself, and then heard Mack's voice.

"I'm cracking up," she said. She really had lost it. She could hear him saying, "No, this is great. Perfect. We don't need a booth."

Maybe it was some trick of her mind, placing the spirit of Mack in this room just to remind her that his voice made her all quivery inside. Or maybe it was another man who sounded just like him. That was possible, right? It's not like she'd heard the guy's voice more than a handful of times.

The voice spoke again: "I hear their seafood platter is really good."

Before she even had a chance to think about it, Holly lifted her head, looked to the right, and locked eyes with Mack, the very real version, who was sitting just one table away.

He looked down at the empty spot across from her and raised an eyebrow. Holly silently cursed the server who'd removed the extra place setting. For a long couple of seconds, she felt frozen, unsure of how to handle this moment. She could pretend like her date was in the bathroom and coming back shortly, to eat with his hands. Without a napkin. She could say something about how he canceled at the last minute and she was craving lobster. Or she could just pretend there was nothing out of the ordinary about her being here, solo.

Before she could decide what to do, though, Mack's date shook out her napkin, making a loud snapping sound, and Holly jumped as Mack looked away. How had Holly not noticed the woman sitting across from him? She was impossibly gorgeous, with impeccable skin and shining chocolate-colored hair that flowed down her back like one of those fondue fountains people had at parties. Of course, while Holly was still staring at her, open-mouthed, the woman redirected her laser-beam glare from Mack's face to Holly's.

Her eyes were a sparkling dark green, like emeralds. Deep in her gut, Holly felt a stab of jealousy, but she wasn't sure whether it was because this woman was drop-dead beautiful or because she was sitting across from Mack.

Not that it mattered. Holly would never be that stunning, and she'd certainly never be sitting across from Mack, giving him (or a female acquaintance at a restaurant) that withering stare.

Now Mack cleared his throat, and when Holly looked at him, she was surprised to see that he was smiling broadly.

"Jess," he said, "this is Holly. She's the sister of one of my former co-workers. Sequoia Carr? Remember her?"

Jess gave Holly an icy look and picked up her menu. "Lovely to meet you."

And ... dismissed, Holly thought. "You, too."

The snooty server delivered Holly's seafood platter, and for a brief moment, Holly considered asking if she could move to a different table. If only she hadn't *oohed* and *ahhed* over the view. She started out with the shrimp, stabbing each one forcefully before dipping it in melted garlic butter and putting into her mouth as daintily as possible. How could she ever eat the lobster without making a complete mess—and a complete fool of herself—in front of Mack and Jess?

At one point, her eyes flitted over to Mack without her consent, and she saw that he was watching her. His gaze followed her movements as she lifted each bite from her plate to her mouth.

Something about this seemed very sensual, and Holly shivered as he watched her lips. Jess, for her part, seemed not to notice. She'd picked up the cocktail menu and was examining it as if it were the map to a secret treasure.

Although she tried to keep herself from looking at Mack—instead directing her gaze towards her food, out the window, or at the empty spot across the table from her—she felt drawn to him, and kept finding her eyes locked with his.

Even when the server came over to take his order, his eyes were on Holly as he spoke. She felt a surge of heat in her lady parts when he said, his voice suggestive, "I'll have exactly the same thing she's having."

At this point, Jess seemed to remember Holly's presence, and looked at her platter with something close to a sneer. An awkward silence fell, and Holly wondered why Mack and Jess weren't talking more, and why he seemed almost jovial at seeing Holly here.

The situation improved slightly when their food arrived, and Holly was able to finish her own within a matter of minutes ...

minutes that felt like hours. She got up to go wash her hands in the bathroom, hating that she had to walk right past Mack on the way. She could practically feel his eyes on her.

Things got even more dicey when she emerged and found him waiting for her.

"So your date canceled, huh?" Mack was standing outside the bathroom door, his hands in his pockets, looking very relaxed and not a little amused. This made Holly nervous. She tried to walk past him, but he moved just slightly so his body blocked the hallway. He smelled so good, like pine and citrus and garlic butter.

"Excuse me," she said, trying again to get past him.

He moved forward, forcing her to back up against the wall. Being this close to him put Holly's senses on high alert and her brain slightly off-kilter.

"I just wanted to talk for a minute," he said.

Holly could feel her heart beating in her chest, in her throat, and, worst of all, in her lady parts.

"Won't Jess be upset if she sees us talking? She looked pretty peeved that we even knew each other."

"Nah," he said. "What happened to your date?"

Why couldn't he let it go?

"Had to work," Holly said. "Unexpected project."

"Oh, really?" Mack said. "What does he do?"

He shifted now, and leaned against the wall, as if they were just having a casual conversation.

"Oh, you know," Holly said, grasping for the job she had assigned to Alejo. She hoped it was a job involving projects.

"Wait," she said, buying herself time. "You already asked me that." Ah. There it was. "He's in finance."

Yes, that's what she'd told Mack at the Broken Egg. It was vague enough. Plausible, even.

Mack leaned towards her then, and for a split second she thought he was going to kiss her. This idea filled her with an anticipation so strong she could practically feel his mouth on hers.

But instead of kissing her, he brought his lips to her ear. His breath danced over her skin, producing a rush of goosebumps.

"Just so you know," he said. "If you and I had planned dinner, I wouldn't miss it. You'd be my only project."

Then he pressed his lips to the spot just below her ear, and they were so moist and soft and warm that she almost melted right there on the spot. At a complete loss for words, she just nodded at him and walked out of the restaurant, keeping her eyes downcast as she made her way through the dining room.

CHAPTER NINE

That night, Holly dreamed of men. Or, more specifically, she dreamed of one man. Instead of dreaming that Mack ravished her between the sheets—which would have been a very nice dream, indeed—she dreamed that she ran into him everywhere she went.

At the grocery store, he was sorting through peaches when she walked into produce. At the bank, he was standing in line for a teller, and turned around when she came through the door. When she got home, he was standing in her kitchen, pouring beer into a frosty mug. She didn't even own a beer mug.

In every one of the instances, he looked up at her, as if she were the one intruding on his life. He never spoke to her or touched her. He just looked at her.

She woke up unsettled and out of sorts. She brewed herself a pot of strong coffee and sat down to check her email. Tristan's name was in the "From" field on the first email that popped up. The subject: *There's a message waiting for you in your Compass Coaching Message Center.* Holly groaned, remembering that she was supposed to check in with him last night. After running into Mack, she'd completely forgotten. She logged into her Compass Coaching account and clicked on the blinking mailbox icon.

· · ·

SUBJECT: Your date.

DEAR HOLLY, I wanted to touch base about last night. Were you able to go on a date with yourself? How did it go?

Also, while I'm here, I wanted to see if you'd had time to think about the answers to the questions I asked you. As I mentioned on our last session, I got the impression you weren't being totally honest about your dating situation. I'd like for you to take a few moments and think about why. I understand if you're not ready to be completely open with me, but I want to ensure you're being completely honest with yourself.

Drop me a line when you can, and I hope you're having a great weekend.

HOLLY KNEW she had to respond. This coaching software probably included some kind of notification so Tristan would know she'd opened the message. But what would she write?

"Aha!" she said, smiling to herself as she imagined a little light-bulb blinking on above her head. She clicked on "Reply."

SUBJECT: Re. Your date. - It was great!

HI TRISTAN,

THANK YOU FOR CHECKING IN. My date with myself was lovely. I had a lovely time. I got a table with a sunset view and ordered the seafood platter. I had some great time for introspection. I found that I enjoy being alone more than I realized.

"THAT IS, before I ran into a very sexy man who distracted me from the business at hand," she said aloud.

. . .

ABOUT THE DATING THING: you're right. I wasn't being completely honest. I am seeing someone. His name is Alejo. He's in finance. I felt like you'd tell me I should stay single for a while, especially because this thing with Alejo is relatively new. I thought you might encourage me to spend more time alone, but I really want to explore where things go with Alejo. The cat's out of the bag. Still, I took your advice and went out alone last night. Hope you're having a great weekend, too. :)

SHE CLICKED, "SEND," and got up to refill her coffee. Before she even sat back down, her computer chimed. It was another message from Tristan.

SUBJECT: Thank you for your honesty.

HOLLY PUT her forehead in her hand and closed her eyes briefly before reading the message. Even as she felt like she was digging herself deeper and deeper, she felt completely unable to stop this train.

DEAR HOLLY,

THANK YOU FOR YOUR HONESTY. I usually recommend my clients in your position "pause" their dating lives during the course of our work together, simply because doing so allows you to spend time really focusing on your own needs and desires at this point. However, if you don't believe your relationship with Alejo is interfering with your self-discovery, then carry on! We'll chat more about this on our next session. Cheers!

. . .

"HMM," Holly said. "That went more smoothly than I expected."

So far, things with Alejo were going swimmingly. He was keeping Mack at bay—well, somewhat—and he was helping to put all the questions about Holly's love life to rest.

Now, all she had to do was keep the illusion alive. If she managed to make everyone believe Alejo was real, she could do exactly what Tristan said, and carry on, without interference. "I can do this."

At least, she thought she could, until she logged into Blackbook.

MESSAGING REQUEST FROM MACK BRAVO.

HER HEART RATE picked up and she clicked *Accept*. Mack had sent the message just after midnight. Probably after dropping the gorgeously snooty Jess off at home. Or after tucking her into the bed they were sharing. Why was he doing this? Why was he kissing her next to the bathroom, showing up in her dreams, and sending her messages after midnight? And all when he thought she had a boyfriend? She should just delete his message right away, and leave him to his beautiful woman. Of course, curiosity won.

HI, Holly,

I DIDN'T WANT to be so forward as to make an official friend request. I wanted to apologize for last night.

"I DON'T WANT you to apologize," Holly said. "I want you to kiss me again, more thoroughly this time."

NOT FOR WHAT happened next to the bathroom.

. . .

"OH, GOOD."

BUT FOR THE looks Jess was throwing you. She's not always the most friendly to girls I meet.

"WELL, FOR GOOD REASON."

Suddenly, Holly's sixth sense woke up, and she wondered if he was angling for a threesome with her and Jess. Why else would he be writing? Holly considered herself open-minded and forward-thinking, but she wasn't into sharing her men.

SHE'S JUST A LITTLE PROTECTIVE. Anyway, I hope Alejo was able to get off work and get home to you so he could enjoy your company. You looked absolutely delicious last night, by the way.

OF COURSE, this last line brought sensory images of Mack kissing her neck straight to the forefront of her mind, and her imagination ran with that. What would he have done if they were alone? In private? Would she like it?

There was no question she would. Judging by that single contact, he'd be an excellent lover. He would probably take his time, lavish attention on every single square inch of her skin.

"And now I'm going to have an orgasm right here sitting at my kitchen counter," she said. "Perfect."

Should she respond to his message? It would be the polite thing to do. But would that be leading him on? Could they be "just friends" at this point? Not really, considering every time she saw him she'd be thinking about that kiss outside the bathroom. She clicked *Reply.*

. . .

HI, Mack,

THAT WAS NICE AND NEUTRAL, right? It didn't scream, "Take off my panties!"

IT WAS nice to see you last night. No need to apologize for Jess's behavior. She seems like a nice person.

HOLLY DELETED that last bit and replaced it with, *I'm sure she's a nice person.*

SHE WANTED TO ADD, *Sometimes,* but she didn't.

YES, Alejo got off work shortly after I got home. We had a romantic evening.

SHE CROSSED out romantic and replaced it with, *nice.* Mack didn't need to know she'd sat alone in the living room without even turning on the TV. She signed off there. She wasn't sure what else to say, and anyway, it was time to get ready for work.

The afternoon shift at the Broken Egg was almost always busy, but more so on Sundays when the after-church crowd merged with the sleeping-in crowd and they all showed up wanting piles of eggs and stacks of whole wheat pancakes. Holly was so busy delivering veggie scrambles and yogurt parfaits and tofu breakfast burritos that she was surprised when Jaclyn Connelly said, "Your fellow's back, huh? Did the two of you make up?"

When Holly finally saw Mack—after he'd been there long enough that someone else had poured him coffee—she blew a stray lock of hair out of her eyes and sighed. He was so … *distracting.*

"Not exactly," she said to Jaclyn.

As she went over to take Mack's order, she said to herself, "And he's not my fellow."

"What can I get you?" she said to Mack.

"Wow, you're not your usual friendly self this morning. Tired from last night?"

Not for the reason you think. It was you who kept me up all night, not Alejo. Oh, and by the way, where's Jess this morning?

She didn't respond out loud, and he shrugged as if to signify he could play this game, too. "The usual."

She wrote his order on her pad, snapped it shut, and was mid-turn when he grabbed her wrist. Even that tiny contact made her skin all tingly and her knees weak, and she hated herself for it.

"Holly," he said.

"Yes?"

"If that Alejo guy is ever stupid enough to lose you, I'd love to take you out to dinner."

He hadn't released her wrist, and Holly found herself wishing he would twirl her right into his lap so she could show him what *she'd* love to do.

"I'll keep that in mind," she said.

"You do that," he said. He finally let go and she was surprised she could still feel the heat from his hand. "In the meantime, I wanted to invite you to my house next weekend. I'm having a big barbecue, inviting a bunch of people over. It's just a drop-in thing, nothing formal. You can come any time Sunday. Before work, after work. Hell, take the day off and come during work. It's kind of like a post-retirement-party party. One where I won't toss my cookies at the end. You know? A different setting. You can bring Alejo. I invited Carr—I mean, Sequoia, too."

"I'll have to see what my schedule's like," she said, even though she knew perfectly well that she had next Sunday off.

Before she had any further interactions with this man, she had to get to the bottom of a little mystery: Why was Mack flirting with her when he was involved with Jess and she was involved with Alejo? Was he just masochistic?

Mack left the Broken Egg without any more conversation, and when Holly finally got a break she texted Sequoia: *Why is Mack flirting with me?*

When Sequoia's response came through, Holly imagined her sister rolling her eyes as she typed: *Because you're a beautiful woman, Holly, and funny when you want to be. Charming, actually.*

She could see Sequoia grinning at her own humor. She didn't find Holly charming at all. If anything, she found her irritating and childish. Still, Holly wrote back: *I mean, doesn't he have a girlfriend? And he knows I'm seeing someone.*

Sequoia responded: *I have no idea if he has a girlfriend. His social life is none of my business. I would say he's quite a catch, though, so probably. I'd imagine he doesn't stay single for long. Also, do you think he believes you're seeing someone?*

"Hmm," Holly said.

She wrote: *Why wouldn't he believe it?*

Sequoia responded: *Why would he?*

Holly gritted her teeth: *Aren't you, like, an observer of human nature, or something?*

Sequoia wrote back: *LOL. Yep. But I don't really see Mack outside of work, and now that he's retired, I have none of his behavior to observe. But I do observe yours.*

Another text came in: *Wait. Why are you so interested in Mack and his social life? Are you INTERESTED in Mack and his social life? You are, aren't you?! I can't say I'm surprised. He is a good-looking guy. I could find out if you want. You know, if he's seeing someone.*

Holly responded: *Well. That would be awkward. That's something you'd never talk to anyone about. You're not exactly a social butterfly.*

Before her text even finished sending, Sequoia sent another: *But… YOU are seeing someone. Alejo, wasn't it? Alejo in finance. What is up with this line of questioning?*

Then another text came in: *No, I am not a social butterfly, by any means, but I could ask around. If you want. Which is weird. Since you're seeing someone.*

A third rapid-fire text came in before Holly could text back: *Oh, he's having this bbq thing next weekend. I could snoop around there if you want.*

Holly realized almost immediately that she shouldn't have revealed her hand. But her fingers flew over her keyboard before she caught her own mistake: *Yeah, he invited me. But I don't think I'll go. I won't really know anyone.*

Her phone rang. It was Sequoia.

"Ugh," Holly said before answering. "She's going to say, 'Of course you'll know someone. You'll know Elijah and me. And wait. How did he invite you? Did you see him somewhere, or what?' I'm not even going to answer."

Compulsion forced her to pick up, anyway. "I just have a minute. I'm on a break and it's almost over."

"Of course you'll know someone. You'll know Elijah and me," Sequoia said, exactly as Holly had known she would. "And wait. How did he invite you? Did you see him somewhere, or what?"

"He comes into the Broken Egg every once in a while," Holly said, then cringed, expecting Sequoia to question her heartily about how often he came in and whether he always sat in her section.

"Hmm," was all her sister said. "Well, that's nice. You should come. We can ride together."

"I've got to go," Holly said. "Break's over."

* * *

MESSAGE REQUEST FROM MACK BRAVO.

HI, Holly,

I FORGOT to mention something when I saw you this morning: you looked exquisite. Seriously mouthwatering.

· · ·

"WHY AM I even entertaining fantasies about this guy? He was at dinner with another woman and he's talking to me like this."

ANYWAY, I know I invited you to come over on Sunday, for the party, but I wanted to see if you want to come over on Saturday for a bit. You know, just to hang out. Totally platonic. That is, if Alejo doesn't mind.

"I DON'T KNOW if Alejo is really the jealous type," Holly said.

Mack inviting her to come over on Saturday seemed a little intimate. Maybe he just liked having lady friends. That would explain Jess, and it would explain why he was inviting her over. And the truth was, she wanted to accept his invitation. She wanted to spend time with him. Alone. She may not know what she wanted out of life, but she knew what she wanted out of Mack. Her inner voice was screaming that she should show up on his doorstep Saturday and spend time being everything but platonic. Tristan would tell her to listen to her inner voice.

Still, she struggled to formulate a response.

Maybe she should just keep it short and simple, like, *Yes, I'd love to. What time?* And then let things play out.

Either Mack was just ballsy, or ... well, she didn't want to think about the alternative. Was his comment, *That is, if Alejo doesn't mind,* tongue-in-cheek? Did he somehow know she had invented Alejo, created him right out of thin air?

Holly decided the safest bet—in order to protect Alejo's true identity—was to go along with the whole "just friends" thing.

So, she clicked *Reply* and asked the other question that was the elephant in the room: *I'll admit your offer sounds intriguing—I'd love to see what Mack Bravo does on the weekends when he's not sitting in my section at the Broken Egg—yet, I can't help but wonder why you're inviting me over.*

She nodded, satisfied with herself for bringing that topic, at least, out into the open. Then she got up to get herself a glass of water and before she even finished filling it, her computer chimed.

The message said: *I want to show off my farm. Oh, and because I find YOU intriguing, Holly. That's why.*

At that moment, Holly told herself she couldn't be held responsible for the way her body reacted: her hands began to shake, heat spread from her face to her lower abdomen, and she felt a broad smile on her face.

She wrote back immediately: *What time?*

He wrote back: *8 am?*

She responded: *I'll be there,* and then she thought, Alejo isn't going to like this one bit.

CHAPTER TEN

"So. Holly. I assume this new boyfriend of yours, Alejo, right? Will be your date at Jasmine's wedding?"

Holly took her time answering. She looked at Sequoia, who was sitting on Jasmine's couch, serene, her feet on the coffee table, as relaxed as could be. How had this happened? Holly felt like she was drowning. And she'd done it to herself. At first, Alejo had been a solution to a problem. His existence would give her the space she needed to remain single and focus on her own transformation. But now, he was a heavy weight, one she'd attached to her own ankles with a thick chain. And she'd hurled herself over the side of a boat and into the deepest part of the ocean.

She didn't *have* an Alejo to bring to Jasmine's wedding, and she had no idea how to respond to Sequoia.

"Wait until I sit down," Jasmine said, saving her. "I wanted to show you guys the playlist Hudson and I came up with for the wedding. Let me grab it."

"What I want to know," Holly said to Sequoia, "is why we're talking about me when we should be talking about Jasmine's big day."

What was taking Jasmine so long? Was her playlist buried in the Sahara, or something?

Sequoia shoved a handful of popcorn into her mouth and spoke right through it as she chewed. "You haven't brought it up to him, have you?"

"I can't understand you," Holly said. "Stop talking with your mouth full."

Sequoia shrugged. "I don't know where she put that playlist, but it must be buried somewhere in the Sahara."

Probably because she was feeling awkward at the moment, Sequoia's comment made Holly giggle. When Sequoia just raised an eyebrow at her, she giggled some more, even snorting as she tried to pick up a handful of popcorn and dropped most of it on the couch.

"Geez," Sequoia said. "It wasn't that funny."

This made Holly snort again, and Sequoia shook her head.

"I think you're cracking up, Holly."

Finally, as Holly regained her composure, Jasmine returned, a notebook in hand.

"Where'd you go, the Sahara?" Holly said, her voice bubbling with humor. Again, Sequoia shook her head, and Holly said, "I can tell you're smiling on the inside, Sequoia."

"What's so funny?" Jasmine said.

This started Holly giggling again, and Sequoia said, "Nothing. Let's see the list."

Jasmine sat down. "So Hudson wants to surprise me with the song that plays when we walk back down the aisle after sharing our first kiss as husband and wife. But other than that, it's complete."

Sequoia pointed at a line about halfway down the page. "So you guys chose *Talk Dirty to Me* for your first dance?"

"What?" Jasmine said. Her voice came out in a shriek and she snatched the notebook from its spot on the table to look at it more closely. She read the list, and then, her face turning red, started flipping through the rest of the notebook.

"Ugh. He stole my playlist. This is a fake! He is *not* walking down the aisle to *Sexual Healing*, and I am most certainly not walking down the aisle to *Let's Talk About Sex*. Where in the world did he put the real list?"

"Wait. So he stole your list and wrote an entirely new one, with all sex-related songs?" Sequoia said. "I knew I loved Hudson from the moment I saw him."

"He probably figured I was going to show this to you guys," Jasmine said. "Funny guy."

Sequoia shook her head. "A gold star for Hudson. I love this guy."

Then she turned her attention to Holly. Again. "So, Holly. Alejo. Your date for the wedding?"

Now Holly shot Jasmine a pleading look, but for once, Jasmine didn't jump in to save her. She just offered a cat-who-ate-the-canary smile.

Did they know what was really going on? Holly felt paralyzed, uncertain of what to say. Of course Alejo wouldn't be joining her at the wedding. She couldn't bring along an imaginary friend and set a place for him at the table, and have her sisters play along—they weren't little kids having tea parties any more.

Before she could come up with a suitable answer, Jasmine said, "When are we going to meet this Alejo guy, anyway? I mean, haven't you guys been dating for a while now? Why are you keeping him a secret from us? You're embarrassed of us, aren't you?"

Sequoia nodded like she'd been wondering the same thing, and she shoved another handful of popcorn into her mouth and wiped her hands on her pants.

"I'm afraid you'll embarrass me, more like," Holly said. "By telling him all about my monochromatic phase."

"That was so cute, though," Jasmine said, and Sequoia said, "And your fashion sense has improved. Obviously."

"I, uh—" Holly said. "He's just really busy, you know. He goes out of town a lot."

There. That would lay the foundation for Alejo's absence at Jasmine's wedding.

"On another note," Holly said to Jasmine, "I hope you're not serving popcorn at your wedding. Your sister over there has atrocious manners."

Jasmine gave Sequoia a once-over, taking in the tiny piece of popcorn stuck to the corner of her mouth, and the stray pieces that had fallen on her shirt.

"What?" Sequoia said, then, and all three of them dissolved into laughter.

Her crisis averted, at least for the moment, Holly stood up and walked into the kitchen to refill her wine and to think of a subject change.

"You're not off the hook, Holly," Sequoia called after her. "Why don't you just bring the wine in here?"

"So, Jas," Holly said as she came back into the living room, "is there anything we can help you with for the wedding? Floral arrangements? Party favors? A menu? Are you feeding people?"

This did the trick. Jasmine began talking, and picked up speed as she went into details. There would be no floral arrangements except her bouquet, no party favors except wine, and the menu was taken care of, thanks to a catering company. The only bridesmaid duties Holly and Sequoia had to fill were helping Jasmine get ready, showing up at the wedding, standing next to Jasmine at the altar, and posing for lots of pictures.

As Jasmine spoke (and spoke and spoke), Sequoia bored holes into Holly with her eyes. Fortunately, Hudson returned home then, and distracted them all with a story about a photo shoot he'd done that day where a great white shark swam with surfers at The Point.

Then, Sequoia got a text that made her ears turn pink. She left in a hurry, muttering about how she had to meet Elijah because he had a special surprise for her.

After she left, Jasmine got the broom and started sweeping up all the popcorn Sequoia had dropped. "She looked pretty dreamy, didn't she?" she said.

"She did," Holly said. "It's so nice to see her like this."

And it was. Sequoia wasn't married—yet—but she was going home to a man who could turn her ears pink with one single text. And Jasmine would be walking down the aisle with the very man who was now playfully swatting her bottom with a dish towel. Holly stood by with her empty wine glass, which served as a sad representation of the empty house to which she'd be returning home.

"I'll take this as my cue to exit stage right," she said, and Hudson laughed wickedly. After setting her wine glass in the kitchen sink, Holly hugged Jasmine and said, "I'm so happy for you."

As she walked out the front door, she heard Hudson say, "She's leaving you alone with me, my pretty lady. Now you're in trouble."

THE WEEK PASSED by so quickly that by Friday night, Holly felt completely unprepared to fulfill the agreement she'd made to go to Mack's house the next day. She sat on the couch with a cup of sparkling water in one hand while the other dipped into her favorite mix of caramel and cheese popcorn.

"What was I thinking?" she said aloud.

Of course, no one answered, and she thought again about getting a dog. Not that a dog would answer, but it would at least make her talking to herself less pathetic. Well, slightly less pathetic, anyway. Why had she even thought it was a remotely good idea to accept Mack's invitation?

She could just pretend she was sick, and hole up inside all day so no one saw her out in public. He'd never know. The doorbell rang, and Holly went to answer it. She and Cara had planned a girls' night, where they'd eat popcorn and watch an action adventure movie without the slightest trace of romance.

"Food poisoning!" Holly said as she opened the door.

"What?" Cara said.

"It's a believable illness, one with a short lifespan," Holly said.

"Oh, yes. That explains everything." Cara gave Holly a strange look, and held up a DVD case. "Indiana Jones," she said. "Action, adventure, and yes, a tiny bit of romance. But I couldn't find anything without that male-female chemistry. Tell me you don't have food poisoning."

"Nah," Holly said. "I was trying to come up with a good excuse for not going to Mack's tomorrow."

"I thought his barbecue was Sunday."

"It is," Holly said. She told Cara about Mack's invitation to spend time alone together the following day. "And if I got food poisoning tonight or tomorrow, I would have returned to normal health for Sunday's barbecue."

"That might work," Cara said, her voice trailing off.

"But," Holly said, letting her voice trail off the same way.

"But why don't you go?"

"Go to his house tomorrow?"

"Yeah." Cara was in the kitchen, making herself tea. "I mean, why not?"

Holly had to admit, even to herself, that she wanted to spend at least part of a day alone with Mack, and she said as much to Cara. "I'm intrigued. He said he was intrigued. He also said I looked mouthwatering."

Cara returned to the living room and set her mug on the coffee table.

"And didn't you tell me he was edible?" she said.

"I did," Holly said. "He is."

"So go," Cara said.

Something in Cara's expression—maybe the way she was avoiding eye contact—made Holly think there was something she wasn't saying.

"But Alejo—" Holly said. "He might not like it if I'm hanging out with another guy. Platonic or not."

"Look," Cara said. "I am not getting the best vibe about this Alejo character. First of all, you mentioned him to us as kind of an afterthought. And you haven't seemed that, I don't know, *taken* with him. He's never around. And Sequoia said—"

"What did Sequoia say?"

"Nothing," Cara said. She took a hasty sip of her tea, an obvious cover-up, and then flinched because it was still too hot.

"You can tell me," Holly said. "I won't be upset."

"That's a lie!" Cara said. "I'm not going to contribute to a sibling argument."

Holly pounced on that. "The fact that you believe whatever Sequoia said will lead to a sibling argument makes me think I'm going to want to know what it is."

Cara just shook her head. "You'd just be going to Mack's to hang out. Platonic. Right?"

"Right," Holly said, drawing it out.

"Well, if, you know, if Alejo won't mind, then you should go. I know what it's like to put all my eggs in one basket," Cara said, "and have it be the wrong basket. The one with the loose handle. That handle breaks and so do all the eggs. Know what I mean?"

Holly nodded.

Yes, if Alejo really existed, he may have a problem with Holly hanging out with Mack. Especially if he knew how Holly's body responded to being close to Mack. But he didn't exist. So what was the harm?

"Okay," Holly said. "I'll go."

"Good," said Cara. "Now let's watch this movie."

"Let's," Holly said.

She could always change her mind first thing in the morning.

CHAPTER ELEVEN

Holly didn't change her mind. She showed up at Mack's house at eight a.m. on the dot, wearing skinny jeans and a tank top with cowboy boots she'd bought more for fashion than practicality. Still, they seemed appropriate since he said he wanted to show off his farm. One of the horses in the corral lifted its head, ears perked, when she got out of the car. It made a kind of huffing noise as it watched her approach.

She couldn't help but notice the clean smell of the fall air. It was so different from the city air outside her own house, which heavily featured the scents of car exhaust, bakery scents, and over-full Dumpsters.

Mack opened the door before she had a chance to knock. His eyes raked over her body, from her face to her boots, before resting on hers. She could have sworn she felt it. She could see his muscles through the fabric of his white t-shirt. And he sure looked good in those jeans.

"Good morning," he said, the corners of his mouth turning up just slightly and his eyes twinkling with mischief.

He stood back and gestured for her to come in, and when she walked past him she could smell his cologne. This made her want to ask him to show off his bedroom rather than his farm. So so she held her breath and switched her focus. Barn wood floors led from the entry to the kitchen on one side and the living room on the other. Cozy furniture sat around a fireplace with a traditional-looking mantle, and a bowl of fruit sat on the counter.

A couple of frames sat on the side table next to the sofa, and they held photos of a couple—one half of which must be Mack's brother or sister—and some kids.

"Cute place," she said. "I can't wait to see the rest of it."

If she could have put her palm to her forehead, she would have. *I can't wait to see the rest of it? Like the BEDROOM? Get a grip, Holly.*

"Thanks," he said. "I like it. Especially now that I'm retired and I can spend more time with the animals. Over the past couple of months, I started building it up. Put up the corral, bought a couple of horses, you know?"

"Actually, I don't," Holly said. "I don't have any animals. Not even a regular animal like a dog. I can't imagine taking care of horses and everything."

"You don't even have a dog? Who do you talk to at night?"

"Who do *you* talk to at night?" She was thinking about Jess, but she managed not to say so.

"Touché," he said.

"Listen, Mack," Holly said. "I wanted to ask you—"

"Oh, real quick," he said, "Because my mother would kill me if I didn't ask: do you want some coffee or something?"

He'd said he wanted to show off the farm. Accepting coffee from him would be more intimate than accepting a simple tour of his property. She'd be obligated to return the favor at some point, maybe even offering him a nightcap. Which sounded great.

"Coffee would be nice," she said. "Thank you."

He pulled out a chair at the dining room table and went into the kitchen, returning a moment later with a mug. Instead of setting it down, he handed it to her. She told herself it was childish to notice the way his fingertips brushed hers ... but she noticed. She also told herself it was weird to analyze the fact that he chose to sit next to her instead of across from her. But she analyzed it anyway. Did it mean he wanted to sit closer to her? Or was it just his regular spot?

"So," he said. "What did you want to ask me?"

Holly cleared her throat. What she wanted to ask him was whether Jess knew she was here, and whether it would bother her. She also wanted to ask him why it didn't bother him that she was seeing Alejo.

"Why a farm?"

She blurted it out before she had the chance to say something stupid. He looked a little surprised, but took a sip of his coffee and recovered well.

"I don't know," he said. "I always wanted horses, but of course, working long hours, I didn't really have the time to take care of them. Plus, I was so into my career. Being a cop was my lifelong dream. And now that I'm done, I guess I'm trying to find myself. Again."

He shrugged. "It sounds stupid, trying to find yourself at age forty, but there it is. Anyway, this is something I always thought I'd enjoy. So I'm trying it."

"It doesn't sound stupid," Holly said. "I still feel like I'm trying to find myself. For the first time. At age thirty. At least you've already found yourself the one time."

It wasn't something she'd usually admit to someone on the first date. But this wasn't a date. Plus, having a pretend boyfriend took away a lot of the pressure Holly would normally feel. She didn't have to impress Mack or try to get him to like her.

"Yeah," he said, "you don't strike me as the type to work at a small-town diner for an entire career. What do you want to do?"

Holly found herself opening up immediately.

"I don't know," she said. "I thought I wanted to become a personal trainer, but my heart's just not in it. I've never really taken the time to explore. I guess I've always just kind of followed in my sisters' footsteps. But when neither of their careers appealed to me, I just started floating along. And now, here I am, thirty years old, without any real sense of purpose. I don't even know how I got here."

Mack held up a finger. "Be right back."

He disappeared into a room off the living area, and returned with a book, which he set down in front of her.

Holly read the title out loud: "The Untethered Soul."

"Want to borrow it? I read it a few months ago when my retirement was imminent. It's a great book."

So Mack goes deep, Holly thought.

"Sure," she said. "Thanks."

A beat of silence followed, and Holly felt she would be remiss not to mention Jess. But the moment she started to speak, prepared to ask about Jess—"Listen, Mack—" he started to speak, too: "So, would you like a tour?"

She could hardly say no, and maybe this was just a sign that she should shut up and not worry about Jess. Jess wasn't here, anyway, was she?

"I'd love a tour," Holly said.

Because it stood just outside the house, the corral was the tour's first stop. The horse that had greeted Holly upon her arrival trotted over to the fence when it saw Mack, and he reached up to rub its face.

"This is Lady," Mack said. "Short for Lady Luck. And that's Miss Fortune over there, but she's not as friendly as Lady is."

"Can I pet her?"

"Of course."

He motioned for Holly to stand in front of him. Just as she did, Lady tossed her head, which startled Holly and caused her to take a big step back. She bumped up against Mack's chest, and he wrapped his arms around her waist. When a rush of warmth ran through her body, Holly reminded herself he'd done this to keep them both from stumbling backwards, not because he knew it would light all of her nerve endings on fire.

He moved his hands to her waist to steady her, and then let go. Holly reached up to pet the horse, which had the good sense to stand still this time.

For the most part, the rest of the tour went without incident. Mack showed Holly the pig pen, where a fat mother pig lay in the mud with five little piglets. They collected eggs from the chicken coop, and then Mack said, "Okay, second-to-last stop."

They were standing outside a small shed, and Mack whistled. Holly could hear rustling sounds inside, and she smiled when a medium-sized dog came out into the sunlight, blinking. The dog nudged Mack's hand with its head, and then did its best to maintain the contact while it stretched.

"Hey, Mama," Mack said, kneeling down and scratching the dog behind both ears. "This is Louise."

Louise's coat was the color of a brand new penny, and her ears looked like they belonged on an elephant. Holly knelt down to pet her, and she leaned against Holly's side, obviously pleased with the attention.

"I know," Mack said. "She's so ugly she's cute, right?"

Holly reached out to pet the dog. "Nah, she's pretty."

So what if her legs were a little too short for her body, and her nose a little too short for her face?

Louise looked back, then, and Holly gasped. Four little puppies came bounding out of the shed after their mother. Louise looked at Mack as if to imply that she'd been trying to get away from them, but still, when they swarmed her, nipping at her ears and tail, tumbling over each other to get to her, she stood there patiently.

"They're so cute!" Holly said.

One of the pups, mostly white with a few brown spots, took an interest in the newcomer, and started to gnaw on Holly's hand. Charmed by a new face, its siblings came over to check her out.

"Looks like you've got a new friend," Mack said. "That's Quimby. He's a chewer. If you don't like it, well, I don't know what to do if you don't like it. He chews on everything. Try this."

Mack handed her a rubber dog toy. Holly offered it to Quimby, who chomped down on it with his back teeth and began yanking on it, his entire body jerking backward.

"He's got some strength," Holly said. "He's about to pull me over."

"He likes you," Mack said. "You should take him home."

"I don't know," Holly said. Quimby lost his grip on the toy and tumbled away, one end over the other. As soon as he righted himself, he engaged in a wrestling match with one of his siblings.

"No, really," Mack said. "You should."

Holly watched the puppies play. The truth was, she'd been wanting a dog. Quimby wasn't white or fluffy, but he was adorable. And he had a lot of personality.

"I have to find homes for all of them anyway," Mack said. "Two months ago, Louise started hanging around. I kept seeing her come out of the shed first thing in the morning when I was feeding the horses. She was timid at first, but warmed right up when I started leaving food for her."

As if she knew what Mack was saying, Louise sat down next to him, leaned against his leg, and looked up at him.

"I always thought she was a voyager, you know? I expected her to move on. But it didn't take long for me to realize she was pregnant. So I bought her a bed and put it in the shed. Within a few weeks, my farm family was five members larger."

Quimby was back, and he'd taken the end of Holly's shirt in his mouth. She disengaged it and reached for the dog toy.

"I was going to find Louise a home as soon as the pups were old enough," Mack said, "but we bonded. I think I'll keep her. These guys will be ready in a week or so, and Quimby's yours if you want him. Think of it as an early Christmas present."

At this point, Quimby flopped down next to Holly and rolled over. He closed his eyes but kept nudging her with his nose. She couldn't resist rubbing his belly.

"Tempting," Holly said.

"See?" Mack said. "He's warming you up. Take him."

"I'll think about it," Holly said.

"You know you want him."

Mack gave Louise one more scratch behind the ears, and then she trotted back to the shed, her little family of pups behind her.

"Ready for the rest of the tour?" Mack said.

Holly nodded and followed him around the other side of the house.

"Here's my pride and joy," Mack said. "The garden."

"It is pretty spectacular," Holly said, and she meant it.

"These pumpkins are growing like crazy," Mack said. "Oh, and look how many cucumbers have grown. That's awesome. I've really been struggling with those. I guess they need harvesting."

"I'll help you," Holly said. "I didn't realize this stuff grew so late in the fall."

"Coastal air," Mack said. He retrieved a couple of baskets from a cupboard on the side of the house and handed her one.

"I'll do the eggplants," he said. "That basket works better for cucumbers."

"Is there any technique involved, or do I just yank them off the plant?"

Mack chuckled. "You basically just break them off at the stem. It's not too technical."

They worked in silence for a few moments, and Holly found herself soothed by the scent of the plants and dirt, and by the rhythm of breaking the vegetables off and placing them in the basket. She moved up the row, and was quite content until she grasped a cucumber and simultaneously got a view of Mack's hand grasping an eggplant.

Why did cucumbers have to look so phallic? And why did eggplants have to be shaped like breasts (well, not exactly, but close enough to her sex-deprived brain)?

"Great," she muttered. "Now I'm thinking about sex with Mack."

Although she was speaking in undertones, and she was almost positive he couldn't make out what she said, he paused, eggplant in hand, and said, "Everything okay?"

"Everything's great," she said, pausing to shoot him a smile. "Just fine."

He gave her a puzzled look and went back to his eggplants. "We don't have to do this now," he said. "We can totally do something different."

Was it her, or did that sound a bit racy?

"I'm fine," she said, yanking a cucumber off the plant. "This is fun. Satisfying."

Oh, geez. That sounded a bit racy, too.

"You know what?" Mack said a minute later. "It's hot. Let's go inside and have some iced tea or something."

"All right," Holly said. "My basket's almost full, anyway. Let me just finish up this row so you'll be able to tell where I left off."

Just as she grasped that final cucumber, she heard a car drive up. It was only natural that she'd stand up. And it was only natural that she'd freeze when she saw Jess climbing out of the car, her long hair flowing down her back like some kind of superhero movie star, before she began walking towards the garden.

"Mack," she said, her voice icy and her eyes on Holly. "Holly. Nice to see you again."

Holly had been worried about the Jess Factor; specifically, that Mack would be thinking about the other woman while Holly was at his house. She had not anticipated, however, that the woman would show up in the middle of cucumber picking. Speaking of cucumber picking, Holly realized too late that when she'd frozen in place, she'd done so holding a cucumber in one hand, right at the spot where her legs came together.

Humiliation washed over her just as Jess noticed the same thing and raised her eyebrows. "Nice, Holly. I see that every one of Mack's girlfriends' secret worries has come true for you, too, and he's holding out on you. A vibrator works better than a cucumber does, I hate to tell you."

It would be childish to react to Jess by moving the cucumber, so Holly took a deep breath and smiled her sweetest smile.

"You know," Holly said, "it's not that he's holding out on me. It's just that it was so good I can't stop thinking about it. I guess I got a little carried away. "

Now she held up the cucumber and shrugged. It was a lie, but the shocked expression on Jess's face was so satisfying that Holly didn't care. Mack's laugh sounded at once amused and uncomfortable.

"What's up, Jess?" His smile was alight with humor. "You didn't say you were stopping by."

Jess gave her head a little shake as if to clear it. "I just got something in the mail I thought you'd want to see."

Mack looked at her empty hands. "Where is it?"

"Oh. I left it in the car," she said.

When she turned around to get it, Mack looked at Holly and winked. Jess returned and handed him an envelope, which he folded in half and stuck in the back pocket of his jeans. He really did look good in those jeans, Holly thought. She licked her lips.

"Is that all?" Mack said to Jess.

"Aren't you going to read it?"

"I'm in the middle of something," he said. "I'll read it later."

"Fine," she said. "Although, it doesn't look like your, um, company … needs you. I'll see you."

She was gone as quickly as she'd come. Holly stood rooted to her spot, cucumber in hand. Mack looked at it, gave her a devilish grin, and said, "Well done. Let's get that iced tea."

Back at the kitchen table, Holly took the plunge. "So, I've been wanting to ask you," she said.

"Jess?" Mack said.

"Yeah," Holly said. "I mean, when I saw you at dinner the other night, she seemed pissed off that you were introducing her to another woman. Then you wrote to me on Blackbook, apologizing for that. And then you invited me over. I mean, I wanted to ask you about her before I agreed, you know? But I figured since I was just coming over, you know, as a friend, that it would be okay. With her."

Mack sighed. "Look, Jess is my ex. My ex-girlfriend and my current business partner. When we were together, we started a business. Then she decided she didn't like dating a cop."

"Why, was she a drunk driver, too?"

"Ha," Mack said. "No. She was a partier and she felt like I was judging her because I wouldn't let her party at my house. Anyway. Water under the bridge and all that. Jess and I are trying to sell the business, but until we do, we're business partners. When you saw us at dinner the other night, we'd met—on neutral ground—to discuss an offer someone made. She's still a bit—well, a bit territorial, I guess you'd call it."

"I should say so."

"And she doesn't mind showing up at my place unannounced."

"Has she ever tried to rekindle the romance?" Holly asked. She hated that the question made her sound desperate, especially because it shouldn't matter to her, since she had Alejo. But she had to know.

Mack looked into his iced tea like he was reading tea leaves. "A couple of times, yes. The bottom line is that we just weren't—aren't—a good fit."

Holly nodded. "So what's this business you two have together?"

"It's a laundromat. I know, it's a weird business, but it's lucrative. And the truth is that Jess is digging her heels in on selling it. She says it's because it brings in such a nice profit."

"Couldn't she buy you out?"

"I think she probably could. But at the same time as she wants to keep the business, she says she doesn't want that constant reminder of how we used to be. So she wants to sell it."

"I can understand that," Holly said.

"Needless to say, she's never satisfied with the offers we receive. And I'm stuck interacting with her until we sell it, or she lets me buy her out."

Holly raised an eyebrow, but didn't say anything. Nothing she could think of seemed quite right.

"While we're on the topic of significant others," Mack said, and Holly froze. He continued, "What does Alejo think about you coming over to another guy's house on your morning off?"

What would Alejo think? The benefit of making up a boyfriend, Holly thought, is that she could make him think whatever she wanted him to think. The drawback, though, was that for every thought she assigned him, Alejo became more complex—and a bigger lie.

"He's a bit jealous," she said, as if she were making a confession. "In general, I mean. I actually didn't even tell him I was coming here."

Again, Holly imagined herself drowning, a huge weight chained to her feet as she sank down into the ocean. She could practically see the bubbles rising in front of her face.

Mack looked as if he wanted to say something, but then he

apparently thought better of it and asked if she wanted a refill. While he was at the counter, tea pitcher in hand, he said, "How serious are things with you two?"

"How serious?"

"Yeah," Mack said.

"Um," Holly said, and when he quirked an eyebrow at her as he returned to the table, she said, "I mean. Is that something you can quantify?"

Mack shrugged. "I guess not. But if you're headed down the aisle, I'd like to know. I told you, Holly. I find you intriguing."

"Yeah," Holly said, "there is something really mysterious about a drunk driver you pulled over one fall evening."

Mack looked taken aback, which made this conversation even more awkward. Her face burning, Holly decided it was time for her to exit. She took a long drink of her tea, set the glass on the table, and said, "I'm sorry for making things awkward. I guess I'd better get going. Thank you so much for the coffee, the tour, and the iced tea. It's been a really nice morning."

Whether he was surprised or not, Holly couldn't tell, but Mack stood up and pushed in his chair. "I'll walk you out."

"It's okay, I can—"

"I insist," he said.

Mack's hand was on the doorknob, and as Holly approached, he put his free arm around her waist and twirled her towards his body so her back was against the door and his face was just inches from hers.

"Before I walk you out," he said, "I wanted to say one more thing."

Her breath was coming fast, and she was afraid her voice would shake if she spoke. So she nodded.

He leaned in closer, and his mouth was so close to hers she could feel the feather-light touch of his lips. He said, "After I make love to you for the first time, you're never going to look at a cucumber the same way."

Then his lips were on hers, and his arm tightened around her waist, and she forgot everything else. Her heart beat against his chest, heat flooded her body, and she wrapped her arms around his neck. Even though she knew she shouldn't, even though she knew she'd never live this down with Alejo, she kissed him back.

Mack leaned against her, deepening the kiss. When he finally lifted his head and stepped back, she wondered if she looked the same as she had a moment ago—because she felt like a whole different person.

He opened the door and gestured for her to go ahead of him. She did, and when they got to her car, he opened the driver's door. When she thought he might kiss her again, he simply gave her a mischievous smile and said, "Give Alejo my regards."

Then he was gone, walking back towards the house with an unmistakable spring in his step.

CHAPTER TWELVE

HOLLY WOKE UP THE NEXT MORNING—THE MORNING OF THE BARBECUE—
feeling like she had made a serious mistake. She lay in bed, unwilling to drag herself into the day. Why had she let Mack kiss her, like *that,* when she was supposed to have a boyfriend?

And why had she kissed him *back*? She groaned and put both hands over her eyes. She didn't even have an answer for that, except —well, except that he'd kissed her first. And he was beyond good at it.

She remembered countless disagreements between her sisters when they were kids, where one of them—usually Jasmine—would whine to their mother, "She did it first! She started it!"

Well, Mack had started it.

"And you finished it," their mom had said innumerable times.

Yes, Holly had finished it. And she'd finished it good. Now she had to face him again. There was no possible excuse for skipping out on today's barbecue. If she did, he'd know she was avoiding him. She supposed that wouldn't be a bad thing. Sighing, she got out of bed and went to brew some coffee. How would she even act when she saw him? Fortunately, since he was hosting, he'd probably be too busy to notice her. She hoped she was right even as she hoped she was wrong.

Holly told herself she shouldn't feel nervous about the barbecue. After all, Mack said lots of people were coming. It was unlikely they'd be alone together at any point. But unlikely was not the same as impossible. If they did end up alone, she'd just apologize.

It had probably been stupid to hope Mack would be too busy to notice her, she thought when she arrived at his house. She walked in the front door and saw him standing in the kitchen with a couple of other guys. He saw her, too. It was almost like he sensed her presence as soon as she entered. The way he looked at her, laser-focused and intense, made her shiver. She gave him a nervous wave and closed the door behind her. Before she had a chance to look for the spot to set her black bean salad, Mack was at her side, taking the bowl from her. His fingers brushed hers and she inhaled the pine-and-citrus scent of his cologne. She could take this opportunity to say she was sorry, but he spoke too quickly.

"Thanks for coming," he said. "Your sister's outside. I'll join you in a minute, but first I've got to prove to these guys that I can eat twelve wings slathered in this new hot sauce. Blazing Bayou."

When she raised an eyebrow at him, he said, "It's an ongoing competition."

"Good luck," she said, and she had to stop herself from giving him a quick kiss. As if they were a couple or something. But her eyes must have betrayed her and sneaked a look at his mouth, because she was staring right at it when it quirked into a smile. He walked back towards the kitchen, and the guys started chanting his name.

Holly shook her head. She was still smiling when she stepped out the back door to look for Sequoia and Elijah.

"Hey, you're looking a little bit twitterpated." Sequoia's voice rang out across the yard. Holly tried to smother her smile, to neutralize her expression, but her efforts failed. So instead, she went for playing dumb.

"What?" she said.

"What do you mean, 'What?'" Sequoia said. "I can read you like a book. I think you need a beer."

"Can we have a beer this early?" Holly said. "It's only, like, noon. Right?"

Elijah piped in: "Of course you can. We're in the p.m. hours now."

He held up a beer of his own, and Sequoia clinked hers against it before walking over to an ice- and beer-filled bucket on a table against the wall.

She handed Holly a can of beer whose label proclaimed it was a "Hoppy Ale."

Holly cracked it open right away and took a long drink.

"So?" Sequoia said. She leaned against Elijah, who put an arm around her neck. "What's got you all twitterpated?"

"What are you talking about?" Holly said.

"I saw the look on your face when you came out of the house. Oh, and where's your boyfriend? What's his name? Alejo?"

"Oh. I was just smiling. Mack was about to eat some hot wings and the guys were all chanting and it was funny. I smiled. I don't think that constitutes twitterpated." She shrugged and took another drink of the beer. "This tastes even better on the second drink."

"Did you see that?" Sequoia said to Elijah. "She's avoiding answering my question."

"Saw it," Elijah said.

The two of them stood there, looking smug. Holly loved seeing her sister like this—so comfortable and in love with another human.

"Which question?" she said.

"The one where I asked you where your boyfriend is."

"Oh," Holly said. She took another drink of her beer.

"And you keep doing that," Sequoia said. "You're going to be drunk before you know it if you keep that up."

"You fired so many questions at me that I couldn't answer them all at once. You asked me why I looked twitterpated, where my boyfriend was, and whether his name was Alejo."

"Yeah." Sequoia drew the word out. "And you're still not answering two-thirds of them."

"Which means," Elijah said, "that you're obviously twitterpated, because you find Mack so good-looking, and also that you don't want to tell us."

Sequoia looked up at him, her expression so adoring Holly had to smile.

"Also," Elijah said, holding up his pointer finger, postulating. "You obviously don't have an actual boyfriend. I'm starting to doubt this Alejo character actually exists."

Holly felt her mouth drop open. How did he *know*? She was about to ask him, but Sequoia elbowed him. Hard. So hard that Holly wondered if they'd talked about Alejo not existing. Elijah semi-confirmed that thought when he mouthed, "Sorry," at Sequoia.

Sequoia made a terrible recovery and after far too long, said, "Stop it, Elijah. She probably just isn't ready for us to meet him yet. She's afraid he'll be intimidated because you've got the whole package. You know."

She moved her eyebrows up and down, and Elijah's face turned red. Holly felt hysterical. She *was* hysterical, with nerves about her secret being exposed, and with fear that she was going to have to produce a boyfriend—a plausible Alejo—at some point. Did Sequoia know? Was it possible? If so, how?

A chorus of cheers floated through the open patio door, and Mack came running out, arms in the air in what Holly assumed was a sign of triumph. He was grinning, and it looked maniacal. He gave Sequoia, Elijah, and her a thumbs-up, and then ran to the beer bucket, grabbed a can, popped it open, and chugged it.

When he was done, he wiped his mouth with the back of one hand and said, "Done!"

"Ah, so you beat Rawlings?" Sequoia said.

"I did! First time ever."

Another guy, who Holly pegged as a police officer based on his haircut, came out of the house and slapped Mack on the back. "Meet the new Seabreeze PD Hot Wings Champion," he said.

"Champion of the Retirees," Mack said. "Which means that since you're still working at the PD, we are co-champions of two different divisions."

More cheering came from inside, and the group of men from the kitchen—all of whom had grown considerably rowdier—came tumbling out. More back-slapping, high-fiving, and cheering, and the group moved on.

"Off to the creek," Mack said. "Want to join 'em?"

"I'm going to grab a plate," Sequoia said. "This guy's upped the, uh, *running* regime and I'm constantly hungry."

Elijah grinned at her, then swatted her on the bottom. "Gotta keep this ass in fine shape."

Sequoia rolled her eyes. Holly was surprised to find herself feeling emotional. She even felt a bit teary as she remembered how Sequoia used to run for solitude. She'd preferred to be alone, until Elijah came along.

Mack elbowed her gently, which reminded her that she hadn't responded to his invitation. He was still grinning.

"Oh!" Holly said, watching her sister's retreating figure. "Sure. I'll go with you. Leave these lovebirds to their appetites."

She could have sworn she heard Mack mutter something about appetites under his breath, but out loud, he said, "All right. I'll lead the way."

The other guys had veered off to the right, and when Mack steered her off to the left, she pointed in the direction they'd gone. "Didn't they—"

"Shortcut," he said, effectively shushing her.

They walked past the shed where the puppies lived, and Quimby trotted out.

"Ah! Your pup knows his new mama's voice," Mack said. "He's following you."

Quimby offered Holly the dog-equivalent of a smile, all big teeth and a lolling tongue, and she knelt down to scratch him behind one ear before they continued to walk. The property began to slope downward from there. The grassy ground gave way to hard-packed dirt, and Mack held out a hand, palm up, in an offer to steady her.

She placed her hand in his and shivered at the contact. There was something about how his callouses felt against her own palm…this ignited that heat in her belly and she decided it was some kind of weird primal urge brought on by his toughness.

Within a moment, she could hear the creek running, bubbling

over rocks in its own soothing song. Mack led her closer, under a canopy of trees. Some of the yellowing leaves had dropped to the ground, and the sun shone through the rest. When they came to the creek's edge, Holly smiled.

"This is so peaceful," she said. "You should set up a little seating area right here."

"I should," he said. "That's actually a really good idea."

"Where are the guys?" Holly said, and then realized she didn't have to ask. She could hear them several yards downstream, hollering like Tarzan.

"I wanted some time alone with you," Mack said. He turned his body towards hers and put his hands on her waist. "Think Alejo would mind?"

It was almost like he said it just to see her reaction, she thought. He was watching her carefully. Had Sequoia or Elijah, or both of them, said something to Mack about Alejo not existing? She shrugged, and was surprised to hear the coy tone in her voice when she said, "Alejo, who?"

Then she realized—immediately—that this was not a good path to go down. Not only would it make her look like a disloyal girl-friend, but it also opened the door for further advances from Mack. Not that she'd mind, but she'd made the decision to focus on herself, and she didn't need Mack distracting her, no matter how much she might *enjoy* that distraction.

"Just kidding," she said. "But I have to admit, you're hard to resist."

He had pulled her close, so their waists were touching. Now he leaned his forehead against hers.

"You're hard to resist," he said. "Especially in that outfit. This Alejo guy must not be very smart, sending you out alone to all these social functions. He has to know you're leaving men at your feet."

"Well, at least I'm leaving them at my feet, and not in my arms," Holly said, before realizing that in her arms was exactly where Mack stood. She'd wrapped them around his shoulders and the two of them were swaying now, so close to dancing that all they needed was music. "Mack," she said. "I wanted to apologize for yesterday."

She should apologize for the kiss. But she found herself saying, "For leaving so abruptly."

Suddenly, as she got a vision of herself palm-to-forehead, Mack's mouth was on hers. She could taste the tang of the beer and feel the warmth of the hot sauce from the wings he'd eaten. She could feel his hands on her lower back, and her skin anticipating their next move. Then, before she thought about what she was doing, she felt herself kissing him back. Her tongue was in his mouth, her hands were in his hair, and her body was pulsing with the need to undress, right here on the bank of this creek.

It was impossible to tell who ended the kiss, but they broke apart, both of them breathing heavily.

"No apology necessary," he said, and then, "Are you glaring at me?"

Before Holly could answer, they heard a shout, Quimby barked, and Rawlings, the guy Mack had beaten in the wing-eating contest, came splashing up the creek towards them, his shirt off and his jeans soaking wet.

"There you are, Mack! Are you comin'? We got a new challenge going. We made a rope swing and Schmidt doesn't think I can jump as far as he can. Weakling."

Mack grinned at Holly, wiped his mouth, and winked.

"Let's check it out," he said.

Rawlings took off the same way he'd come, splashing through the shallow creek like a little boy. Mack walked alongside. Holly found herself smiling as she followed them, but she wasn't sure if it was because their competition was entertaining, or because of that kiss.

Speaking of that kiss, she thought as Quimby nipped at her fingertips, *I'm going to have to do something about the Alejo problem.*

Then, she got an idea.

HOLLY'S IDEA hadn't formed completely, but she had a good first step in mind. Because she was still a bit tipsy from the barbecue (enough that Elijah had driven her car home), her inhibitions were slightly lowered when she sat down at her computer and entered her search terms into Google's search bar: *Male escort services Seabreeze, CA.*

It was the perfect solution.

If Holly could find an escort to ... well, to escort her to some of the important upcoming social functions, she could make her sisters and Mack believe Alejo was real. And then, when it was all over, she could pretend they'd broken up.

Jasmine and Sequoia would get off her back. Mack would stop hitting on her. He'd stop kissing her like he had on the bank of the creek, for goodness' sake. She could stop thinking about him.

And she could focus on herself. Just Holly.

Google presented her with a long list of search results. Some of them touted "straight male companions for women," and others went so far as to advertise "male strippers" and "intimacy experts."

"Well, I don't need that," Holly said. "But I do need another beer."

When she returned to the computer, beer in hand, she clicked on the first search result, where the company promised its escorts would meet the expectations of even the most discerning woman.

Holly snorted. She certainly wasn't that discerning. All she needed was an Alejo.

She clicked on the "See Photos of our Escorts" box and gasped when the page loaded.

"Why did I wait so long to think of this marvelous idea?"

The men were gorgeous. Maybe they looked a little glamorous for small-town Seabreeze life. But she could dress her companion down, couldn't she? Anyway, one of the main events for which she needed company was Jasmine's wedding, and weddings were always at least a little bit glamorous, weren't they?

The website allowed her to narrow down search results by age and interests, but not by physical characteristics.

"So I'll just browse," she said. "It's not like I mind looking at a bunch of hot men in boxer briefs."

Even though she found this browsing quite enjoyable, perusing dozens of photos was also tiring. Her eyes burned by the time she'd gone through all of them and narrowed the choices down to three dark-skinned men who could pass for Alejo.

Each of the escorts had a screen name, and she'd chosen Cowboy Carl, Alex the Adventurous, and The Incredible Hugo.

Cowboy Carl had longish hair and wore chaps in his photo, and his profile said he lived on a ranch. Holly doubted that was true, but she liked the idea that he was rugged and worked with his hands. Plus, she'd always had a thing for cowboys. Holly told herself this had nothing to do with the fact that Mack was building his own little ranch.

Alex the Adventurous was a self-proclaimed outdoorsman, with the tan lines to prove it. He'd take her kayaking, hiking, or zip-lining, and all with that sexy stubble on his face.

And The Incredible Hugo was huge.

"He should really call himself Huge Hugo," Holly said as she admired his muscles, which spanned the entire frame of the photo. His skin was smooth and possibly oiled. He'd listed his interests as reading and yoga, but somehow she couldn't see him sitting on a couch with a book or stretching his body into a Downward Dog. Still, she was a good conversationalist. She could find things to talk to him about. Like muscles and baby oil.

"So many men, so little time," she said, massaging her neck and shoulders as best she could.

She put in a "Request for an initial encounter" for each of the three men, and now all she had to do was wait. She'd meet with each of them before selecting one to accompany her to Jasmine's wedding and possibly to a few pre-wedding festivities.

This plan was perfect, she thought, and she had a feeling it was going to turn out to be fun.

CHAPTER THIRTEEN

HOLLY CHECKED HER EMAIL FIRST THING MONDAY MORNING, BUT THERE were no responses to her requests. This meant she'd be checking her phone compulsively throughout the day. She was already looking at the blank screen when Mack texted her at eight: *Working today?*

Her mouth worked itself into a smile. Involuntarily. Holly forced it back into a straight line and responded: *Yep, 10-6*. He wrote back with a smiley face, and she wondered if that meant he was going to come in. Before the daydream reel could start playing, Holly shook her head. For now, it was time to focus on herself. Her next call with Tristan was scheduled to begin, so she logged into her video chat and waited for his image to materialize.

"Have you spent any more time alone with yourself?"

Tristan Compass blinked at Holly from her computer screen, and she smiled back, thinking of all the fantasizing she'd done last night after kissing Mack at his barbecue.

"Yes," she said. "And it's been quite enjoyable."

"Good," Tristan said. "I think it's time to talk about your plan for moving forward."

Holly nodded.

"I have an exercise for you to complete before our next session. It will help you identify your values, and then prioritize them. So many of my clients say they want to do more of this or that, or spend more time doing one thing or another, yet, when they complete this exercise, they realize how much time they're spending on activities they don't like, or with people they don't enjoy. There's a quote I like —it's 'If you're not moving toward your goals, then you're moving away from them.' I encourage all of my clients to spend time only on things that align with their values or move them towards their goals."

Of course, an image of Mack popped into Holly's mind, then, and she thought that she'd like to spend more time enjoying him, doing activities they both liked. *How scandalous, Holly Carr*, she thought.

Tristan explained the exercise, which required Holly to make a list of the activities she did over the course of each week, and the people with whom she spent time. She was then supposed to prioritize the list according to what or who she enjoyed most. Finally, during the next week, she was to track how she spent her time.

Then, when she met with Tristan again, they would compare her prioritized list to the way she actually spent her time.

"This is one of my favorite exercises," Tristan said, his voice gushing enthusiasm. "It's so revealing. I'll bet you're going to be surprised. This is a game-changer, Holly."

She smiled at him, but all she could think about was how this exercise would be completely skewed. She'd told Tristan she had a boyfriend, and she didn't. Where she should have some sort of column for spending time with Alejo, she wouldn't. Worse, she was spending time with Mack, which only confused matters. Not only was that was time she couldn't label (what would she write down? "Chemistry-saturated time with non-boyfriend"?), but also, Holly had a feeling Tristan would tell her it was unwise to be spending time with another guy.

She could label Mack "Alejo," and pretend he was her boyfriend, but that seemed even more dishonest. Therefore, to make life simple, she wouldn't put it on her tracking sheet. Which would leave her with a bunch of empty time slots she'd have to fill in with work, sister time, and time with Cara.

Not for the first time, she questioned her decision to fabricate

Alejo. Now she wasn't sure whether the escort idea would help or hurt.

"You look worried," Tristan said.

You don't know how right you are.

"Oh!" Holly said. "I'm not worried. I just realized how late it is. I should probably go. I need to get ready for work."

Of course, she thought of Mack's message from this morning, then. She felt her face flush, but this time, Tristan didn't seem to notice.

"Okay," he said. "I guess I'll catch you later. Sounds like a busy day. This would be a perfect opportunity to start tracking your time."

Holly nodded, and hoped Tristan read her quick, jerky movements as excitement.

"Thanks," she said. "Great idea. I'll talk to you next week."

"Same time, same place," he said.

He disconnected and Holly felt her posture droop. What had she gotten herself into? This was possibly the stupidest thing she'd ever done.

"See?" she said to herself. "On my own, I'm an idiot."

In a moment of cruelty, Holly's mind flashed back to the time she'd started a fire in the toaster. She was eight. The night before, she'd been sitting with her parents and sisters in the living room. They'd stayed up late watching a movie—was it The Sound of Music? Holly's parents had joked that the girls should get up early and make them breakfast in bed, and Holly was the only one who took them seriously. While everyone in the family slept, Holly crept into the kitchen and began to prepare an elaborate breakfast of scrambled eggs and toast. At first, things went well: she turned on the stove, cracked the eggs into the pan, and added salt and pepper, all without incident. She stirred the eggs, watching as their liquidy insides became increasingly solid.

And then she smelled it: the toast!

While the eggs hypnotized her, the toast toasted. It toasted so much that tendrils of smoke were now rising from the openings in the toaster. Panicked, Holly dropped the spatula, and it clattered to the floor, leaving a trail of half-cooked eggs in its wake.

She turned the dial to pop the toast up, away from the heating elements (which were now glowing with evil glee), but nothing happened. Smoke continued to rise from the toaster, and was now hanging just below the kitchen ceiling. She had to get that toast out of there.

So Holly did what any dumb eight-year-old would do: she grabbed a fork and began using it to pry the burned toast out of the toaster.

Sparks flew, and caught on the very last bit of un-burned toast, igniting a fire. Flames came up out of the slot. Holly screamed, waking Sequoia, who ran into the kitchen, and of course, who had the calm and confidence to unplug the toaster and blow out the fire.

This whole situation, Holly thought now, with Mack and Alejo and Tristan, was just like that toaster fire. It was out of control. Someone needed to put it out—and this time, Sequoia couldn't come swooping in to save her. She was the only one who could do it. Which, of course, spelled disaster. She put her elbows on the kitchen bar and her forehead in her hands.

Then she remembered she didn't have time to wallow. She had to go to work. She groaned and grabbed her keys.

Naturally, her thoughts drifted to Mack as soon as she got in the car. The chemistry between them was simmering, there was no doubt about that, she thought as she drove across town. She felt like she couldn't resist it. Something about Mack made her stupidly needy. Alejo would never make her feel that way. "What a great guy," she said to herself.

As usual, coffee refills and pancake deliveries kept her busy for the first hour of her shift, leaving her barely any time to think about her escort encounters. Or encounters with Mack.

Until he walked in.

How the man engineered such good timing, she'd never know. But a couple of ladies having coffee vacated a two-person booth in Holly's section just as he entered, and he slid into it as if Holly had saved it for him.

"Morning," he said when she approached with the pot of coffee.

"Well, aren't you bright-eyed and bushy-tailed?" Holly said, pouring his coffee.

"I had a great time yesterday," he said. "Thanks for coming. Did you get the same gene as Sequoia? The one that makes you disappear from social events without saying good-bye?"

"Funny," Holly said. "I guess I did."

She started to walk away, but he stopped her by asking, "Did you have a nice time?"

Although she didn't turn completely around, she did look over her shoulder to smile at him.

"I did."

Then, walking back to the kitchen to put in one order and pick up another, she did another mental forehead slap. Why had she said that so coyly? She'd just given him confirmation that she'd enjoyed that kiss. That very knee-weakening kiss.

She *had* enjoyed it but she didn't want him to know. Why did his presence render her brain dead?

This had to end. He had to stop showing up at her work, inviting her over, and, of course, kissing her. And the only way to accomplish those things was for her to bring Alejo into the picture. She checked her phone while she waited for the final plate in an order. Still no emails about the encounters.

"Come on," she said.

One of the cooks, Johnny, shot her a questioning glance, and she smiled, way too brightly. "Not you," she said. "Just waiting on an important email."

"Must be important," Johnny said. "It's got you talking to yourself."

"If only you knew," she said.

He winked at her. "Order up."

THE EMAILS ARRIVED THAT EVENING, a full twenty-four hours after she'd sent the requests.

And as she'd found was often the case when she anticipated something all day long, the messages were kind of a letdown. She expected something personalized from each Alejo. But instead, she received three separate, automated emails:

HI, Holly Carr,

WE'RE pleased that you've requested an encounter with Cowboy Carl. He looks forward to meeting you. Schedule your appointment at this link, and he'll join you at a location of your choosing:

MEET COWBOY CARL <<< Schedule Your Encounter

TO MAKING your fantasies come true,

Robin Kreger
   Escort Coordinator
   Escorts for the Discerning Woman

HOLLY SCHEDULED the appointments for the upcoming Friday evening, Saturday morning, and Saturday evening.

Then, Sunday, she'd make an official decision about which man would become her Alejo. So, six days from now, her problem would be solved.

Feeling satisfied with herself and her innovative thinking, Holly closed her laptop and went to bed.

CHAPTER FOURTEEN

NEVER HAVING MET A MALE ESCORT BEFORE (OR, AT LEAST, NOT THAT SHE knew of), Holly wasn't sure how to greet Cowboy Carl when he arrived at Beachside Pizza. Fortunately, he must be accustomed to these situations, because his eyes found her face immediately, and he shot her a dazzling mega-watt smile that showed off straight ultra-white teeth. She had to tone down her own smile as she stood up to shake his hand.

"You must be Carl," she said.

"And you, Holly," he said. "It is absolutely my pleasure."

His jeans had probably cost more than her entire outfit, and she immediately questioned her choice of a meeting spot. Now that she thought about it, his typical clients probably selected swanky bistros with menu items Holly couldn't pronounce. But when they sat down at the corner table she'd snagged and she thanked him for being there, he exhaled loudly and said, "Thank *you*. You have no idea how nice it is to meet somewhere so casual."

When she asked if she could buy him lunch and he suggested a vegetarian pizza, she knew there was friendship potential. They made small talk while they waited for the pizza, and then he dove in as he lifted slices off the pie stand and onto plates.

"So, Miss Holly, what does a lovely woman like you want with an escort? I mean, I assume it isn't romance, or you would have asked me to meet you at the Bayside Hotel or something."

Holly nodded. "It's funny you say that. Earlier this year, my sister's high school boyfriend tried to reignite their romance, and he took her there. It was kind of a disaster. I may never look at it the same way again."

"Didn't work out?" Carl said.

He'd taken a bite of pizza while she spoke, and now he wiped the corners of his mouth. She noticed how clean and shiny his fingernails were, and wondered if he got manicures. Probably. Men didn't have hands like that unless they visited the nail salon. Which was weird. Sequoia would definitely pick up on it and most likely, make fun of it. He *had* looked pretty rugged in that photo on the website, though, so she figured he could play that up if he wanted to.

Holly realized she'd taken just slightly too long to answer, so she pretended she was still chewing.

"No," she said. "He showed up in her life a little too late. She'd already fallen for someone else."

"Ah," Carl said. "Classic love triangle."

Holly nodded. "I always had kind of a crush on Parker—her high school boyfriend. But she fell pretty hard for Hudson, the guy she's marrying in a couple of weeks."

Carl held up a hand, pointer finger extended into the air. "And that's why you need an escort. You need a date for the wedding. One who can disappear from your life afterward without any heartbreak."

His eyes gleamed, and for the first time, Holly could see the humor in the situation.

"Pretty much sums it up," she said. "The thing is, I've been focusing on myself lately. Avoiding romance all together. But I made a mistake. I told my sisters—I have two of them—that I have a boyfriend. I thought it would save me from having to find a date for the wedding. I thought I could say he was busy that day. But now I've backed myself into a corner. He can't possibly be busy for all the wedding festivities. So I need him to make an appearance."

Carl leaned back in his chair and crossed his arms. He really was handsome, and she'd feel good about having him on her arm at Jasmine's wedding.

"Why didn't you just say you wanted to stay single?" he said.

Holly shrugged one shoulder. "I mean, that's the thing. My oldest sister, Sequoia, was trying to set me up with one of her co-workers. Which is so not like her. And because she was being so—well, so normal, I didn't want to burst her bubble. I couldn't just say, 'No, thank you.' I felt like I had to have a real reason not to date him. So now …"

"Here we are," he said. "Well, I've been a wedding date before. It's actually fun."

"Perfect," Holly said. "So. Are you really a cowboy?"

No, he wasn't a real cowboy. Carl's friends had always told him he looked like a cowboy, like someone who'd spend his days on horseback, lassoing cattle, and his nights sleeping under the stars. So when it came time to develop a persona for his career as an escort, Cowboy Carl seemed like the natural choice.

The bottom line, he said, was that he could be anyone Holly wanted him to be.

She supposed he used that line with a slightly different undertone when he interviewed with women who were looking for encounters of the sexual kind. But when he said it to her at Beachside Pizza, he said it so affably she felt confident, too. As Holly drove home, she reviewed the conversation in her mind. If she had some kind of score sheet, Carl would get tens pretty much across the board. She might ding him on the shiny fingernails.

He was a perfect gentleman, had good manners, and seemed genuinely interested in her, as if he'd actually enjoy being her fake boyfriend during the wedding festivities.

Holly pulled up in front of her house and was surprised to find herself smiling. Strangely, she thought, this process was pretty enjoyable. In fact, she was starting to think she could just date escorts for the rest of her life. Although that would get expensive. She would have to settle for a couple of weeks with a professional boyfriend, and then kiss that concept good-bye.

Next up: Alex the Adventurous.

When Holly first spotted Alex at the Sand Dollar Park that afternoon, she gasped, loudly, and then clapped a hand over her mouth. He certainly looked like an outdoorsman: he wore hiking boots and a knit sweater, probably made of wool. Straight out of a fancy clothing catalog.

"I might have to abandon ship on this one," she said to herself. A little boy playing at the edge of the fountain looked up at her and said, "Stay the course, mi'lady."

Amused, she decided he was right. Still, she approached Alex with caution, just in case *he* wanted to abandon ship once he saw her and realized how much higher he was than her on the "Hotness Scale." The term, of course, came from Sequoia and Jasmine who, as high schoolers when Holly was still in junior high, would gossip about different couples they knew, comparing their rankings on the Scale.

"She's, like, a three," Sequoia would say, "and he's probably an eight. Maybe even a ten. That's a huge discrepancy."

"Yeah," Jasmine would say. "There should be a two-point spread, max."

Alex the Adventurous was definitely a ten. Maybe even an eleven. And Holly was a strong six or, on a good day, when her face was cooperating, a weak seven. Still, when she approached him and stuck out her hand to shake, he smiled as if she were the most beautiful thing he'd seen all day. Little lines crinkled the edges of his eyes, which Holly found adorable.

"Holly," he said. "Lovely to meet you."

"Likewise," she said. "Thank you so much for coming."

She hadn't been able to tell from the photo on the website, but his hair was thick and curly, and his eyes were the nicest shade of moss green.

"I admit, I don't often meet women at parks," he said. "They typically prefer a much more … intimate setting."

Holly smiled. "I guess I'm not your typical client. Want to get a coffee?"

They bought coffees from the kiosk, and sat down on a bench

next to the fountain. The little boy who'd advised her to stay the course glanced over and gave her a thumbs-up.

"So, what brings you to Escorts for the Discerning Woman?" Alex said.

No small talk, then. She could deal with this. He was a straight shooter. Sequoia would appreciate it, and Jasmine would think he was prickly. Holly nodded. She could do straight shooting.

She explained the situation, conscious of keeping her volume down so the little boy wouldn't hear her. "So basically, I need a date who can make all the right moves and then disappear when it's all said and done."

Alex nodded and sipped his coffee.

"I work with a lot of clients who need boyfriends for the weekend," he said. "Weddings, parties, you know, special events. They just want someone to hang out with. But none of them hire me because they're worried about what their sisters think."

"How do you know?" Holly said. "Maybe they're just not being honest with you."

"Or maybe you're not being honest with yourself," Alex said.

Wait. Had her sisters secretly set her up with this guy? And did he want to get hired, or not? Maybe he needed to be honest with himself and admit that he preferred clients who preferred intimate settings. Holly felt herself getting edgy.

"I *am* being honest with myself," Holly said. "And I know that I made a mistake by telling them I had a boyfriend. Now I just need to ride this story line out, to the last chapter."

"Why don't you just go to the wedding stag?"

"Like I said, my oldest sister is trying to set me up with one of her co-workers. He keeps showing up. And he's very tempting. But I need to focus on myself."

"So if you have a fake boyfriend," Alex said, "you think he'll leave you alone?"

Holly nodded. "He's very … persistent."

"Doesn't look like you mind it. You're blushing. I grew up with four sisters, Holly. I know how women work. You like this guy."

She could say the cold weather was putting some pink in her

cheeks. She could say the coffee was warming her up. Or she could tell him to beat it.

But she didn't.

"Maybe I do," she said, instead. "But I can't date him—or anyone —right now."

Before he had a chance to answer, Holly had a revelation: "Wait. I am just now noticing this. You're the argumentative type, right? You're the guy a woman hires when she wants a companion who can participate in debates and deep conversations. Like at dinner parties."

He shrugged. "It's kind of a specialty."

This could be perfect. Alex could match Sequoia, argument for argument, question for question.

"Do you really think hiring an escort is a bad idea?" Holly said.

"Why do you care what I think?"

WELL, that was interesting.

Hiring Alex could go either way, Holly thought. On one hand, she wasn't sure whether he'd give his full participation, since he thought she should go to Jasmine's wedding alone.

On the other hand, he was a professional. He'd be getting paid. And, judging by the way he talked to her at their initial meeting, he could rival Sequoia in a debate, which was rare. If the two of them got into a conversation, the pressure would be off of Holly.

Because Jasmine would be busy getting married, her communication with Holly's date would be limited to a quick introduction. Alex's green eyes and very nice smile would charm Jasmine immediately, and then she'd be on to something else.

Holly had to admit his smile had bordered on icy by the end of their time together, but still. If she hired him, she'd be paying him to be pleasant.

If she was using the same imaginary score sheet for Alex that she'd used for Carl, she'd have to score him slightly lower in certain areas. He wasn't quite as friendly, and she didn't like how he turned the spotlight on her. But he got bonus points for his ability to debate, and to maintain control of the conversation. Not that she'd want that in a real boyfriend. In fact, she'd probably mark him down in that area if she were considering real boyfriends. But as a companion who could keep up with her sister, he got twelve out of ten. If she were forced to choose between Carl and Alex right now, she'd probably wind up a hung jury. Maybe meeting Hugo would make the decision a little easier. Or maybe not.

If worse came to worst, she could always draw a name out of a hat.

THE CAPTION under The Incredible Hugo's profile picture should have read, "Warning: Muscles larger than they appear." Hugo was huge. It really *was* incredible. Sequoia would assume he was on steroids. When he walked into the Burger Shack and Holly stood up to greet him, he wrapped her in a giant hug and immediately felt like an old friend.

"Holly!" he said when he stepped back and held her at arm's length. "They didn't tell me how beautiful you are."

Holly felt her eyes dart to the teenaged girl behind the hostess stand. Hopefully she assumed this was a blind date, not a woman meeting an escort for the first time.

"Aw, you're blushing!"

His voice boomed throughout the reception area, and even though she'd typically be mortified, she found it endearing. This guy would definitely take the attention off Holly at Jasmine's wedding and anywhere else they ended up together.

The hostess was smiling at them, and Holly wondered briefly whether it was because she thought they were cute or because she thought this situation was strange.

Once they were seated, Hugo said, "So, what do you order here? I usually get the triple veggie burger."

When Holly raised her eyebrows, Hugo said, "I know, I know, it's a lot of food. But the patties are delicious, and they're packed with protein. The owners of this place, Zeb and Susan? They make the patties from scratch, and they're—they're just so good. I mean, off the charts."

His massive muscles dwarfed the table and the menu. He reminded Holly of Popeye.

"Actually, I usually get the veggie burger, too," she said. "But just the single."

Hugo laughed, one of those head back, mouth-open laughs. Of course, it was loud, too. A few of the other patrons craned their necks to see what was so funny, and Holly was surprised that none of them looked annoyed. In fact, they looked amused and were smiling, themselves.

So he was a charmer. Where Alex the Adventurous would use his brainy debate skills to keep Sequoia on the edge of her seat, Hugo would entertain her. And Carl the Cowboy would put everyone at ease.

Too bad she couldn't use all three of them as her Alejo.

"What are you thinking about?" Hugo said. "You drifted off."

Holly put her menu down. "I did, I'm sorry. When you first meet a new client, do you wonder why she's hiring you?"

"I usually wonder," he said, rubbing his chin with one hand. "But I don't often ask. I figure, if you want to tell me, you can. Otherwise, I just enjoy my time with a lovely woman. And you *are* lovely, Holly. I can't imagine you need to hire a man to spend time with you."

Holly sighed. "Thank you for saying so. And it's not that I *need* to hire a man to spend time with me. It's just that I'm not in the place to seek a real boyfriend or companion. You know? But I need a plus-one for my sister's wedding and all the related events."

Hugo nodded. "This problem is more common than you may think," he said. "Not that it makes you feel any better, but lots of women have told me the same thing. There's a lot of pressure on you all to settle down, get knocked up, and live barefoot in the kitchen making meatloaf every night."

"You're preaching to the choir," Holly said.

By the end of the meal, she was pretty smitten with Hugo, who listened attentively, laughed in all the right places, and shared his seasoned fries with Holly, who'd ordered a salad with her burger.

She learned that in addition to weightlifting, he enjoyed hot baths and gardening.

"You're a pretty well-rounded guy, Hugo," she said. "If I weren't in the solo category, I'd want to date you."

"I got news for you," he said.

"What's that?"

"I'm gay. So I have a feeling I wouldn't be in your market."

That explained the hot baths.

So. Hugo was charming but gay, Alex was argumentative, and Carl got manicures.

Sunday morning, Holly promised herself she'd make her choice before going to work at noon.

Each man had a list of pros and cons, and each one seemed like a fine companion for a wedding and a few wedding-associated festivities.

Hugo would undoubtedly call the most attention to himself, with his mere size and that loud laugh. But that meant he'd draw the attention away from her … and Holly wasn't sure if her sisters would spot any indicators of his sexuality.

And Alex would be able to handle a discussion with Sequoia, no problem. But would he take Holly's side if Sequoia started in on her usual nonsense?

Carl was rugged and polite, and a great conversationalist. But was he tough enough to withstand anything Sequoia threw at him? Because she would throw something.

Holly decided to think it over in the shower. She must have sent some weird vibe out to the universe, because just as she turned on the hot water, she received a text message from Mack: *Hey there. Just thinking about you. And a club sandwich. You working today?*

Why was he sending her these messages when he believed she had a boyfriend? Was it possible—no, there was no way he could know Alejo was make-believe. And anyway, Alejo would appear, in the flesh, in a matter of days.

Even though she was supposed to be thinking about Carl, Alex, and Hugo while she was in the shower, she found herself thinking about Mack. Every time his imaginary hands slid over her breasts or dipped below her waistline, she kicked him out of the shower and forced herself to redirect.

By the time she got out, she had made a decision. And it felt good. Alejo would make his debut soon, and everything would be okay.

CHAPTER FIFTEEN

IN ALL THE EXCITEMENT OF SELECTING A REAL-LIFE PERSON TO PLAY THE
role of her fake boyfriend, Holly had forgotten to track her time. So
she woke up in a panic Monday morning, realizing that because she
had a meeting with Tristan, she had only an hour to come up with a
completed time-tracking chart. Worse, the chart couldn't include the
escort selection process. And she'd certainly spent several hours on
that.

"Escort selection process," she mumbled to the coffee maker as it
gurgled to life. "Never thought I'd say that."

As had become a regular occurrence recently, her mind drifted to
thoughts of Mack. He'd come into the Broken Egg at the start of
yesterday's shift.

As she'd taken his order, her eyes had shifted downward to look
at his mouth, and her brain reminded her that she'd really enjoyed
kissing him on the bank of the creek, all hot sauce and beer and hard
muscles, the yellow leaves fluttering down around them.

And then she reminded herself that she had to shut this thing
down, now, since Alejo would be making his appearance, soon.

She kept her tone playful when she said, "Don't you get tired of
the Broken Egg?"

"Nah," he said. "Anyway, I needed to talk to you about your new puppy."

"We'll talk about the puppy later," Holly said. "And I've heard Burger Shack is pretty good."

"I've heard that, too. But you don't work there."

That was all the time she had, because the cook called, "Order up."

When she passed his table, delivering a French dip and a barbecue chicken wrap to another table, he said quietly, "Say you'll go to dinner with me. Burger Shack."

She just shook her head and kept walking.

He tipped her forty dollars and wrote on the receipt: *Take me to dinner.*

And now, not even twenty-four hours after that, she was still thinking about him. The coffee maker gave a final, loud sputter. Holly jumped, realizing she'd just stood there for twelve minutes, reliving that hour Mack was at the Broken Egg the day before. She now had forty-five minutes to prepare for her coaching call. She threw together the time-tracking sheet, washed her face, and put on some mascara and lipstick.

"Good morning," Tristan said at eight a.m. on the dot.

Because she was nervous about being outed for faking her time-tracking sheet, Holly infused her voice with extra cheerfulness and wished him a good morning, too.

"So, let's talk about your prioritized list," he said to her.

Shit. The prioritized list. She'd totally forgotten to write it down.

"Oh!" she said. "I was so busy finishing my time-tracking sheet that I forgot to bring it. It's in my bedroom. Hang on. I'll be right back."

She got up from the table as calmly as possible, and when she was certain she was out of the range of the webcam, she ran to her bedroom and grabbed her journal. On the way back to the table, she began scribbling down her prioritized list, certain Tristan had intended for her to put a little more energy into it.

By the time she sat back down, she had a few items:

• • •

Sisters
   Work
   Cara
   Home stuff
   Alejo
   Self-Care Time

"SORRY ABOUT THAT. So I don't have very many items, I realized. And even for this one, Self-Care Time, I'm not sure what I'd put there. But I know self-care is important."

Now, she hoped the things she'd written down on her time-tracker sheet had something to do with the items she'd written down on this list.

Holly held her journal up to the webcam so Tristan could see it, and he leaned forward, eyebrows drawn together.

"So you're right," he said. "That's a pretty short list, which is actually a good thing. The items you have there are foundational, and I'm glad you've chosen to focus on them. So let's see your time-tracker."

Miraculously, most of the activities there matched up with the items on her list.

"Great first steps," Tristan said.

Holly felt herself beaming. Maybe she was doing something right. Of course, she'd fake-tracked her time with the escorts, writing it down as Alejo time. And she hadn't had any activities to put down as self-care. But still.

"I have two new assignments for you," Tristan said. "I want you to explore what self- care means to you. Maybe it's a hobby or an exercise routine, or yoga. Or maybe it's getting a massage. But if you believe it's important to you, then you need to spend some time on it. Right?"

Does fantasizing about Mack count?

"Right," she said.

He nodded. "The second assignment is to begin making a list of what you're really good at. What comes so easily to you that when other people compliment you on it, you feel like you have to turn those compliments down?"

"I guess you're not talking about my waitressing skills," she said. "Because I am a really good waitress."

She'd been joking, but Tristan didn't even crack a smile.

"Actually," he said, holding up a pointer finger, "the skills you use as a waitress can transfer over into other fields. So it's possible you're being too specific when you categorize certain skills—like communication, memorization, teamwork, observation. You may be putting them into the waitressing category, neglecting to see where they could play a role in a different capacity."

"Wow," Holly said. "That's pretty deep."

"But it makes sense."

"Yes, it makes sense."

Holly actually experienced a little hope. She might have more skills than she realized. And she might be able to translate those into the first steps on a different path … a path that fulfilled a calling to do something more meaningful.

Tears sprang to her eyes, and she found herself saying to Tristan, "Thank you so much."

"For what?" he said.

"For helping me realize that I have something to offer. I think I've been hiding behind waitressing because it does come so easily to me. But I never realized that it is easy because I have skills."

"Mad skills," Tristan said.

Holly spent the rest of the day glowing.

The remainder of the week passed in a blur, like a montage of video clips that would show her waking up, getting ready for work, and coming home to flop onto the couch, exhausted. Of course, any good video montage would also include scenes where she tried out new and different hobbies as she strove to find something about which she felt passionate. Unfortunately, this would end up playing like a blooper reel.

First, she tried running. She followed Sequoia's advice and got a new pair of high quality running shoes. She followed Elijah's advice and got a pair of running tights just like Sequoia had. And she followed Jasmine's advice and brought a bottle of water with her. But no one prepared her for the fact that running would make her so tired that she'd end up fast-walking most of the time.

Next up: biking. Holly had fond memories of riding her bike along East Cliff Drive. But people were lying when they said, "Just like riding a bike." Unless they meant that the rider would be nervous, shaky, and swerving between people with absolutely no finesse. The sound of the little bell on her handlebars grated on her nerves by the time she'd gone two miles, and she still had to make the return trip.

Gardening could be fun, she thought, and starting with a few small houseplants seemed like a good idea. Holly bought several brightly colored pots and fern plants to go in them, and then she displayed them in her kitchen window. Only, they wilted within a few days.

"What do people my age even *do* for a hobby?" she growled one day as she realized she was lost while hiking in the redwood forest, a painful blister forming on her left heel.

For now, she could cross off running, biking, hiking, and gardening.

She could cross off yoga, where she'd caused an unfortunate incident, toppling over during a lunge, creating a domino effect with the women next to her.

And drawing and painting, where her failed attempts at creating anything remotely pleasant to look at left her frustrated and near tears.

Google provided a long list of possible activities: chess, amateur radio operation, model car or train building, blogging, board games. Beat boxing.

"Beat boxing! Who knew?"

She imagined herself wailing to Tristan: "The problem is that I'm not good at *anything* that's supposed to be fun!"

Not that one had to be good at a hobby to like it. But hobbies were done for enjoyment, according to the dictionary. And it was hard to enjoy something at which you were terrible.

Finally, even though she'd been resisting it, she decided to use her go-to solution: she asked her sisters.

"I think you should give running more of a chance," Sequoia said, stretching her long legs as if to illustrate how much they loved the activity.

"You should play a musical instrument," Jasmine said. "I hear it's good for brain development."

Holly cringed as she imagined the cacophony that would undoubtedly result from that.

"Yeah," she said. "I'll keep thinking."

And then it was Friday, the day before Jasmine's wedding. The rehearsal dinner would take place at four p.m., which also marked the time of the Big Moment: Alejo's first appearance.

CHAPTER SIXTEEN

HOLLY PACED THE HOUSE, WAITING FOR "ALEJO" (SHE HAD TO GET accustomed to calling him that) to arrive to pick her up. She was nervous. Not about spending the evening with a male escort, a virtual stranger she was paying to hang out with her, but because she hoped beyond hope that they'd be able to pull this off.

She didn't want anything (especially a fake-boyfriend scandal) to take away from Jasmine's special day. On a compulsion, she checked the time again. He'd be here in seven minutes. Surely, timeliness was one staple of his profession. Even though she hated being early— because she hated waiting—Holly had been ready at three, a full forty-five minutes before the time on which they'd agreed.

When she'd called to tell him he'd won the selection process, they'd laid some ground rules, creating a backstory and a "couple persona," which outlined how they'd act together.

"We met at a bar," Holly said, and she knew she'd made the right choice when he said, "No, not a bar. It's not classy enough. Your sisters will never take me seriously. Let's say we met at the gym."

"Perfect," she said.

Now, as she remembered that moment, she took a deep breath to calm herself. She'd made the right choice. Everything would be fine. Then she checked the time. Five more minutes. The doorbell rang and Holly jumped. He was early. It was as if he'd read her mind. She opened the door, already smiling. When she realized it wasn't, in fact, her Alejo, she felt her face fall.

"Mack," she said. "What are you doing here?"

If he noticed her disappointment, he didn't say so. He took a step back, then whistled. "You look really nice."

"Thanks," she said. "But you've got to go. *I've* got to go. I was just leaving."

She backed into the house, in search of her keys and purse, and because she left the door open, he followed her in. So casual, as if he belonged there. And the funny thing was, he *looked* as if he belonged there. Still, Holly thought, she couldn't linger on that idea. She grabbed her things off the table, and Mack said, "Don't you want a sweater? It's feeling chilly already."

He stepped closer to her, so quickly she didn't have time to move away, and he ran a fingertip down her bare arm.

"Look," he said. "You have goosebumps."

She couldn't tell him that was only because he'd touched her.

"You're right," Holly said. She practically dashed into her bedroom to grab a cardigan, and when she came back out, she brushed right past him to the open front door.

"Thanks for stopping by," she said, holding the door to shoo him out. She didn't even think about asking him why he was there.

Fortunately (or unfortunately), her Alejo chose that moment to show up. Three minutes early, which really was perfect. Yes, she told herself again. She'd made the right choice. The car was a Jeep, dark gray with oversized tires and shiny fenders. Holly nodded. Definitely the right choice.

She sneaked a glance at Mack's face and almost laughed when she saw that he looked surprised. He covered it up quickly, and whistled again. "Nice wheels," he said. "This your date? Alejo?" He enunciated each syllable.

Holly grinned. "Yep. And we've got to go, or we're going to be late."

Mack had pulled her front door closed, and she locked it before giving him the sweetest possible smile. "Nice to see you."

Alex the Adventurous, brother of four sisters, great debater, and extremely good-looking Alejo, strolled up the walkway and extended a hand, without blinking an eye at the fact that another man was standing in Holly's doorway.

"Shall we?" he said.

Holly felt herself relaxing right away. "Yes," she said. "Absolutely."

She couldn't help but throw a glance over her shoulder as Alex pulled his Jeep away from the curb. Mack was standing on her front step, smiling a strange smile and looking into her eyes. A scary thought skittered through Holly's consciousness: what if Mack knew? If Sequoia knew, and Elijah knew, then it only made sense that Mack knew, as well. And what if that strange smile meant, *Challenge accepted*? Because that is certainly what it looked like.

"DO you want to go over our story one more time?" Alex asked as they turned off of her road, yanking Mack out of her field of vision.

Bringing her attention back to her driver required some hard work, but Holly managed.

"Sure," she said. "We met at the gym. After a spin class. That was the week after Labor Day, so we've been dating for two months."

Alex nodded. He said, "Your favorite food is tofu burritos, and mine is—"

"Yours is veggie pizza."

"Yes," he said. "And our first date was a walk on the beach, which got rained out due to an unusual September rainstorm."

"Remember that one?" Holly said. "Seaweed washed right up to the parking lot at West Cliff Beach."

Again, he nodded. "Who was that guy at your house?"

Well, this was an interesting dynamic. Alex sounded genuinely curious. How refreshing. Holly could answer honestly since this was strictly a business relationship. Now that she finally had the opportunity to talk about it, Holly found the words tumbling out of her mouth as she explained everything, from Mack pulling her over for drunk driving to Sequoia's obvious and out-of-character attempts to set the two of them up. She told Alex how Mack kept showing up at the Broken Egg and making romantic overtures even though he thought she had a boyfriend. Then, she threw in the part about her fear that her sister, Elijah, and Mack had realized she was making Alejo up. Throughout Holly's retelling of the entire chain of events, Alex listened attentively, nodding here and there.

"So, why was he here this evening?"

"I have no idea!" Holly said, throwing her hands up in exasperation. "I didn't even give him the chance to say. He showed up right before you did. He recommended I grab a sweater, which I did, and when I came back out of my bedroom, you were here."

"Well, it doesn't take a rocket scientist to know he's got a thing for you."

"That's true," Holly said. "But why? And why is he being so persistent even though he believes I have a boyfriend? And, if he knows I'm making up my boyfriend, he should think I'm a lunatic. So why is he being so persistent?"

"Good question," Alex said. "I mean, you have a lot going for you, Holly. I can see why he'd be interested. But you're right. It seems strange that he'd keep pursuing you, in either case. If you were one of my sisters, I'd ask you if you think this guy is a creeper."

Holly sighed. "I don't think so. I mean, he worked with my sister for years before retiring recently. And I think she'd be getting creeper vibes if he was a creeper."

"Maybe it's a case of wanting what he can't have. Some guys are like that, you know. As soon as he believes you're single, he may very well disappear. Or, like you said, maybe he knows your relationship with Alejo is fake and, in his eyes, your good qualities outweigh your lunacy. I mean, you obviously have a thing for him. Maybe he's just banking on your story running its course so he can go full throttle."

By now they'd pulled into the parking lot at Harbor Park, where Jasmine and Hudson's wedding would take place. As planned, they'd arrived a few minutes early. Her sisters' cars were already there, and Holly felt the nerves building up again.

"You know," Alex said, "I hate to be the one to say something so obvious, but it would explain why he keeps coming back." He cleared his throat. "Your feelings for him are pretty obvious."

Holly's mouth dropped open, and because she didn't know what to say, she closed it again.

"Sit tight," Alex said. "I'll get the door for you."

He came around the front of the Jeep and opened her door, offering a hand to help her down. She smoothed her shirt and grabbed her purse. And her sweater. It was a bit chilly.

"Nervous?" Alex said.

She nodded, lips pressed together. She was glad the gazebo was on the other side of a small bluff, so her sisters couldn't see her.

"Here." Alex spun her around so her back was to him, and began massaging her neck and shoulders. Meanwhile, he spoke in a calm voice, his breath warm in her ear. "Remember, it's just a few hours. We can get through this. A few hours today, a few hours tomorrow, and this whole thing will be over. It's, what, like seven hours of your whole life?"

Surprisingly, this perspective did make Holly feel calmer, and she nodded as he massaged the tops of her arms. He gave her shoulders one final squeeze, and then said, "Showtime."

When he took her hand and started walking up the path that led to the gazebo, Holly felt almost normal. Sequoia actually looked surprised to see them, and Jasmine bounded over from where she was standing. She was practically squealing when she reached them, and she pounced on Alex, wrapping him in a tight hug.

"Alejo!" she said. "It's so nice to finally meet you."

Sequoia's approach was much calmer. She meandered over to them, and while Jasmine hugged Holly, Sequoia introduced herself. Her eyes bordered on steely, but Holly noticed they softened a bit when Alex directed his charming smile at her.

"I've heard so much about you," he said to Sequoia. "And I would have said it was statistically impossible, but you're as beautiful as Holly is."

Sequoia blushed, an occurrence so rare Jasmine froze and pointed at her face. "She's blushing! Holly, your boyfriend made Sequoia blush!"

This cracked the ice, and it broke completely when Hudson came over with a beer for Alex, Elijah in tow. "Nice to finally meet you, man," Elijah said. "Sequoia was starting to think Holly'd made you up."

Holly froze, her mind going crazy. Fortunately, Alex handled it like a pro. Because, she reminded herself, he *was* a pro. She was paying him to handle things like this.

"I can see why," he said. He winked at Holly. "I've just been so busy with work lately."

"What do you do again?" Hudson asked.

"Finance," Alex said, before expertly steering the conversation back to Hudson. "I hear you're a photojournalist. Holly tells me your photos are amazing."

"Don't make me blush, too, dude," Hudson said.

Jasmine clapped her hands together. "This is going to be so much fun! So. We're just waiting for the officiant, and then we'll get started with the rehearsal. It should only take a half-hour, and then we'll head over to The Galley and chow down."

This kind of situation—one where they all stood around with time for small talk—was exactly what Holly dreaded. What if the conversation veered into dangerous territory? But Alex managed to gain and maintain control of the entire conversation, asking lots of questions and following people's answers up with even more questions. Only once was he required to talk about himself or his relationship with Holly, which was when Sequoia asked, "So, how did you and Holly meet, again?"

"At the gym after a spin class," he said. "I was admiring her backside during hamstring curls."

He shot Holly a wicked smile and redirected, asking how Sequoia met Elijah. Of course, Elijah, being the self-proclaimed hero of that story, loved telling it, and played up the part about how he'd melted Sequoia's icy heart.

By the time he got to the part about how he'd brought her pumpkins to carve, the officiant showed up and started the wedding rehearsal. Alex stood off to one side, giving Holly a smile here and there. While she stood next to Jasmine, Holly thought about how insightful Alex was. He'd said she had a thing for Mack, and he was right. She could admit that. Plus, what he'd said about Mack rang true: he wanted what he couldn't have. He'd never really date a drunk driver, and he'd probably lose interest as soon as she lost Alejo.

When she got back into Alex's car to drive to The Galley, Holly put a hand on his arm. "You're perfect," she said. "I'm so glad I chose you."

He winked at her and said, "I'm a professional."

"Well, we still have to get through dinner," she said. "So keep it up, would you?"

The Galley's best feature was an expansive window that took up an entire wall and overlooked the Seabreeze Harbor. Their table had a view of Harbor Park, which looked picturesque in the pastel light of the setting sun. It was going to be a lovely wedding. Holly thought that if she ever got married, she'd choose an outdoor location, too.

"Everything okay?" Alex spoke quietly, and intertwined his fingers with Holly's on top of the table. "You're so quiet."

Holly smiled at him. "Everything's fine," she said. "It's great. I'm just so happy for Jasmine. It's making me a little misty, you know?"

"Women," he said, giving her hand a little squeeze. "Crying all the time."

This produced a watery laugh. Holly took a sip of her water, trying to dislodge the lump in her throat, and was relieved when Alex ordered a glass of wine for her. That sense of relief lasted only a second, though, until Sequoia turned her entire body to face them and said, "So. Alejo."

Holly sat up a little straighter. She had to resist the urge to send him some kind of warning signal, like a knee-bump or an elbow in the ribs. Then she reminded herself that he had four sisters, and at least one of them had to have personality traits like Sequoia's. Like a Rottweiler's.

"So. Sequoia," he said.

"Why has it taken you so long to meet Holly's sisters? Were you afraid of us?"

"Actually," he said, "I was really excited to meet the two of you. My work has just been non-stop lately. I've been out of town a lot."

"What kind of finances require out of town meetings?" Sequoia said. "You've got me curious."

"Curious like a tiger stalking a bunny rabbit," Holly said.

Alex smiled. "No, no, I'd be curious, too, if my baby sister's boyfriend was out of the picture all the time. We're involved in a big merger." He shrugged. "It's boring stuff, really, but it's taken up a lot of my time." Now he leaned closer to Holly and kissed her on the temple. "I've really been missing my girl, here."

Sequoia raised an eyebrow and Holly felt her own shoulders tense. Sequoia continued in interrogation mode.

"What kind of merger?"

Alex took a sip of his beer. He waved a hand. "It's boring, seriously."

As always, Jasmine jumped in. "Sequoia, don't make the poor man talk about business at my rehearsal dinner. This is supposed to be a festive occasion."

Sequoia gave Alex a dark look. Then she transferred it to Holly, and finally, to Jasmine. "Fine," she said.

"So, Alejo, where do you live?"

Jasmine guffawed, loudly, and said, "Sequoia!"

Holly panicked. They hadn't talked about this. She had to give Alex credit, though. He just smiled and said, "Over at North Point."

North Point was a high-end apartment complex, all steel and glass rising into the sky on the north end of town. The least expensive units sold at the million-dollar mark. Under any other circumstance, Holly would be surprised. No one she knew could afford a place like that. But she'd done the math, based on how much she was paying for Alex to be here with her. He had to make upwards of high six-figures every year. Maybe even seven figures.

His response seemed to satisfy Sequoia, for the moment. Holly was sure she would come up with further questions.

"Which way does your apartment face?" Sequoia said.

Ah. So she was trying to catch him in a lie. She thought she'd get him on the details.

"It's one of the end units," he said. "So it has windows on the east, south, and west. Awesome views."

Now Holly was sure her face revealed her surprise.

"Oh, you lucky!" Jasmine said to Holly. "I've never been inside one of those apartments, but I've always wanted to. What's it like? Is it super fancy?"

Holly nodded and swallowed. "It's amazing," she said. Then she remembered her sisters would never see the inside of Alex's apartment, so it was probably safe to elaborate. Or, maybe not. Sequoia may have been in one of the apartments on a call for work or something. "Great views. In fact, he can see Harbor Park from his living room."

That, at least, was probably true. Sequoia twisted around in her chair, trying to get a look at the North Point building. "So which one's yours?"

Holly rolled her eyes. "Enough, okay, Sequoia? I'm sure Alejo would like to retain at least some semblance of privacy. He doesn't need you stalking him. Next thing we know, he's going to come home from work and walk in on you snooping through his silverware drawer."

"Junk drawer," Sequoia said. "It's way more revealing."

At this, Alex laughed out loud. At least he found it entertaining, Holly thought, because she found it humiliating. "All you'd find in my junk drawer is a few stray pens and loose change," Alex told Sequoia. "Oh, and takeout flyers."

"Huh," Sequoia said. Then she looked at Holly. "So how many times have you been to his apartment?"

"What? I don't know. I'm not keeping track."

This time, Elijah stepped in.

"Seriously, Babe," he said. "Stop giving this poor guy the third degree. He's going to think you're interrogating him."

"She *is* interrogating him," Holly said. "Take the night off, Sequoia."

"It's fine," Alex said. "I totally understand. Did Holly tell you I have four sisters? I think most families have one sibling who feels responsible for the rest of them. That's you, right? You want to make sure no one is going to take advantage of your little sister. I get it. And it probably seems unrealistic that your youngest sister would meet someone who can afford to live at North Point. Totally reasonable. But I can. I'm very good at what I do, and it enables me to live well. Very well. I made my first million five years ago and I haven't looked back. That being said, Holly's a grown-up. I think she can handle herself, and me." Here, he turned toward Holly and winked at her. Then he looked at Sequoia again. "Did you have any other questions before our dinner gets here?"

Sequoia looked at Elijah, who was giving her a funny smile, and said to Alex, "No, I guess I don't."

"Perfect timing," Elijah said. "Food's here. And now we can enjoy our meal. Right?"

"Right," Alex said. "It looks spectacular."

"Right," Sequoia said, her voice more of a mumble than anything else.

This little exchange left Holly more impressed with Alex than she was before. She'd never seen anyone shut Sequoia down quite that quickly. Then, throughout the meal, Alex was attentive and pleasant, asking thoughtful questions and making jokes in all the right places. Holly could see how he'd become a millionaire. Now she just had to hope his professionalism stood up to a wedding. She'd find out tomorrow. But first, she had to face her sisters alone, tonight.

THE THREE CARR sisters had decided to spend the night before Jasmine's wedding at Holly's house, since she was the only one who didn't cohabitate with a male.

Sequoia had driven them home from The Galley after each sister said good-bye to her significant other. Holly wondered whether Jasmine and Sequoia noticed the lack of passion in her kiss with Alex. Well, strike that: she knew Jasmine didn't notice, and she knew

Sequoia did. She hoped her oldest sister attributed it to "Alejo" being shy since it was the first time he'd met Holly's sisters.

Jasmine, who was sitting on the couch, taking up all three cushions like she had since she reached double digits and grew legs long enough to do so, nodded so vigorously her bun tumbled loose and her hair draped over her back.

"I never thought you'd be getting married first," Sequoia said to Jasmine. "I thought it would be Holly, for sure."

"I thought so, too," Jasmine said.

The doorbell rang and the door opened before any of them had a chance to open it. "The party's here," Cara announced, holding up another bottle of wine. At first, Holly was grateful for the distraction. But then Cara said, "Tell me! How was it meeting Alejo? He's hot, right? I mean, Holly just keeps talking about how hot he is."

"Why do we always end up discussing my love life?" Holly said, her voice somewhere on the spectrum of whine-to-moan.

Cara shrugged and went into the kitchen to open her wine.

"I'm just surprised, that's all," Sequoia said. She'd taken the arm chair, and leaned forward to refill her wine glass from the bottle Holly had brought. When only drops plopped into her glass, despite her tapping the neck of the bottle on the rim, she hollered, "Cara, bring that bottle in here, would you? We just ran dry on this one."

Cradling the empty bottle in her lap, she said, "I don't know, Holly. You've always been so boy-crazy. I thought planning a big wedding would end up being more important to you than, well, than anything else. I mean, I always figured that's why you didn't have much direction—because you'd end up being someone's wife. Like, that was your main life's calling."

Of course, the comment stung. At that moment, Cara came back in and made a round, refilling glasses. Holly took a gulp of her wine, hoping it would help her let Sequoia's comment roll off her back.

"Geez, Sequoia," Cara said. She set the wine on the table. "Some of us don't find ourselves until we're a little older. Wisdom, maturity, all that. Not all of us know our calling when we're toddlers."

Holly thanked the universe that she'd been smart enough to sit on the floor. It gave her the opportunity to pick at the carpet rather than make eye contact with Sequoia, who drained her glass and said, "But do you have to wait until you're in your thirties? Give me some more wine."

Jasmine had stopped at two glasses, determined not to be hungover, dehydrated, or to have bags under her eyes on her wedding day. Now, she gave Holly a pointed look, inclined her head toward Sequoia, and took the open bottle of wine off the coffee table and into the kitchen.

"Where are you going with that?" Sequoia hollered.

Holly and Cara giggled.

Sequoia took advantage of Jasmine's absence to bring up the topic Holly had been dreading: "So, your new boyfriend, Alejo—"

"Yes, Alejo," Holly said.

She was determined not to let Sequoia get to any item of substance before Jasmine returned to referee.

Sequoia waved her off and said, "I like the way it rolls off the tongue. Anyway."

"Anyway," Holly said, feeling a little boost of confidence because her wits were sharper than Sequoia's right now. "I don't want to be interrogated any further. Alejo's a great guy. I don't need you to question me on my relationship with him."

"Geez," Sequoia said, her lip pouty and her eyebrows drawn in an overdone expression of hurt. "All I was going to say is that he seems pretty nice."

"Okay," Holly said. "Thank you."

"So, are you bringing Al—sorry, I won't say his name," Sequoia said. "Are you bringing your new boyfriend to the wedding?"

"Um, yes," Holly said. "Unless something comes up for work."

"Speaking of work," Sequoia said. "I don't think you ever said what he does for a living. Like, specifically. I mean, he said he works in finance. But that's so … vague. Like, what's his actual job? What are his *duties*?"

She lifted her wine glass to her lips before realizing it was empty.

Cara smiled. "Yes, Holly. What are his actual *duties*?"

Sequoia gave Cara a dirty look, and Jasmine saved Holly by coming back into the living room then, a mug of tea in her hand.

"First of all," she said, "even if Holly did believe being a wife or mother was her life's calling, what would be wrong with that? We need more people in this world to focus on raising nice children. Second of all, Sequoia, stop being such a bitch. It's my night. Let's talk about me."

Jasmine, ever the peacekeeper, winked at Holly, who flashed her a grateful smile in return.

"Fine," Sequoia said. "Just saying. Anyway. What do you want to talk about, Jas? Did you get a sexy outfit to wear tomorrow night? I mean, I know you and Hudson have heated up the sheets already, but you've got to have lingerie."

Color seeped up Jasmine's neck and into her face, which made Sequoia, Holly, and Cara chuckle.

"I got you a present," Sequoia said. "While we're on this topic."

She leaned over the side of her chair and dug a book out of her purse, then tossed it across the couch to Jasmine. If it were possible, Jasmine's face became even redder when she read the title aloud: *"Kama Sutra to Light Your Sheets on Fire."*

Holly raised her eyebrows and went to sit next to Jasmine, who, of course, was already flipping through the new book.

"Did you get a copy for you and Elijah?" Jasmine said to Sequoia.

Now it was Sequoia's turn to blush. "Maybe."

"You *did!*" Cara said.

"Any recommendations?" Jasmine said.

Sequoia looked down, staring into her empty glass like it held the answer to the secrets of the universe. Then she said, "Check page forty-five."

As Jasmine found the page, Holly considered this strange turn of events. Sequoia had used a Kama Sutra book? What was happening here? Her sister was usually so rigid, so aloof. Holly couldn't imagine her actually trying out a somewhat acrobatic sexual position.

"Wonders never cease," Holly said.

Sequoia shot her a dirty look, but a gasp from Jasmine stopped any possible conversation before it could start.

"Sequoia Carr! I can't believe you *did* this with Elijah! How scandalous!"

Holly leaned over to see the page, and was surprised that it showed a photograph rather than a drawing. So real people got into these positions and held them while a stranger snapped photos? Unbelievable. Then, not for the first time, an image of Mack floated into her consciousness, out of nowhere. And not just any image—an image of Mack, with her, in that same position.

To distract herself, she said, "How do you even *do* that?"

"Well, I guess I'll find out tomorrow night," Jasmine said.

"Well, I've just gotta say, it's worth the hard work," Sequoia said.

This had Jasmine, Holly, and Cara in stitches, and Sequoia, for once, was frozen in place with nothing to say.

When they finally quieted down, Holly said, "So, Jas, how are you feeling on this eve of your marriage? How does it feel to know that tomorrow, you're going to commit to being someone's life partner?"

Jasmine shut the Kama Sutra book and picked up her tea. To Holly's surprise, Jasmine's eyes filled with tears. "It's so amazing, you guys. It's just so wonderful. I never thought it was that important to me to get married, you know, at a certain time or whatever. I just always figured it would happen whenever it happened. But now that it's here, it's like—I don't know how I lived without him before."

Holly felt her own throat tightening with emotion. She was so happy for Jasmine, of course, but she also realized there was a pretty significant void in her life … one she couldn't fill with her fake boyfriend, Alejo.

She put her arm around Jasmine and Sequoia joined them, holding hands with both of her sisters.

"We're both so happy for you, Jas," Sequoia said. "We can't wait to watch you walk down the aisle tomorrow."

CHAPTER SEVENTEEN

WATCHING JASMINE WALK DOWN THE AISLE WASN'T THE ONLY THING ON Holly's mind when she woke up on the wedding day. She was also thinking about Alex and Sequoia, and how she'd keep them apart as much as possible. Holly imagined Elijah sitting with Alex during the wedding. Elijah would make small talk, joke about hiding a flask under his jacket, things like that. But he wouldn't ask inappropriate questions or make Alex feel like he was under a microscope. Guys were so much cooler. Why couldn't she have had brothers?

Sequoia and Cara were still asleep in the guest bedroom, but Jasmine, who was sleeping in Holly's bed with her, had sighed so loudly upon waking up just after six that she'd woken Holly, too. Now, Holly was setting Jasmine's favorite coffee—a scoop of French roast and a scoop of Dark Colombian—to brew while Jasmine showered.

It was the reception that really worried Holly, she thought as she assembled the gift basket she'd picked up for her sister. That's when things always got crazy. Jasmine would be occupied and unable to run interference, and Sequoia would have time to grill Alex, or to listen to everything he said, looking for inconsistencies. Not that he and Holly had lied about anything other than the nature of their relationship, but Sequoia had already decided something was off, and she'd be on high alert, looking for something—anything—to prove Alejo unsuitable.

Maybe she could call it an early night after they had cake. Jasmine would understand. Or maybe she could sweet-talk Cara into helping her out.

At this point, Sequoia came into the kitchen, squinting, her hand on her forehead. "Aspirin? Coffee?"

"I don't feel even a tiny bit guilty for taking pleasure in your discomfort," Holly said. "But because I'm a good sister, I will get you three aspirin and pour your coffee."

"Oh, thank goodness," Sequoia said. She sat down on a barstool and laid her head on the counter. "Why do you take pleasure in my suffering?"

"Because you take pleasure in mine, of course," Holly said. She took four mugs from the cupboard and set them on the counter, then turned to get some aspirin. "Otherwise you wouldn't give my boyfriend the third degree at Jasmine's rehearsal dinner and then cross-examine me afterward. Can't you just let me be happy?"

"Coffee," Sequoia said. "Coffee first, talk second."

"A little hair of the dog?" Cara had walked in, her bright red hair standing on end. She held up last night's bottle of wine, which was still half-full.

Sequoia pretended to gag, and Holly chuckled as she set the aspirin in front of Sequoia, along with a glass of water. As she poured the coffee into the mugs, Jasmine walked into the kitchen wearing a robe, a towel on her head, and an easy, brilliant smile.

"Morning ladies," she said.

"Coffee?" Holly said, handing her the cup and then sliding one over to where Sequoia sat and handing another one to Cara.

Jasmine sat down next to Sequoia, who seemed to forget she was supposed to be answering Holly's question. Holly was certain she'd forgotten on purpose, and she didn't want to bring it up now that Jasmine was here. So she slid the gift basket across the counter to Jasmine and then busied herself cracking eggs into a bowl for breakfast.

"Holly!" Jasmine said. "This is so sweet! You got me lip balm and hand cream!"

"Jasmine scented," Sequoia said. "That was so sweet!"

"And the vodka shooter is a nice touch," Cara said.

"Take the edge off if she gets nervous," Holly said.

Jasmine's eyes filled with tears and she got up and came around the counter to hug Holly. "Thank you so much," she said. "That was so thoughtful."

Back to business, she sat back down and said, "Okay. We have a lot to do today. I think we're right on schedule; that is, if you hurry up and shower, Sequoia. I can tell from your countenance that you're going to need extra time to get ready. A little too much wine last night?"

Her tone was a knife's edge dipped in honey, which made Holly smirk as she whipped the eggs.

"Let's go over the schedule," Sequoia said, "because I know going over the schedule was the first item on it."

Her tone was a lot nicer than her words were, and Jasmine said, "True. Okay. Ready, Holly? Ready Cara?"

"Ready," Holly and Cara said.

Jasmine listed off the day's activities, item by item: "Eat breakfast, get dressed, pack the car, drink water—"

"Drinking water?" Sequoia said. "You put that on our schedule?"

"I can't have any of us getting dehydrated," Jasmine said.

Holly set out plates. Jasmine continued with her schedule: pick up the wedding favors, eat lunch, and drive over to Harbor Park, where they would set up for the reception. Cara would remain at Harbor Park as the unofficial wedding planner and the Carr sisters would head back to Sequoia's house to get dressed for the wedding. The photographer would meet them there, and Alex and Elijah would pick up Hudson and they'd all meet back at the park at 2 p.m., just before the wedding started. Cara was in charge of making sure Hudson was on time, even if she had to go pick him up, herself.

"Breakfast's ready," Holly said. "How am I on the schedule?"

"You're perfect," Jasmine said. "Let's eat."

Holly took advantage of the relative silence to think about Alex.

She hoped he would remember to show up. She could send him a text message, but she didn't have his phone number. His company sent her an "appointment reminder" email, but she knew it was automated. Hopefully he'd received one, too. Not that he should forget, considering they'd just been together the night before. But still. It would look really, really bad if he wasn't there.

The doorbell rang and Holly jumped. Was it Alex? He wasn't supposed to be here. Or, what if it was Mack, who showed up whenever and wherever he pleased? Sequoia would take notice of that. And not in a good way. Holly's heart leapt into her throat.

"Aren't you going to get that?" Sequoia said.

"Oh. Yeah," Holly put down her fork, wiped her mouth, and stood.

"Are you expecting someone?" Jasmine said.

"Nope, are you?" Holly said, looking around.

"Nope," Jasmine, Sequoia, and Cara answered together.

Holly looked through the peephole. "It's UPS," she said. "And Sequoia, I know how much you love a man in uniform."

Jasmine cackled as Holly opened the door.

"I have four packages." The delivery man held out the first package, which was addressed to Jasmine, and the second, which was addressed to Sequoia. "Be right back," he said, the East Coast accent thick in his voice. "The others are in the truck."

"Aw, I'm sure this is from Hudson, Jas," Holly said.

Jasmine came to get it, just as the UPS man came back up the walkway, one package under one arm.

"Don't usually get four packages in one day at a residential address," he said. "Special occasion?"

"My sister's getting married," Holly said, taking the packages. "Jasmine."

Jasmine gave a little wave from the table, where she was using her keys to open her box.

"Hey!" the UPS man said. "Wonderful! Congratulations! My wife and I just celebrated our thirtieth wedding anniversary this month. Feels like yesterday. Finding your one true love is the best thing that will ever happen to you. Congratulations, Hon."

Again, Holly felt herself getting emotional.

"Thank you so much," Jasmine and Holly said at the same time.

The UPS man nodded and walked away, and Holly closed the front door.

"Looks like this one's for you," she said to Sequoia, holding out one of the packages. "One for you, Cara. And one for me."

"Did you order something?" Sequoia said. "Are we sure these aren't explosives? Or Anthrax?"

"Always thinking worst-case scenario," Holly said. "I didn't order anything, but I'm sure they're not explosives. Jasmine's, anyway."

Jasmine got her box open first, and said, "Awwww!"

She withdrew a small bouquet of sunflowers, daisies and mums, tightly packed into a round glass vase.

"Who's it from?" Sequoia and Holly said.

"Well, it's from Hudson, of course," Jasmine said. She read the card: *"Can't wait to see you later today, as it's sure to be the best day of my life. I love you. Love, Hudson."*

Holly gasped when she saw what was in her box: a miniature planter filled with tiny cacti. The card simply read: *For a beautiful woman on a beautiful day.*

Sequoia, of course, was peering over her shoulder when she read it. "No signature," she said.

"Thanks," Holly said. "I saw that."

Before Sequoia had the chance to start giving her the third degree, Jasmine jumped in. "What about yours?" she said to Sequoia.

Sequoia blushed, closed the little card she'd removed from her own bouquet, and put it into the pocket of her pajama pants.

"Come on! I told you what was on my card!" Jasmine said, and Holly said, "Yeah, and you snooped and read mine. Spill it, sister."

"Why are we not trying to solve the mystery of who sent Holly her plant?" Sequoia said.

Why, indeed, Holly thought. "What does yours say, Sequoia?"

"I can't say. Okay?"

"Can't, or won't?" Jasmine said.

"Both," Sequoia said.

Her face was now a fierce red. Cara, smiling, opened her own box.

"Aw, how sweet," she said, reading the card. "It's from Hudson, too. How did he know I love blue lilies?"

"I may have mentioned that," Jasmine said. "What does the card say?"

"It says, *Thank you for running the show today. I know things will go spectacularly.*"

"He's so sweet," Holly said, and Sequoia, obviously groping around for something to talk about (other than her own card) said, "That Hudson. He's a great guy, isn't he? The greatest."

"C'mon, Sequoia," Jasmine said. "It's my wedding day, which makes it, like, my day a million times over. Like a birthday on steroids. You have to tell us what your card says because I say so."

If they'd been teenagers, Holly was sure this would have broken into a wrestling match in which Holly and Jasmine would take Sequoia down and pry the card out of her pocket. Now that they were older, they'd have to use their wits instead of force.

"If you don't tell us, I'm going to ask Elijah," Holly said.

Sequoia snorted. "Go ahead. He won't tell you any more than I will. You're wasting your breath. Why don't you tell us who sent you the cactus?"

Holly didn't know. She had an idea, of course. It was either Alex or Mack. But since she hadn't paid for Alex to send her anything, and she doubted she was such a special case that he'd send it on his own, she could only bank on the cacti being from Mack. The girls didn't have to know that.

"They're from Alejo. I don't know why you think it's such a big mystery. Who else would send me a plant?"

"Who, indeed?" Sequoia said.

Jasmine shrugged. "We can't let this so-called mystery get us off-schedule, ladies. That was sweet of the guys to send us flowers, right? Let's put this behind us. We have to load the car."

"Fine," Sequoia said, and Jasmine, Holly, and Cara said, "Fine."

Sequoia didn't look convinced the plant was from Alejo. She shot

Holly one final look, and Holly imagined her thinking, *I'll get you, my pretty.*

Rather than feeling relief that Jasmine had so quickly dismissed the mystery of the identity of the plant sender, Holly experienced a new wave of stress. Sequoia had been acting so strangely about Holly's love life lately, from taking an interest in it in the first place to interrogating "Alejo" at the rehearsal dinner.

So Holly knew she wouldn't let this one go, even though Alejo being the sender of the plant seemed plausible, practically non-questionable. As long as Sequoia didn't say anything to Alejo, everything would be fine.

DESPITE HARBOR PARK being the ultra in casual, the setting looked elegant in the late afternoon sunlight. Wispy gray clouds stood out against a candy-colored sky so that the backdrop was swirls of gray, pink, purple, and orange. Hudson had been in charge of stringing lights on the gazebo, and they twinkled in a way that made the whole place feel like a fairy garden. Holly half-expected to see a live gnome under a mushroom somewhere.

A dozen white chairs were set up next to the gazebo, with a view of the water and the harbor, and when Holly and her sisters got there, Alex was sitting in one of them, cool as a cucumber. He turned around when he heard Sequoia's car pull up, and then he sauntered over.

"May I offer my assistance to the lovely bride and her gorgeous sisters?" he said. "You really do look radiant, Holly."

He kissed Holly on the cheek, and for a moment, she felt a stirring of pride. Then she remembered he wasn't her real boyfriend.

"What a gentleman," she said, taking the hand he offered. "If we can get the bride out of this car without getting her dress dirty, we'll be in good shape."

"I think we can manage," Alex said.

Holly hoped so.

Because Jasmine was so intent on a simple, frills-free wedding, she had kept most of the planning so low-key that she hadn't dragged her sisters dress shopping or to a fitting. So this afternoon had been the first time they saw Jasmine in her dress.

Of course, when she emerged from the guest bedroom in Sequoia's house, both Holly and Sequoia gasped.

"It's perfect!" Holly said, pulling her sister in for a hug. "You look like a princess."

"It is perfect," Sequoia said, her voice thoughtful, and Holly cringed, bracing for some critical remark. Sequoia added, "I'm just not sure how we're going to fit you in the car."

Up to this point, they'd been right on schedule. At exactly twelve minutes to two p.m., they stood beside Sequoia's car, ready to leave —fully dressed, hair and makeup done. Now, it seemed they'd hit a roadblock: fitting Jasmine—and her skirt—in the car seemed nearly impossible.

"You obviously didn't think this part of the day through very well," Sequoia said.

After several different attempts, each featuring a unique configuration, they managed, lifting Jasmine up in a horizontal position and then shoving her, feet first, into the backseat.

By the time she was in, they were laughing so hard their mascara threatened to run. Now, Alex gasped when he opened Jasmine's car door, which put all four women in hysterics again.

"We've got to lift her up and slide her out," Holly said.

"And someone's got to grab her legs so they don't flop down," Sequoia added.

To his credit, Alex just shook his head, and smiling, said, "On three?"

They hoisted Jasmine up and out of the car, and set her on her feet.

"Spectacular," Alex said to Jasmine. "You look just incredible. I've never seen a more beautiful bride."

Even Sequoia seemed pleased to hear his compliment, and Holly hoped this would bode well for the rest of the evening. Of course, that hope was short-lived. By this time, Holly had almost forgotten about the mystery identity of the houseplant sender. Sequoia had not. And naturally, she had to bring it up.

"Beautiful flowers you sent Holly this morning," she said, and neither the pointed, snarky tone in her voice nor the purposeful factual error (it was cacti, not flowers) escaped Holly's ears.

"It was cac—" Holly began, trying to throw Alex a bone while simultaneously wondering, *Who* did *send it, anyway?*

Alex was close to perfect, Holly thought, but everyone knows perfection is a myth. His face registered surprise, for just one fraction of a second, but Holly didn't miss it, and she was positive Sequoia hadn't, either. Now she knew: Alex hadn't sent the cacti. Which meant only one thing: Mack had.

"Ah, yes," Alex said. "I chose a living plant so it would last longer."

"As long as I don't kill it," Holly said, squeezing Alex's hand and realizing too late that her voice was infused with way more excitement than the situation called for.

"I'll remind you to water it," Alex said, and Sequoia said, "Oh, perfect."

"Shall we?" Holly said. "We need to get Jasmine to the safe point so Hudson can't see her when he gets back from the reception tent. I think we're three minutes behind schedule now, thanks to the dress debacle. Which means he's changing at the moment, but he'll be back in—"

"Two minutes!" Cara said.

"Assemble!" Sequoia said. "We've got to get Jasmine behind the screen."

"Yeah, we didn't leave much of a cushion for this part of the day, did we?" Jasmine said.

"I can only hope the safe point is big enough to hide your gigantic skirt," Holly said.

"So Holly and Sequoia will wait with Jasmine until the ceremony," Cara told Alex as they walked up the hill to the screen, Jasmine clutching her sisters' arms for balance.

"And then I'll be able to sit with you during the reception," Holly said.

Alex nodded and gave Holly a quick kiss on the temple. "Have fun. And Jasmine? You look stunning. Just beautiful."

She really did, Holly thought. Then, as Alex walked away, offering Cara his arm, she wondered if she, Holly, would ever get the chance to hear a man say she looked beautiful on her own wedding day. It was questionable.

Her mind took this opportunity to show her an image of Mack. Mack, who had sent her a cactus on the morning of her sister's wedding. *For a beautiful woman on a beautiful day.* Mack, who thought she was beautiful. Mack, who was so persistent despite his believing she had a boyfriend. Mack, who kissed her like he meant it, and who she actually *liked*, despite herself.

Mack, who she could never be with.

"Whoa," Jasmine said, cutting into her thoughts. "Where'd you go, Holly?"

"Oh, I was just thinking about our schedule for the rest of the evening," Holly said. "Wedding at two-thirty, photos at three, cocktails at three-thirty? After that I'm just going with the flow."

"Your toast is ten minutes after cocktails start," Jasmine reminded her. "You can go with the flow after that."

Holly nodded. "Got it."

Sequoia said, "Liar."

"What?" both Jasmine and Holly said.

"She's lying," Sequoia said to Jasmine. "She wasn't thinking about the schedule. She was thinking about whoever sent her that cactus."

"It was Alejo," both Jasmine and Holly said.

"Liar," Sequoia said.

"Stopit," Holly said, running the words together like Sequoia always did when she got irritated.

This earned her a smile from Sequoia and a reprimand from Jasmine: "May I remind you ladies that this is my wedding day?" she said. Her voice sounded syrupy sweet, but Holly heard the edge underneath it. "There will be no bickering. Lying, sure. Bickering, no."

Sequoia huffed out an impatient sigh. "Fine."

Holly smiled at her, and the look Sequoia sent back said, "This isn't over."

THE WEDDING CEREMONY was short and sweet, and the first nuptial kiss was long and deep. Even Sequoia had tears in her eyes when it was over. While Jasmine and Hudson stayed behind for newlywed photos, Holly ventured into the reception tent to find Alex. He greeted her at the bar with a glass of white wine, which she consumed in two long gulps.

"Want another?" he asked.

"After my toast," she said. "I just needed a little something to calm my nerves. I've been worried about the reception. Making a toast would be nerve-wracking enough. But Sequoia's probably going to grill you about that damned cactus."

Alex smiled. "She caught me off guard when you guys first showed up. She's good."

"She's a cop," Holly said, "and even at her sister's wedding, she can't stay in regular human mode."

"Oh, she's fine," Alex said. "She just cares about you, that's all. It's sweet. Like a mama bear."

"Sweet like a mother gorilla, more like."

Holly watched Sequoia now. She stood next to Elijah and leaned up against him, her head on his shoulder. His cheek rested on the top of her head, and his hand made circles on her lower back. They weren't speaking, but the connection was so strong Holly could practically touch it from here. The moment seemed so intimate Holly felt like she should look away.

"Don't let her get to you," Alex said. "And don't worry about me. I can fend for myself. She just wants you happy. She can probably sniff out that I'm not the real thing, but she doesn't realize I have good intentions. Maybe she thinks I'm playing you."

"That actually makes a lot of sense," Holly said. "Although, I don't know why you'd be playing me. It's not like I'm a real catch."

"Yes, you are," he said. "You're beautiful. You're smart and witty and so caring. You're a great catch. And right now, you're vulnerable and you're suddenly dating this guy—me—who, I'm guessing, gives her strange vibes. I'm sure your sister doesn't want some guy swooping in and breaking your heart."

"Wow," Holly said. "You can really read her like a book."

"Remember," he said. "Four sisters. I've got one just like her. Go easy on her."

"*Me*, go easy on *her*?"

Now Alex chuckled. "Yeah. Don't paint her as a villain, even in your own mind."

"Great," Holly said. "Now I'm picturing her in a black catsuit with a cape and a mask. The Great Caped Sister-Villain."

"Really?" Alex said. He gestured toward Sequoia and Elijah, who were now slow dancing, foreheads together. "Look at her. She doesn't look even remotely like a villain."

It was true. She didn't. She looked like a beautiful, tender, sentimental woman, in love with a man who was also very in love with her.

"Fine," Holly said. "You're right."

Alex gave her a smug smile and said, "Now. If I didn't send you the cactus, who did?"

"Top-secret information," Holly said.

"Okay," Alex said. "Your choice." He held out a hand. "Shall we dance?"

They joined Sequoia and Elijah on the dance floor, and Holly made a decision that she would enjoy this evening with "Alejo." She could enjoy the no-strings-attached companionship, the friendship, the good manners, and the great dancing. He twirled her around the dance floor, making her feel like she knew what she was doing. And even though their relationship wasn't real, she found herself taking quite a bit of pleasure in it. When it came time for "Alejo" to leave—Holly's money for this project having run out—she felt a little sad. It had been so fun playing his girlfriend. And even though she hadn't been able to relax completely, thanks to Sequoia's continued questioning, it had been nice to join the in-crowd as one half of a happy couple. Holly insisted on walking Alex out, in part because she wanted to thank him for a great evening and in part because she could use the fresh air.

"You're a great boyfriend," she told him as they walked. "Even if you're a fake. Lending me your arm as we walk to the car ... the chivalry never ends."

"Heels in grass?" Alex said. "Every woman's arch-nemesis."

When they got to his car, she thanked him again and gave him a hug. Before he got in, he said, "Oh, and Holly? Try giving that guy a chance. The one who pulled you over for drunk driving and sent you a cactus on the day of your sister's wedding."

Then she watched, mouth open, as he drove away. "How did he know?" She shook her head. It didn't matter how he knew. "It's almost like the end of an era," she said, and then, when she realized the scene before her—the twinkling lights of boats in the harbor—was getting a bit misty, she said, "Get a grip, Carr."

Because she wasn't quite ready to go back inside, Holly walked past the reception tent to the walkway that ran the length of the bluff overlooking the harbor. She leaned against the railing and let her mind drift as she watched the boats bob in the inky black water.

She jumped and simultaneously thought she'd been stupid to come out here alone when she heard a voice behind her: "Beautiful woman. Oh, and beautiful night, too."

The saner part of her mind recognized the voice, but her heart was still beating fast when she turned around.

"Mack. Number one, you startled me. Number two, are you crashing my sister's wedding?"

He smiled. "Sorry. And no. I was driving by and I saw you out here."

"You can't see this spot from the road," she said.

"I saw you in the parking lot with your boyfriend," he said. "Why'd he leave so early?"

"Is it just me, or did I detect a weird emphasis on the word, 'boyfriend'?"

Mack smiled, and in the semi-dark she couldn't read whether it was a kind smile. He said, "Is he really your boyfriend, Holly?"

"What? He came to Jasmine's wedding, didn't he?"

"But is he really your boyfriend?"

"What were you doing out, just driving by?" She hoped he heard the emphasis on *just driving by*, like she'd heard the emphasis when he'd said *boyfriend* the first time.

"Why didn't you kiss him goodnight?"

Why, indeed. If she had kissed him goodnight, this conversation would not be happening.

"Were you watching me?"

"I was just driving by. I saw your very friendly hug and wondered why it contained less passion than the kiss you and I shared at my barbecue. I mean, if I were going to kiss you goodnight, it wouldn't be quite so chaste. Who is this Alejo guy?"

"He has an early work meeting."

"On a Sunday?" Mack said. He raised an eyebrow at her.

"He's leaving early tomorrow. Meeting's on Monday morning."

"Really?"

"Why are you doing this?"

"Why are *you* doing this?"

Holly said, "This is strangely reminiscent of conversations I had with my sisters when we were in elementary school."

"Come home with me."

"What?" Holly was incredulous, even though her lady parts had jumped to attention and were now begging her to accept his invitation.

"You heard me. Call it a night. Alejo, or whatever his name is, left. And you've put in your time at the wedding. Come home with me."

"I can't, I—Alejo … Anyway, you never said what you're doing out at this time of night."

"First of all, it's not that late," Mack said. "It's only seven. I had to run to the store. I was going to make dinner and I realized I'd forgotten to buy wine."

"Wine? For a solo dinner?" Holly said.

"Yeah. To deglaze the pan. For the sauce."

"Seriously? Deglaze the pan?" Although, to be fair, she'd pegged him as a man who could cook since the first time she saw him in the Broken Egg.

"Yeah. Seriously. Why are we talking about this for so long?"

He was adorable when he was exasperated, Holly thought.

"Why are you eating dinner so late?"

"Long day," he said. "Come home with me. I'll feed you spaghetti with a killer wine sauce."

"Fine," she said. "But only for dinner. I have a—"

"I know. You have a boyfriend. Whom you hug like he's your brother."

Holly told herself she shouldn't be charmed by the way he ordered her around. She told herself accepting his invitation was stupid, and a big mistake. A big, stupid mistake. Nevertheless, she told him she'd go, and she was more charmed than ever when he took one look at her heels, scooped her up in his arms, and carried her to the car.

Alex had said heels and grass were a woman's arch-nemesis. Right now, they felt like Holly's long-lost BFF.

SOMETHING ABOUT BEING next to Mack in his car, something about the scent of his cologne and his profile in the lights from the dashboard, made Holly jumpy.

"So, you were making a fancy spaghetti with wine sauce, just for yourself?" she said, in what was probably an obvious attempt at making small talk.

He looked sideways at her, grinned, and focused on the road again. "Yep."

"Why?"

"Why not?"

When she didn't respond right away, he said, "I love spaghetti with wine sauce. Now that I'm retired, I have more time for cooking. So I cook myself spaghetti with wine sauce."

"Seems reasonable," Holly said. "But it also seems like a lot of work for one person."

"How very fortunate that I ran into you tonight, then," Mack said.

"Indeed," Holly said.

"And I like leftovers," he said.

"Mm-hmm," she said.

They rode in silence for a few minutes, until Mack turned on the radio. It was tuned to a classical station, which Holly found somewhat surprising. As he drove, she looked out her window, watching the moonlight race across the water, following them.

After a moment, she realized she could also see his reflection, and she stole this opportunity to look at him without him knowing. His features looked almost chiseled, like an artist had sculpted the planes of his face. He had both hands on the wheel, and he looked alert and focused.

Later, she'd reflect on this moment and blame the classical music. Before she realized what was happening, she'd slipped into a daydream where he took his right hand off the wheel and put it on her leg, running it up her thigh, back down to her knee, and back up to her thigh. While her imagination took off on that little side trip, she watched his reflection as he licked his lips.

Of course, this made her imagination go a little wild: it had him pulling the car over, putting it in park, and turning towards her. In her daydream, he took her face in his hands and kissed her, and he tasted like wine sauce. Suddenly, they were in the backseat, and she was on top of him, sliding her body along his.

She shifted in the real-life passenger seat. Things were getting a bit warm.

"Could we turn on the AC?"

Her voice sounded strangled, and she was sure he noticed. Within seconds, she was on top of him again, and he'd undone his pants and pulled up her skirt.

She almost cried out before she realized the car was coming to a stop. He'd pulled up in front of his house. Weak in the knees, and warm and tingly in her lady parts, she got out and followed him into the kitchen.

"I've got to open this anyway," he said, holding up the wine, "so would you like a glass?"

She nodded, and slid onto a barstool with the hope that doing so would stop the throbbing that had started up during her little fantasy. It didn't seem to be working, so she stood up and accepted the glass from him.

"This will just take me a half-hour or so," he said. "But I like to let it simmer for at least an hour after that. So we can find something to do to pass the time."

"I'm sure we can," Holly said.

"What do you like to do?"

Well, that certainly stopped the throbbing. She knew the question was innocent, but it was a stark reminder that she was having some kind of life crisis and had no idea what she liked to do. She sighed.

"You know … the usual stuff. Watching movies, reading, drinking wine."

"Ever play ping pong?"

"Ping pong?" she said.

"Yeah," he said. "You know, table tennis, whatever you want to call it. You hit a ball with a paddle, and the other person hits it back to you?"

"Yes, I've played ping pong. But it's been awhile."

He looked up from the saucepan with a wicked gleam in his eye. "Okay, I challenge you to a round of ping pong, then. We'll go to twenty-one."

Although her vision of "finding something to do to pass the time" included the two of them getting hot and heavy on the couch, and going to home base instead of twenty-one, she thought playing ping pong sounded much more friendly and acceptable, given her (fake) status as someone else's girlfriend.

"You're on," she said.

For the next few minutes, she watched him cook, chopping vegetables, browning meat, stirring in wine and tomato sauce. He looked good in the kitchen. He looked good in a uniform. He looked good in the Broken Egg.

This was ludicrous.

"Okay," he said. He wiped his hands on a dish towel and turned down the flame on the stove. "Are you ready for this?"

"Ready," she said.

Leaving her glass on the counter, she followed him into the garage.

"I hope you know what you're getting into," he said.

She said, "Me, too."

An hour later, the two of them were sweaty and exhausted, and Holly's face hurt from laughing so much. He'd beat her, but only by a point. They'd matched each other, score for score, throughout every game, and ended up going for best out of five. Mack won the tie-breaker, and now he was gloating as they walked back into the kitchen.

"I knew I could take you down," he said. She elbowed him, and he rubbed his arm as if it had hurt.

"I worked up a good appetite," she told him.

Of course, her mind caught the innuendo after it had already slipped out, and her face immediately flushed. She wondered if he could tell, since her cheeks were surely rosy from all the jumping around she'd just done. If he could, he didn't say so. He had already set water to boil for the pasta, and was taking bowls down from the cupboard.

"Good thing, too," he said, "because this spaghetti is going to be delicious."

She leaned against the counter and sipped the wine. She let it sit on her tongue for a moment and enjoyed the peppery taste of it.

"Here," he said, setting a cutting board next to her on the counter. "Would you mind slicing this bread?"

He put the loaf on the cutting board and pulled it out of its paper wrapper. Holly froze. Shared kitchen duties were a symbol of a shared life. Preparing food together, eating food together, cleaning up together ... this led to some kind of couple bliss, didn't it? Did this *mean* something? No, she told herself. It was just cutting up some bread. She drained her wine, took a deep breath, and picked up up the knife.

"Probably not the best idea to finish off that wine before handling a sharp object," Mack said to her.

"True," Holly said. She thought, *and that's exactly why we could never be together, slicing bread in couple bliss. It wasn't the best idea for me to drive home after all those margaritas the first time we met and now I'll never live it down.*

Suddenly, he was behind her, and had wrapped his arms around her waist in a very un-friendlike way. She half-expected his hands to travel up the front of her body, but they didn't.

"I was just joking, you know," he said.

Then he kissed her neck, and her traitorous body betrayed her by responding like he was water in the middle of a desert. She kept slicing, concentrating especially hard on making all the pieces of bread the same size. He ran his lips along her neck, from her collar bone to the spot just beneath her ear, and she shivered. She felt him smile against her skin, and then he stepped away.

"I'm hungry," he said. "Ready to eat?"

He refilled their wine glasses, and in a rhythm so fluid it felt like a choreographed dance they'd been doing for years, they brought everything to the table.

"Best spaghetti ever," Holly told Mack after taking her first bite.

He nodded. "This might be my best attempt yet. I've been working on this recipe for months."

"I'd say it's pretty near perfect," she said.

Maybe if they kept making small talk, he wouldn't find time to ask her about "Alejo" again. She dreaded that, because she felt so weird about lying to him.

"So, besides reading and watching movies, what else do you like to do?" Mack said.

Okay, so this was almost as bad as talking about her boyfriend. She set down her fork.

"I'm not sure I'm cut out for a hobby," she said. "I've tried several things, but I'm at a loss. I'm thinking of beat-boxing or macramé, next."

"Well," Mack said. He took another bite of spaghetti, and waited until he'd chewed and swallowed to respond. "Maybe we could explore new hobbies together."

"Mack," Holly said. "Why do you want to spend time with me, like this, when you know I have a boyfriend?"

"Do you?" he said.

Well, what was she supposed to say to that?

"Wait," she said. "I asked you a question, first."

"Why do I want to spend time with you, like this, when I know you have a boyfriend?"

"Yeah."

She watched as he wound spaghetti around his fork. He had nice forearm muscles.

"I told you." He shrugged. "You're delicious."

"That's not something you say to a woman you view as a friend."

"True," he said. "Maybe I don't."

This was infuriating. And again, her body betrayed her, thrumming now like she was a guitar and he'd plucked her strings. Of course, that analogy made things even more exciting. She took a gulp of wine. Then she reminded herself she'd better slow down on the wine.

"You haven't answered my question," he said.

"Do I have a boyfriend?"

"Yeah," he said.

"Well, that's a silly question," she said.

"So let's talk about something else."

"Like hobbies?"

"Yeah," he said. "I think we should explore hobbies together. Since, as you know, I'm on the hunt for a hobby, as well. What about hiking? Biking? Do you consider yourself outdoorsy? If not, maybe we could try something else. Painting?"

Holly held up a hand. "Wait," she said. "I need to think about whether it's even appropriate for me to explore hobbies with you."

"Of course it is," he said. "We're friends, aren't we? I'd say so, since you've now eaten at my house more than once. Also you picked cucumbers in my garden."

This reminded Holly of the moment she'd been holding the

cucumber just below waist level, which was obviously Mack's intention. She blushed, yet again. "I do like your cucumbers. Maybe we should try gardening."

He laughed, then, and some of the tension dissipated.

"That reminds me," he said. "Did you like the cactus I sent you?"

"That was you?" Holly said, even though she'd already figured out that it was.

"Who else would it be?"

Holly decided not to answer that one.

Instead, she said, "Have you ever gone to one of those painting parties?"

He scoffed. "Nope. Doesn't seem very manly, does it? Have you?"

"No," she said. "I always thought those looked fun, though. But I don't know if it would be a good hobby."

"True," Mack said. "I'm sure they're not cheap. What about chess?"

"I'm not sure that could become a bonafide hobby. I don't even remember all the rules."

"You know: king, queen, pawn, rook. One person makes a strategic move. Then another person makes a strategic move. As long as the queen doesn't get hurt, you're okay."

Was he still talking about hobbies?

"Chess sounds okay," Holly said. "But it seems pretty serious."

"Okay," Mack said. "Chess is too serious. What about building model cars or trains?"

Holly waved a hand. "Maybe I need to sleep on it," she said. "Let's revisit this. I can tell this talk isn't going anywhere good. I don't have room for model trains. Haven't you seen those train rooms people have? Jasmine wrote a feature story on it once. This guy built a miniature town train. It was incredible. It took up an entire room, and the train track ran through his whole house. He'd put holes in the walls and everything."

"Intense," Mack said. "But not as intense as my ping pong skills."

"Nor as intense as your spaghetti-cooking skills," Holly said.

"That was really good. Probably the best spaghetti I've ever had. Since you cooked, I'll do dishes."

"Want to stay for a movie?"

Her mind was telling her that was a bad idea. Possibly a terrible one. But her body was at it again, practically vibrating at the thought of sitting in close quarters with Mack's body on the couch. Grateful she was already walking into the kitchen with an armful of dishes so he couldn't see her face, she said, "I shouldn't."

"But do you want to?"

She put the dishes in the sink and turned on the water. "Maybe. I mean, yes. I do. But I really shouldn't. The truth is, Mack, I shouldn't be spending all this time with you. Dinner was pushing it. But a movie? That's taking things right over a line I don't want to cross."

Her scrubbing had become over-vigorous. This lie was out of control. It had grown, morphed into a huge, slimy monster. Why she couldn't just *tell* him she didn't want to date because she was focusing on herself?

There were two reasons: first of all, she actually liked him. And, secondly, it sounded stupid, that's why. Not only should a grown woman not need to figure out her life purpose at age thirty, but she also should be able to figure it out while dating, shouldn't she?

"Suit yourself," he said. "I'll drive you home. But not until you finish those dishes. I'll be right back."

Holly assumed Mack was going to the bathroom, but he returned with a wiggling puppy in his arms. "Your new dog wanted to see you before you go."

Holly gasped. "Quimby! You've grown since I saw you last."

If it was possible, the puppy wiggled even more, and Mack had to set him down. Legs scrambling on the smooth floor, he dashed over to Holly, who dried her hands before kneeling to pet him. He put his paws on her knees and gave her face a thorough washing.

"Wow," Mack said. "I think he knows who his mama is."

"Wait," Holly said, "I haven't even agreed to take him yet."

"Doesn't matter," Mack said. "You're his."

The puppy flopped onto his back, his tongue lolling out of a wide open mouth while Holly rubbed his belly. "It appears that way, doesn't it?"

"Sure does. He'll be ready to go next week. Just in time for us to begin Hobby Exploration. He can be your sidekick."

Holly stood up and walked over to where she'd left her purse, and Quimby followed along, nipping at her heels. "I thought you were my sidekick," she said to Mack.

He just shook his head. "So. Next weekend? Hobbies?"

Holly answered before the rational part of her brain could stop her: "Okay. As long as we can bring Quimby."

The drive back to Holly's house was pretty much silent, except for the classical music. Quimby rode with them. Exhaustion having taken over, he climbed onto Holly's lap, curled up, and slept as they drove. When Mack pulled up at the curb, he said, "I'll walk you to the door."

Holly felt a mix of relief and disappointment when he didn't turn off the car. Disappointment took the lead when his good-bye consisted of a quick squeeze of her arm and a cursory, "Good night, Holly."

From inside the front window, she watched him drive away. The silent house felt so empty that she flipped on every single light and turned on her own music—twangy country heartbreak songs. Then, she realized she hadn't checked her phone all night, and when she dug it out of her purse, she gasped at the message waiting from Sequoia: *Gig's up. I know Alejo is not your real boyfriend. It's time to come clean, sister.*

Stomach in knots, Holly turned off her phone. "I'll deal with this tomorrow," she said to the empty space.

CHAPTER EIGHTEEN

Circumstances forced Holly to deal with Sequoia's message much sooner than she would have liked to. Her sister, who'd always been the early riser of the three, knocked on the front door at seven a.m. Holly didn't even have to open her eyes to know who it was. She slid out of bed and shuffled to the door. When she opened it, Sequoia held out a to-go cup of coffee and a white bakery bag.

"You can't avoid me forever," she said.

"Good morning to you, too," Holly said.

"Fun night last night, right?"

Holly shut the door and followed Sequoia to the dining table. She sipped her coffee and nodded. "Fun night."

Sequoia had busied herself pulling out two chairs. She gestured for Holly to sit down, and Holly obeyed.

"I guess Jas and Hudson are already in full-on honeymoon mode," Sequoia said. "They're probably halfway to San Diego by now."

"Doubt it," Holly said. "They probably slept in. Like normal people."

Sequoia opened the bag she'd brought, took out a breakfast sandwich, unwrapped it, and took a bite before shoving the bag across the table at Holly. "I never claimed to be normal."

"Stop talking with your mouth full. It's too early for this."

"Too early for friendly conversation between sisters?"

"This conversation is going to be anything but friendly," Holly said, "and you know it."

Sequoia swallowed her food. "So why don't we cut to the chase."

"Why don't we."

"Why are you going around with a fake boyfriend?" Sequoia said.

"Why are you so interested in my love life?" Holly said. "I mean, it's usually Jasmine who's grilling me about getting a boyfriend. You're the one who's telling me to get a life."

Sequoia shrugged. For the briefest moment, Holly thought, *She is really beautiful.* For once, she wore her long, dark hair down, and her light eyes looked clear and bright despite the early hour.

"I have my reasons," Sequoia said.

"And what are they?"

"None of your beeswax."

"Um, actually," Holly said. "I think your reasons are my beeswax. Since we're talking about my love life."

"You're not answering the question," Sequoia said. "Don't think I'll let you get off track, here."

Holly rubbed her hands over her face. "I haven't even finished this one cup of coffee."

"Fine," Sequoia said. "We can talk about the weather until you do. I'll make more."

She went into the kitchen. Holly could hear her rinsing and filling the pot, pouring the water into the coffee maker, and scooping grounds into a new filter. "Beautiful day," she said, her voice cheerful.

"Humph," Holly said.

"I heard they're expecting a storm, end of this week."

"Maybe you'll melt if you stand outside. Like the green witch in the *Wizard of Oz.*" This made Holly laugh.

"Uncalled for, Holly," Sequoia said. "Completely uncalled for."

She returned to the dining table, and Holly smelled the fresh coffee brewing.

"Don't you love a good storm?" Sequoia said. "Remember how we used to make those little paper boats and float them down the creek behind the house when it rained?"

Holly nodded. "Yeah, and I'd always cry because mine would get soggy."

Actually, she remembered now, that wasn't true. The soggy boat and the crying had happened only once—the first time they floated paper boats. Her sisters, busy with their own boats, didn't realize that Holly hadn't waterproofed hers. Yes, tears were shed. But the next time it rained, Sequoia took Holly's finished boat and covered the entire thing with tape, all the while explaining how important it was to protect the paper.

"Only happened once," Sequoia said, and Holly knew she was remembering the same chain of events.

"You saved my boating experience," Holly said. Distracted, she tipped her coffee cup upward, revealing she'd finished. Simultaneously, the coffee maker finished brewing. Sequoia got a gleam in her eye, then went into the kitchen to pour them each a fresh mug.

"Now," she said when she sat back down. "Dish. Why the fake boyfriend?"

"Wait," Holly said. "What did your card say? The one on your flowers?"

"Oh," Sequoia said, a brilliant pink making its way up her neck and into her cheeks. "That."

"Yes," Holly said. "That."

"It's private. Between Elijah and me. Why the fake boyfriend?"

"Why do you think he's fake?" Holly said.

Now that she was fully awake, her wheels were turning. Maybe she could hire Alex the Adventurous to come back and play Alejo for a couple more functions. It would be too obvious if she came up with a break-up story at this point.

"What do you mean, 'Why?'?" Sequoia said. "It's obvious, Holly."

"Is it?" Was it?

"I mean, when we finally met him in person, Alejo seemed like a perfectly nice guy," Sequoia said. "But I noticed right away that the chemistry just wasn't there."

What could she say to that? She went for a humorous tone of voice: "Oh, just because we didn't, you know, disrobe and get it on right there at Jasmine's wedding?" Then, to give "Alejo's" character some depth, she added, "Alejo's not that in to PDA. You know?"

Sequoia nodded. "Remember I said he seemed like a perfectly nice guy? He was. But almost too perfect. Too smooth, you know what I mean? I've seen these guys in action, Holly."

"What guys?"

For a moment, Holly thought Sequoia knew she'd hired a male escort. She thought the cat was out of the bag. And in a way, it felt like a relief to know she could stop this façade and spill the whole story.

But then Sequoia said, "Fake boyfriends."

"What do you mean, fake?" Holly said. "You saw him, in the flesh. He was as real as they come."

"Was he?" Sequoia sipped her coffee, all the time maintaining eye contact with Holly.

"Stop interrogating me. I'm not a criminal."

"You may not be a criminal," Sequoia said. "But there is something going on that you're not telling me. And I intend to find out what it is. Right now."

"Why do you care so much? Even if he was a fake, why out me?" Holly said. "Why not let the whole thing take its course?"

"You and I are not the only ones involved in this story," Sequoia said.

"What? What do you mean?"

"I mean, we're not the only characters in this story. We're not the only bulls in this china shop."

"Why are you being so cryptic?" Holly said. "It's not like you. Also I'm not sure about the bull-in-a-china-shop analogy. Come out with it."

"Don't try to turn the tables on me," Sequoia said. "I know what you're doing. Tell me why you have a fake boyfriend."

Holly unwrapped her own breakfast sandwich and took a bite

while Sequoia stared at her. What could she say to get Sequoia off this trail? She was like a bloodhound. Maybe she could say Alejo was actually a government spy and she couldn't reveal his true identity, but that she'd begged him to come to her sister's wedding festivities so her other sister would stop bugging her about her boyfriend. Was that too much?

She could say he was really shy, but that wouldn't jive, considering the way he hadn't even blinked when Holly had asked him to help them get Jasmine out of the car at the wedding, and the way he'd called Jasmine—who was practically a stranger to him at the time—"spectacular" when he saw her in her wedding dress. He wasn't even close to shy.

She could say he was in the witness protection program, but that would be too easy for Sequoia to check out.

Or maybe she could give him some kind of disease. A sexually transmitted disease. And she could say she'd just found out and they'd broken up. That didn't seem fair, though. Alex the Adventurous was a perfectly nice guy. If Sequoia ever ran into him on the street, she wouldn't hold back from saying something snarky.

Before Holly could answer, Sequoia, having apparently decided to jump to a different track, said, "Who sent you that cactus, Holly?"

"What? Why are you asking me that?"

"I will not be derailed," Sequoia said. "Who sent you that cactus?"

Uh oh.

"I—I don't know. I thought Hudson sent it."

"What do you mean, you don't know? There was a card."

"It didn't have a signature. So I assumed Hudson sent it, along with Jasmine's flowers, so I wouldn't feel left out. Besides. You haven't told me what your card said. So why should I tell you who sent my cactus?" She realized her mistake as her words screeched to a halt, so she quickly added, "If I even knew, that is."

A triumphant light switched on in Sequoia's eyes as she made eye contact with Holly. "It said, *'Let's try page ninety-six. Tonight.'*"

"Ah," Holly said. "The Kama Sutra book. Well, that's disappointing. I thought it would be a lot juicier."

Sequoia shrugged.

"Well? Did you try it?"

Sequoia looked at the tabletop. "I answered your question. Now, you answer mine. Who sent you the cactus?"

"That's it?"

"That's it. And yes, we tried it. And it was good. Really good."

"Oh, geez, Sequoia," Holly said. "Enough already."

"You asked," Sequoia said. "Your turn."

"I can't tell you," Holly said. "Okay?"

"Why?"

"Because."

"Because why?"

"Because I said so, that's why."

"Are you kidding me, right now?" Sequoia said. "I can't believe we're doing this."

"It takes two," Holly said. "If you'd stop pestering me, we could stop doing this."

"You're making it such a big deal," Sequoia said. "Now it's this big thing. If you'd just answered in the first place, we wouldn't have gone through this. Which makes me wonder why you're hiding the identity of the person who sent you that cactus."

Holly knew she should just say it. She should just tell Sequoia it was Mack. Was it really that big of a deal? So what if he'd sent her a plant? Even if Sequoia knew that, she wouldn't know how the thought of Mack made Holly weak in the knees, warm and liquidy inside. Would she? And Sequoia was right. This conversation had snowballed into something way bigger than it should have.

"Fine," Holly said. She held up both hands. "Fine. It was Mack. Okay?"

Sequoia looked surprised, which Holly had expected. Even if she had her suspicions about Alejo being a fake boyfriend, it was unlikely that she thought Mack was the secret sender of that plant. Or, maybe she was just surprised Holly had revealed his name so quickly.

"I thought so," Sequoia said.

Now Holly was surprised. If Sequoia wasn't surprised Mack had sent her the cactus, what had caused that brief flash of shock to cross her face?

"You did?"

"Yeah," Sequoia said. "You can't tell me you didn't realize he has a thing for you, Holly."

"Did *you* realize he has a thing for me?"

"It's so obvious. Of course I did."

"Did he say something to you?" Holly said.

"Of course not," Sequoia said. "Everybody knows I'm not into that social stuff. And besides, that would be weird."

"That *would* be weird," Holly said. "We're all adults, here."

"Enough, already," Sequoia said. "I just don't know why you were keeping it a secret that Mack sent you the cactus. I know you've gone over to his house. More than once. I know the two of you have kissed. And I know he fed you spaghetti last night. Despite the fact that you have a boyfriend. Supposedly."

"What? How did you know he fed me spaghetti?"

"He told me. And he also told me he's giving you a puppy."

"Why?"

"He really likes you, Holly," Sequoia said. "He really wants to see where things could go between you."

"No, I mean, why did you talk to Mack about me?" Holly said.

"Technically, he talked to me about you, first," Sequoia said. "After he pulled you over. And then, yes, I participated in a conversation."

"A conversation about me."

"Yep. There have been several conversations, actually. He's really interested in you. Meanwhile, because I thought your boyfriend was a fake—which you basically confirmed by eating spaghetti at Mack's house after giving *Alejo* a platonic good-bye last night—"

"How did you know I—wait. Did Mack tell you he saw me saying good-bye to Alejo and then invited me over for spaghetti?"

"He did," Sequoia said. She lifted her chin just a little. "And someone else confirmed it."

"Wait. What?"

Sequoia nodded, but made a lip-zipping motion and threw away the key.

So Holly went on. "And so, because you thought my boyfriend was a fake, you …"

"Oh. Right," Sequoia said. "I looked him up. Your "Alejo" is actually David Alexander McCormack, also known as Alex the Adventurous with Male Escorts for the Discerning Woman."

Holly felt her mouth drop open before she could stop it. She felt her eyes become saucer-sized, and her fists curl into balls on the surface of the table. "You checked up on my boyfriend?"

"Your *fake* boyfriend, yes. I had to know who you were spending time with, didn't I? I had to make sure you weren't going home with some felon, didn't I? What if he was a serial killer? I'd feel responsible since I have the tools to research these things. I had to check, didn't I?"

"Well, no! Not really. You didn't tell Mack about it, did you?"

"I'd just be confirming what he already suspected."

"So did you tell him?"

"Did you?" Sequoia said.

"No! I told him I had a boyfriend," Holly said.

"Why are you doing this, Holly? It's really strange."

And they were back where they'd started. Holly wondered how Sequoia would handle it if she took her by the shoulders, spun her around, and marched her right out the door. The two of them sat there at the table, staring at each other. Sequoia drummed her fingertips on the tabletop, and Holly jiggled her leg. Sequoia stared hard at Holly, and Holly looked at her lap. Neither of them broke the silence, and by Holly's calculations, at least two minutes passed. During that time, Holly pressed her lips together, reminding herself that no one could make her answer.

"This is childish," Sequoia said, finally. "I can't believe you're just not answering me."

"I know," Holly said. "It is childish. But at least I haven't tried to change the subject."

"Not yet, you haven't. Holly, if I could at least understand why you're doing this …"

Her sister's voice trailed off.

"Then, what?" Holly said. "If you could understand why I'm doing this, you could think I was even more of an idiot?"

"Ugh. No. If I could at least understand why you have a fake boyfriend, I could help you."

"I don't want *help*!" Holly heard the tone of her voice rising towards shriek mode, and she took a deep breath. Sequoia really was trying to help her.

"I don't want help," she repeated, more softly this time. "I just need some space to focus on myself. I want to spend some time getting to know *me*, figuring out what I want. I realized that ever since we were kids, I've just followed along with whatever you guys are doing. And now that we're all adults, I'm just drifting. You know? But for my whole life, every time I've tried to do something on my own, I've failed. That talent show dance, the paper boats, the time I cooked breakfast in bed for Mom and Dad and lit a fire in the toaster."

Sequoia smirked.

Holly went on, "When Mack pulled me over that night, and you were so concerned, I had an epiphany. And I realized I needed to get my life off the dead-end path it was on, and put it on a new one. And then you started hinting that Mack was interested in me. First of all, things could never work between us because he'll always view me as a criminal. Second of all, I knew I needed to focus on myself. But I didn't want to disappoint you. So I told you I was dating someone. And then it turned into this big lie, and I had to keep it going. It's out of control. But, I really need this space, this time, to figure myself out. Just me. Just Holly."

When she finished, Holly realized she was breathing hard and her hands were shaking. Across from her, Sequoia was sitting up straight, her mouth in a tiny "o" and her hands folded on the table.

"I never knew you felt that way," she said. "Like you fail at everything you do on your own."

"Of course I did!" Holly took another deep breath. "Of course I did. I mean, even now. You're here because you want to help me. You and Jasmine are so happy! And I know you want that for me, too, but I think I'm realizing that happiness is going to look different for me. I don't even know what it's going to look like. But I'm trying to figure myself out, here."

Sequoia nodded. "I know you are. And I'm sorry, okay? I'm sorry for making you feel like you were disappointing me."

"Hold it right there. Did the phrase, 'I'm sorry,' just leave your lips?"

One side of Sequoia's mouth lifted in a smirk. "It did. And I *am* sorry. I'm sorry for pressuring you. I just see what a smart, talented, beautiful woman you are, and I want the best for you. I've always wanted the best for you in terms of your career, and after I found Elijah, I started wanting the best for you in love, too. But I know I can be a bit overpowering at times."

"A bit," Holly said. "At times."

Holly thought her admission would put an end to this conversation, and she felt her heart rate decreasing, settling back to normal. She should have known Sequoia wouldn't let things go.

"Here's the thing," Sequoia said, and Holly felt her stomach lurch. "I don't think what you're doing is fair to Mack."

"But he knows I have a boyfriend. So how is it not fair?" Holly said, the logic falling flat even in her own mind.

"He knows you have a fake boyfriend," Sequoia said. "But he has real feelings for you. And judging by the way I saw the two of you dancing at his retirement party, and by the fact that you went to his house last night, I think you have feelings for him, too. Whether you want to or not. I'm not saying you have to act on them. I'm just saying it feels like you're leading him on. You're saying one thing and doing another, you know? You're saying you have a boyfriend and can't take things farther with Mack, but you're eating his spaghetti."

"Friends eat each other's spaghetti, don't they? It's not like we're doing that pose from page forty-five."

Sequoia smiled. "True," she said. "Friends eat each other's spaghetti. But they don't kiss like long-lost lovers next to the creek."

"How did you—"

Sequoia held up a hand.

"All I'm sayin', my sister, is that you should come clean with Mack."

"But why? What will it change?"

"It may not change anything," Sequoia said.

"All it will do is make him think even less of me," Holly said.

"What is that supposed to mean?"

"It means," Holly said, "that we're completely unsuitable for each other. No self-respecting cop wants to date a woman he pulled over for drunk driving."

"He's retired," Sequoia said. "And don't you think it's up to him to make that call?"

Holly shook her head and looked down at her lap again.

"So do you have any intentions of giving him a chance?" Sequoia said.

Holly shrugged, out of answers or explanations.

"You need to tell him. Full disclosure. Especially if you don't plan on giving him a real chance. He really likes you. And he deserves to know the real reason you're keeping him at a distance—which isn't because you have a boyfriend. I've seen the way he looks at you. I've seen the way he kisses you. And I think he's just biding his time. But if you don't intend to give him a chance, then you need to end things. If you don't tell him, Holly, then I'm going to."

"What?" Holly said. "Now who's being childish?"

"It's for your own good," Sequoia said. "Now, thank me for breakfast. I've got to get going."

"Thank you for breakfast."

Sequoia kissed Holly on the cheek, then picked up the empty bakery bag and paper cups and walked to the front door. Before letting herself out, she said, "You know, Holly? You should give Mack a shot. Actually, you should give yourself a shot. I know you created Alejo and hired Alex the Adventurous for a reason. But this isn't going to work forever. You won't be able to afford it, for one thing. And for another, you have this perfectly nice guy who wants to spend time with you. Why wouldn't you give a real relationship a chance?"

Could this get any worse? Holly thought as Sequoia closed the door behind herself. Then, she realized, of course it could. She had no choice but to tell Mack about Alejo. Yes, it would be humiliating. Yes, it would probably mean Mack backed off completely and avoided her forever. But isn't that what she wanted? A voice somewhere in the recesses of her brain answered that no, it wasn't what she wanted, but she hushed it.

Besides, if she didn't tell him, Sequoia would, and, if it was possible, that would be even more humiliating.

CHAPTER NINETEEN

Are you ready for an adventure?

Mack's text message came in shortly after Sequoia went out, which made Holly suspicious. Had Sequoia called him to let him know Holly was alone?

Still, she wrote back almost immediately: *What do you have in mind?*

She'd already tapped *Send* when she realized that may sound indecent.

"I should have written something else," she said. "Something like, 'Are you?'"

Although that sounded provocative, too, she thought, but only because she wanted an adventure with Mack.

I'll pick you up at noon.

Wait. Had she told him she wasn't working today? How did he know she wasn't busy? It didn't matter. It was too late for her to decline now. She thought about texting him, *I'm getting in the shower*, but she didn't. Instead, she wrote, *Okay. See you then.*

At noon on the dot, he knocked on her door. Holly had spent the entire morning trying to come up with ways to tell him Alejo was a fake. On the surface, it seemed so simple. All she had to do was blurt it out. But then, because she was Holly, she felt like she had to offer some sort of explanation as to *why* she'd faked having a boyfriend. It's not like that was something normal people did. And how would she explain her reasons? They sounded stupid to her, and they'd certainly sound even more stupid to Mack.

"I want to focus on myself."

"I wanted to spend time alone, to figure out what I want."

"I was afraid I would fall for you, but that you'd never be able to love me."

"Actually, I don't even know how to spend time alone. So under the guise of wanting to, I hired a fake boyfriend."

If he thought she was a loser before, he'd think she was a double loser when he found out she'd not only dated a nonexistent boyfriend but that she'd also hired a male escort so she could perpetuate the lie. It didn't even matter why she'd done it.

So when she opened her door to greet him and was tempted to kiss him long and deep, she resolved to tell him all about Alejo—but not today. She could spend today crafting her explanation, and she could present it to him the next time they were together. For now, she'd just enjoy his company … since it might be the last time they spent together.

"You look way too sexy for someone who's wearing a pair of shorts and a t-shirt," he said.

"Is that how you greet all your lady friends?"

"Nope."

Now he stepped forward and put his arms around her waist, the movement slow and fluid and sensual. Holly told herself that her reaction—to wrap her arms around his shoulders in the same way— was only natural. If they were together, or even if they were dating casually, he would have kissed her. But instead, he nuzzled her neck.

"You smell good, too," he said.

"So what's on the schedule for today?" she said, easing out of his arms.

"I thought we could check out the Skyline Trail. Ever been?"

"If I have, it's been so long I can't remember," Holly said. "Should I grab some water bottles?"

"I've got it covered," Mack said, jerking a thumb towards his car. "Water, snacks, a birdwatching book, and binoculars. Oh, and a puppy."

"Birdwatching, huh?"

"Don't look so incredulous," Mack said. "It's not just for senior citizens. Are you ready?"

At first, Holly thought Skyline Trail was a misnomer. The trail-head was wedged between two wooden posts in a dusty parking lot at the edge of a meadow, and the trail itself wound through waist-high, amber-colored grass and out of sight. She doubted Mack would get any use out of his binoculars; any nearby birds were probably hiding in the grass.

Still, when they got out of the car, she said, "This is nice."

Quimby, floppy ears and oversized paws, tumbled out of the car and made a few laps around Holly's feet before sitting down and leaning against her leg.

"I know," Mack said. "It doesn't look like much. But don't worry, there's more to this trail than meets the eye."

Holly took the water bottle he offered, curiosity sufficiently piqued. "Let's get to it."

They walked in silence for a few minutes, Quimby darting from one side of the path to the other, pulling hard on the leash.

"You're going to have to train your puppy," Mack said.

"He's not even my puppy, yet."

Still, she took a firmer grip on the leash and told Quimby to heel. He looked up at her every few seconds, as if to ask whether he was behaving appropriately.

"I think he *is* your puppy," Mack said.

Holly realized the trail's simplicity really was beautiful in its serenity. It came to the base of a hill, and Mack offered his hand. Holly pretended to be distracted by the puppy, who had gripped the leash between his teeth and was pulling her along ... even though she could already feel Mack's skin on her palm. She couldn't see the ocean, but she could hear the tide swishing in and out, and gulls calling. She hadn't realized they were quite this close to the coast.

The trail became steeper and narrower, and Mack gestured for

Holly and Quimby to walk in front of him. She knew he was being chivalrous, and she did love good manners, but she also didn't want his face level with her rear end as he walked behind her. Wouldn't it be leading him on, to let him walk behind her like that? Sequoia would be scandalized.

The shuffle that resulted from her indecision was awkward, especially since all three of them ended up tangled in the leash. But Mack's comment was even more awkward: "You don't want me at butt level, do you?"

This made Holly relax, just the tiniest bit.

"I didn't, no," she said. "But it's fine. I'm just being shy, I guess."

Mack let her pass, and of course, with Mack walking behind them, Quimby could barely contain himself bounding back and forth between them.

"Wow," Holly said when they came to the top of the hill and saw the panoramic view.

"Yeah, I know," Mack said. "That's what I was thinking all the way up that hill."

"Funny guy," she said. She meant to bump her shoulder against his, but somehow she found herself leaning against him, instead. Apparently worn out, Quimby flopped down on the ground and rolled onto his back.

The view really was breathtaking. The hill swept out below them, steep and golden, joined at the dark blue ocean with a strip of nearly-white sand in a crescent moon shape. The water in the cove sparkled in the mid-morning sunlight, and emerald green ice plant crawled up the bank to the right.

"It's so peaceful," Holly said. "I can't believe I've never been up here."

"You're welcome," Mack said.

Then, all business, he retrieved the binoculars from his backpack and spent a long moment looking through them, sweeping them from one side to the other.

He was concentrating hard enough that she was able to take the opportunity to admire his profile, the way his jeans fit, and the way his hands looked. His skin was so clear and smooth, and she found herself wanting to take him right here on this bluff.

"Did you happen to bring a blanket?" she asked, not realizing she'd spoken aloud until he looked at her.

He asked if she was cold, but she could see something else glinting in his eyes. Could he read her mind?

"No," she said. "I just thought we might, you know, sit down for a while."

Until that moment, he'd been holding the binoculars in both hands, his arms still raised. Now, he took them off and set them on top of his pack. He turned toward Holly and she felt her body go on alert: her heart rate picked up, her skin tingled in anticipation, and her stomach fluttered. Her lady parts even stood at attention. He took her hands, and his gaze was intense.

"I'd like to, you know, sit down for a while with you, Holly," he said. "That is, whenever you're ready."

Then he leaned forward, and she thought he was going to kiss her. Her entire body thought he was going to kiss her, and it liked that idea.

Instead, though, he put his cheek up to hers and his lips near her ear. "I'm ready, anytime."

Holly considered the hike a success. She'd spent time with a very handsome man. She'd seen new scenery. Mack even found a blue heron to look at, and the moment they shared watching it walk along the beach and then fly off—long legs, elegant wings—was breathtaking. At least, until Quimby woke up on full alert, barking at the huge bird as it flew overhead. The three of them walked back down the hill, the ocean breeze cooling Holly's fired-up libido, even as she daydreamed about declaring herself ready right then and there so Mack could throw her down on the hood of his car and take advantage of her.

Instead, she thanked him for the hike, and was surprised when he said, "We're not done yet. We have two more stops to make."

"Another hobby?" Holly said.

She wondered whether buying stuff at the sex shop around the corner counted as a hobby.

"You bet," Mack said. "It's got kind of a different vibe. But I have a feeling you'll like it. I'm going to feed you, first. I was going to ask where you want to eat, but I changed my mind. I'm taking you to my favorite spot."

"Is Quimby coming along?"

"Nah, we've got to drop him off."

As they drove back to Mack's house, Holly thought nothing could live up to her idea of picnicking—on Mack—atop that hill overlooking the ocean. Still, after they dropped off Quimby and Mack announced he was taking Holly to Mama Rosa's, a traditional Italian restaurant that touted the best meatballs in the state, she was delighted. They could share a huge plate of spaghetti, just like Lady and the Tramp.

"Best meatballs in California," Mack said as they walked to the front door, which he held open for her.

"I've heard," she said. "I always get the pizza."

"That's a travesty," he said. "We're getting meatballs."

Apparently, Mack was well-known at Mama Rosa's. The hostess smiled warmly at him when they walked in, and signaled for them to go into the dining room.

"Do you bring all your lady friends here?" she asked when he pulled out a chair for her.

"Absolutely not," he said, his serious tone not matching her playful one at all.

When he sat down across from her, she realized that he seemed nervous, which was totally out of character. He licked his lips and fidgeted with his linen napkin. His eyes darted to a spot somewhere behind Holly's left shoulder.

"Are you okay?" she said. "You seem kind of on-edge."

He smiled at her, but it was forced. He wiped his forehead with the back of his hand. "I'm fine."

"Really?"

In her mind, Holly ran through a list of possible scenarios that could be making him sweat. Was that hostess an old girlfriend? Or had he seen an old flame in the dining room? Was his blood sugar low after hiking? Was that snake, Jess, hiding somewhere around here? What could it possibly be? A server brought them water, and Mack gulped his down. On high alert and trying to be as dainty as possible in case he had seen a woman from his past (or present! She hadn't thought of that), Holly sipped hers.

"Really," Mack said. "I'm fine. Completely fine."

This was weird. Holly sipped her water again.

A moment later, the first clue presented itself.

"Hi, Mack."

Judging by her outfit, pants, a button-up shirt and an apron—all black—and the way she was holding her notebook and pen poised to take their order, Holly deduced this must be their waitress. Judging by her smoky voice, she'd seen her fair share of late nights and shots of whiskey. Finally, judging by her knobby knuckles, the wrinkles around her lips, and her bright blue eyeliner, she was old enough to be Mack's mother.

"Hi, Phyllis," Mack said.

He took a deep breath. Holly couldn't be sure whether he was feeling more or less nervous. She gave him what she hoped was a reassuring smile. He picked up his napkin again and started twisting it.

"Are you going to introduce me to your lady friend?" Phyllis said, putting one hand on her cocked hip like she planned to stay a while.

"This is Holly," Mack said.

Phyllis turned to Holly and gave her a smile that was somewhere between sweet and skeptical. "Lovely to meet you," she said in a tone that suggested it actually wasn't.

"You, too, Phyllis," Holly said.

"What can I get you?"

They ordered meatballs, Phyllis walked away, and Holly exhaled the breath she was holding. Mack did the same.

"What was that all about?" Holly asked. "Is Phyllis one of your old flames, or what?"

"Nah," Mack said. "It's worse than that. She's my aunt."

"Ah," Holly said. "That explains the once-over."

"She means well," Mack said.

"I'm sure she does," Holly said. "She seems nice."

"Ha!" Mack said. "She does not. She probably thought it would be fun to intimidate you. This isn't even her section. I sat here on purpose, but she probably bribed one of the other servers to let her wait on us."

Holly had questions, but Aunt Phyllis returned with a bread basket and a bottle of table wine, and when she left, Mack had regained his composure and control of the conversation.

"So, what do you think? Could we add hiking to your permanent hobby list?"

"Yes," Holly said. "As long as the view is always as good as it was today."

"I agree," Mack said. "My view was damned good, especially coming up the first half of that trail."

"Thank you, I think," Holly said. She wished she could immerse her entire body in her glass of ice water. Some outrageous figment of her imagination had Mack's foot running up the inside of her leg under the table. *Get a grip, Carr*, she thought.

"I should be thanking you," he said.

"Nice one," Holly said. "Put that in a little book of one-liners. You could sell it."

He smirked, and she was relieved to see that some of the tension from earlier had dissipated.

"So are you going to give me any clues about our next round of hobby exploration?" she said.

"I was hoping to surprise you," he said. "But I will give you a hint. It's within walking distance."

"Are we going to the mall?"

"Nope," he said. "I picture you as a big shopper, but I am not. Guess again."

"Wait. I feel scandalized."

"What? Why?"

"Because you think I'm a big shopper."

"Aren't you?"

"Yes!" Holly said. "But I feel like you thinking I am means that you also think I'm shallow."

"Are you?" he said.

"I like to think I'm not," Holly said. "But I do enjoy shopping."

"What do you enjoy about it?" he said.

This couldn't go anywhere good. Holly enjoyed lots of things about shopping. She thought about her answers, though, and worried that every one of them would seem materialistic or flighty.

"Wow, I never imagined you'd be so conflicted about answering that question," Mack said. "I mean, most women love shopping, right?"

"Right," Holly said, drawing the word out. "But I feel like it's always associated with shallow women. You know? At least, my sister always hints that I'm shallow."

"Carr?" Mack said. "I mean, Sequoia?"

"Yeah," Holly said.

"Well, she would. That woman would wear workout clothes twenty-four seven if she could, just so she never had to shop for real clothes. My guess is that she always goes for comfortable and practical, right?"

"You sure know women," Holly said. Then she wondered if that was offensive.

"I'm just observant," he said. "So tell me why you love shopping."

Before she could answer, Aunt Phyllis returned with their plates. She gave Holly a smile that bordered on evil, and said to Mack, "The chef will be out shortly to make sure your food is satisfactory."

If Mack had seemed nervous before, he looked downright terrified now.

"I swear I can see sweat beading on your forehead, and seeing as how my sauce isn't particularly spicy, I don't think yours is, either," Holly said. "What's up?"

Mack gulped down all the wine in his glass, but he didn't answer. Instead, he picked up the bottle and poured himself a refill.

"I guess it's good our next destination is within walking distance," Holly said.

Now he smiled at her.

"We could always dine and dash," he said. It sounded like he was speaking more to himself than to Holly.

"Are you feeling okay? Are you sick? I could drive you home. Although, you probably wouldn't have downed that wine if you weren't feeling well, right?"

"Actually, that first glass is hitting my bloodstream. I think I'll be all right. It's just the chef. She—well, let's just say she frightens me."

"Why did we come here, then? We could have gone anywhere."

"I know, I know. You're right. We should have gone somewhere else."

"Did you have a bad experience, or something?" Holly said.

"Not exactly."

He was wiping his hands incessantly, and when he saw that Holly had noticed, he put the napkin back on his lap.

"Look," he said.

But before he could explain, a voice reverberated through the restaurant. "Mack, my boy! Elusive as a panther, this one."

The voice increased in volume and proximity, and then the body to which it belonged came around the corner behind Mack. The woman was about six feet tall, with long, slender arms and legs. She was dressed in a black chef's uniform, complete with a hairnet that covered her bun. Her skin was the color of caramel, and her eyes sparkled with a mixture of good cheer and … and intensity that strongly resembled the intensity in the eyes Holly had been looking into throughout this meal.

"Oh," she said, understanding dawning like the fog rolling out to sea on a late summer morning. "This must be your—"

"My mother," he said. "In the flesh."

She was table-side now, and looked even taller up close. Mack had stood up and she had folded him against her body and was kissing his temple.

"Ma," he said, "This is—"

"Oh, you've brought a lady friend," she said. "How wonderful. You must be Jess's successor. What shall I call you?"

"Ma," Mack said again. "Don't call her—"

"Call me Holly," Holly said. She stood up and extended a hand, and Ma shook it.

"Call me Annamaria," she said. "Let me get a look at you."

She held Holly at arm's length, and examined her from head to toe as if she were a cow at market.

"Nice eyes," she said, "and a lovely bone structure, Mack. Good, spacious hips. And wonderfully long legs."

Now, she released Holly's shoulders and turned to Mack. "She'll do. Much better than that other viper of a woman you insist on doing business with."

"Ma," he said again.

"Don't 'Ma' me," she said. "I'm your mother. This is my duty. Sit down, the both of you."

They obeyed. She smiled. "Enjoying your meatballs?"

"Very much," Holly said.

"You know, my Mack can cook, too," Annamaria said.

Mack put his forehead in one hand and closed his eyes.

"I know he can," Holly said, and she felt the air next to her leg move as if Mack had tried to kick her, and failed. "You must have taught him well. He made me spaghetti just the other night."

Annamaria's eyes widened and her lips pursed. "You made her spaghetti, son?"

Eyes still closed, head still in his hand, Mack nodded. "I did."

"Oh," she said. Her eyebrows were raised, practically into her hairline.

"Well," Holly said, feeling she should clear this up. "He didn't make it for me, specifically. I just happened to be leaving my sister's wedding and he saw me and invited me over. He'd already planned on spaghetti. Right, Mack?"

"Dessert's on the house!" Annamaria said, before Mack could answer. "This is a special occasion, no?"

She bustled away as quickly as she'd come, and Holly gave in to the urge to giggle. "Seems like you just got railroaded. What's the special occasion?"

Mack sighed. "My mom thinks me cooking a woman spaghetti is a special occasion. She says it's my signature dish, and, you know, in our family you cook your signature dish only on special occasions. Or for funerals."

"Haven't you ever cooked spaghetti for a woman, before?"

Now Mack looked up and Holly saw that intensity again. And again, before he could answer, his mother emerged from the kitchen, this time carrying a platter of desserts. Holly assumed she and Mack would select the one they wanted, but Annamaria set the entire tray on the table between them and walked away—after giving Mack an ultra-obvious wink.

"We're supposed to eat all of this?" Holly said.

"Yeah, Ma doesn't believe in take-home boxes."

"This might take a while."

"Dig in," Mack said.

As Holly followed his order, taking bites from the chocolate torte, the ricotta cheesecake and the tiramisu, she said, "So why did you bring me here, if you're so scared of your mother? Which, by the way, I can totally understand."

"She made me," he said.

"She made you?"

"Yeah. If I hadn't brought you in, she would have come into the Broken Egg without me. Which would have completely removed any control I had over the situation."

"What situation?" Holly said.

"The one where you met my mother for the first time."

"Huh," Holly said. Her verbal response had been minimal, but her mind was churning out tons of thoughts: He had planned that she'd meet his mother? He figured she'd meet his mother more than once? His mother knew she worked at the Broken Egg? Had he talked about her?

"I can see your mind spinning," Mack said. "Go ahead. Ask."

"I just—did you—I mean, did you know I'd meet your mother?"

"Yes," Mack said. "I knew. She made me."

He sounded so much like a pouty little boy. When he responded only by glaring at her, she brought her expression back to neutral and took a sip of wine.

"Why did she make you?" Holly said.

"She knew I'd been spending time with a woman, and she insisted on meeting you, as soon as possible."

"But, why? I mean, you have it going on. I'm sure you've had occasion to spend time with lots of women, right?"

"She said, 'I can see the light in your eyes, Mack. You must introduce me.'"

"Was there a light in your eyes?" Holly said. "Now I'm intrigued."

For a moment, she forgot that she shouldn't be flirting. She shouldn't be intrigued by a light in Mack's eyes, and she shouldn't be charmed that his mother had wanted to meet her. She definitely shouldn't be relieved that his mother had found her suitable.

Mack put his head in his hands again. "Finish your dessert. We have a hobby to explore."

Holly was surprised when they left the restaurant and, rather than heading to the parking lot, Mack led her around the corner to the bowling alley, which squatted on the corner, its peeling white paint and small, dark windows giving it a spooky vibe in the midday light.

"We're going bowling?" Holly said. "I've never even seen this place in the daytime."

"Yeah," Mack said. "There's actually a bowling team. So if you liked it, we—or you, I guess—could join. You know? Great hobby. You could get a ball to match your hair."

She elbowed him. He opened the door for her and winked at her as she walked in. As she allowed all of her senses to adjust—her eyes to the darkness, her nose to the grease, and her ears to the cracking of ball on pin—she thought about how this had been the scene of one of Jasmine's first serious news stories and the beginning of a budding romance between Jasmine and Hudson. A young guy had committed suicide on lane twelve, Jasmine had passed out cold when she saw the scene, and Hudson had brought her coffee laced with whiskey.

It didn't seem very romantic now, Holly thought. But Jasmine still pointed to it as a defining moment in their romance.

"Shall we get some shoes before I beat you at bowling?" Holly said.

Mack smiled. "My kind of woman."

The bowling alley, with its background of colored lights and loud hard rock music, certainly didn't provide the typical backdrop for amorous events of any kind. Yet, Holly felt herself falling for Mack even more than she already had. He kept finding ways to touch her or smile at her. When she bowled a strike or a spare, he'd squeeze her arm or give her a high five. Between turns, he sat next to her so they touched from shoulder to knee.

Her body reacted without her approval; skin tingling, stomach fluttering. Still, she reminded herself, they were just friends. This hobby exploration was nothing more than what it looked like on the surface: two people, each at a crossroads in life, exploring new activities to enjoy. Yes, they were exploring together, but they'd enjoy the activities separately.

After two games, Holly's right arm and left leg ached. Triumph was worth the pain, though. In the final frames, she bowled two strikes, and then a third to end the game. She beat Mack by a dozen points and did a victory dance. At the end, she threw her arms around his neck.

She meant the gesture to be friendly. She would have hugged her sisters, had they been here. She would have hugged Alejo. Or Alex the Adventurous. She would have hugged anyone. But she probably wouldn't have felt the heat in her lady parts if she'd hugged just anyone. She could feel Mack's stubble on her face, and she could feel her body pressing against his.

Before she even realized what was happening, her lips were on his, her hands were in his hair, and her legs were wrapped around his waist. Her tongue was in his mouth, and he responded with such fervor that she continued kissing him. That little voice in the back of her mind, the one admonishing her about kissing someone when she had a fake boyfriend? She stomped it right down. Why had she lied to Mack? Why had she lied to herself? She wanted him. She wanted to hike with him, and bird watch, and bowl, and eat Italian food and meet his mother. All the time.

Then the group of guys in the next lane started clapping. And she remembered that she was kissing someone other than her fake boyfriend. In the bowling alley.

"Let's take this somewhere else," she said, surprised at the sultry, breathless quality her voice had taken on.

Mack was still breathing fast when he said, "Let's. Somewhere close."

CHAPTER TWENTY

A walk back to the car, and a subsequent drive back to one of their houses would definitely give the passion time to fizzle out, Holly thought. Mack must have thought so, too, because he took her hand and pulled her around the side of the building, where he leaned her against the wall and kissed her some more. Her hands curled into his shirt, just near the waist, and she pulled him towards her so their hips touched.

Someone whistled from across the street and then hollered, "Get a room!"

Mack, his lips still on hers, laughed deep in his throat, and said, "This could be public indecency. Maybe we *should* get a room."

Holly was reluctant to break the spell. But it was probably for the best.

"I guess we should go," she said.

He gave her one last, hard kiss that made her entire body scream for more, and then he took her hand again and started walking back to Mama Rosa's, where his car was parked. Holly could feel the electricity between their palms and crackling in the air around them, and she wondered if any of the drivers passing by could sense the tension. They didn't speak. Typically, Holly would chatter like a bird in an effort to soothe the friction. But at the moment, words escaped her.

"I guess the backseat isn't going to cut it," Mack said when they finally arrived at the car. "There's no doubt my mother would catch us."

"Sounds like you have some experience in that department," Holly said, eyeing the backseat, which was too small anyway.

"Teenage trauma," he said.

For some inexplicable reason, Holly found this amusing. She started to laugh and, probably because of the tension, she kept laughing as he opened the door for her, walked around to the driver's side, and started the car, and kept right on laughing as he shifted into drive and peeled out.

He gave her a sidelong glance and said, "Where to?"

She threw up her hands as tears leaked out of her eyes. "Anywhere."

Now he shook his head. "The moment is gone. I can feel it. All that good energy has been zapped."

For some reason, this made Holly laugh even harder, and Mack said, "I should have taken you right there, against the bowling alley. It's not romantic, but it would have relieved this pressure."

His hands gripped the steering wheel so hard the veins in his arms stood out. Holly stroked his forearm, and noticed that as soon as she touched him, goosebumps rose on his skin. She found this reaction incredibly arousing, and she no longer felt like laughing.

Of course, Mack noticed the change, and he grinned at her—a cocky, meaningful grin that turned her insides to Jell-O all over again. Holly hadn't even realized they were so close to her house. Mack parked at the curb and was out of the car in less than a second. He opened the door for her and extended a hand. When she placed hers in it, he yanked her to standing so quickly that before she knew it, their bodies were pressed together and they were kissing.

He picked Holly up and flung her over his shoulder, only to stop again at the front door when he tried to open it and it was locked. He put her on her feet, and then attacked her again, this time using his body to pin her against the door so his hands were free to roam her body. They started at her waist, but moved quickly up to her breasts. Of course, by now, her nipples were standing at attention, and she could feel them hard against his thumbs. He continued kissing her while he caressed her nipples, and when she would have started begging him to take her inside, he ran his hands down her torso. One hand braced against the door, he used the other to begin unbuttoning her shorts.

At this point, she could think of nothing other than him inside of her. The only way to get to that point was to find her keys and unlock this door. It was a small miracle that she managed to dig them out of her purse while Mack kissed her neck and collarbone, unzipping her shorts and sliding his hand inside her panties. She almost exploded. She would have, if her struggle with the deadbolt hadn't distracted her. As soon as she turned the key, Mack had his arms around her waist and was carrying her to the couch. He laid her down and stretched his body out over hers, sliding his hands under her shirt again.

Holly moaned, with pleasure, with anticipation, and with frustration. This shouldn't be happening. Mack still didn't know Alejo was a fake boyfriend. So right now, to Mack's knowledge, she was betraying her boyfriend. She'd always known things couldn't be serious or long-term with Mack, and this situation only made things worse. Not only would he always think of her as a drunk driver, but he'd also think she had the capacity to be unfaithful.

An unfaithful drunk driver. A cheating jailbird.

"This will never do," she said.

"I know," Mack said. "Should we take it to the bedroom?"

"No, not that," Holly said. She sat up, and he sat back.

"What's wrong?" he said.

Holly put her face in her hands. "It's just—"

This would be the perfect time for her to come clean. If she took this opportunity to tell him about Alejo, to tell him that she was really single and very available for dating, at least he wouldn't think she was a cheat. But he *would* think she was strange. It was very strange to make up a fake boyfriend just to avoid getting a real one. Wasn't it?

"I'm sorry," Mack said. "I'm rushing you."

"Not, it's not that," Holly said.

Her inner voice (which sounded an awful lot like Sequoia's voice) was whisper-yelling, *Tell him. Just tell him.*

Holly opened her mouth. She closed it again. "It's just—"

"It's just that I'm not really your type? You're not attracted to me?"

"No, it's not that at all," Holly said. "I find you very attractive."

"I find you very attractive as well," Mack said. "And I've always believed that if two people find each other very attractive, they should absolutely pursue that attraction."

It sounded reasonable. In fact, pursuing a mutual attraction sounded more than reasonable. It sounded downright delectable. But she had to come clean, first.

"So?" Mack said.

"I just can't do this. This has been a really fun day. I've had a great time with you. But I can't."

"YOU DON'T SEEM like your typical chipper self today," Tristan said.

If only you had seen me five minutes ago.

Holly had almost forgotten about her appointment with Tristan, so ushering Mack out the door instead of starting a hot and steamy sex session with him had worked out for the best on more than one level.

"Just tired," she said.

Then she saw the little square on her screen that showed her what her webcam was picking up. It showed her what Tristan was seeing. And he was seeing post-sex hair. No, she hadn't had sex with Mack. But her hair wanted Tristan to believe she had. It stuck up at odd angles on one side, and it stood straight up in the back.

Her attempts to smooth it, nonchalantly, didn't work. This was going to require a comb.

"Today, I want to talk about honesty," Tristan said, and Holly didn't even have time to stop her knee-jerk reaction, which was to look wildly around her house as if it were bugged. Did Tristan know about Alejo? Had he hired someone to spy on her and see what she was up to? Of course, he couldn't know. And it was unlikely he'd gone to the trouble or to the expense of hiring someone. Unless... Unless Alex the Adventurous was really a spy for Tristan. Was that even possible? Tristan definitely lived somewhere with a beach. His Blackbook advertisement had featured wide beach views. Seabreeze was a beach town. Tristan could live right next door. He could be spying on her, himself. He could have seen Mack leave just now.

Too much time had passed since Tristan had spoken. Holly cleared her throat and said, "Okay."

She drew the word out, something Sequoia would have done when she anticipated being forced to talk about a topic she'd rather avoid.

"Are you being honest right now, Holly?"

Well, of course she wasn't. What was she supposed to say to that?

She nodded, her head moving up and down at warp speed. "Yeah. I'm being honest. Why?"

"Honesty is critical during periods of personal growth," Tristan said. "Especially honesty with yourself."

Holly licked her lips and nodded again. "Of course."

"Last time we met, we talked about your unique strengths. Have you thought about what those are?"

During the past week or so, she'd thought of little other than her situation with Mack and Alejo. And Holly wasn't sure what her unique strengths had to do with honesty. Still, she'd better come up with something, here.

"Well, I've been thinking mostly about my waitressing skills. And I totally get how you said these same skills may be applicable in other ways. But I could use some help with that. I'm great at helping someone decide what to order. I can chat with someone for a few moments and then choose the perfect dish, even if it's one I wouldn't order, myself. I'm also good at making people feel welcome, like they're part of a family, just from a single experience at the restaurant. Lots of my regulars, like this couple, Jaclyn and Phil Connelly, for example, have told me that's why they come back to the Broken

Egg over and over again. I'm fairly organized, but lately that's not been my strongest attribute."

Tristan nodded. "Okay. So, you're good at reading people, right? You're good at communicating with them. And you have a knack for making people feel special. It's a connection thing, isn't it? You're great at connecting with people."

Holly nodded. It was true. She was great at connecting with people. But what did it mean for her future?

"I'm also good at fashion, but I'm not sure that's really a strength."

"I admit, I've noticed your hair color changes from time to time."

"Great."

"No," Tristan said. "It's a good thing. I think some people might assume it speaks to lack of identity, but after talking with you, I think it speaks to your adventurous nature."

"Hmm."

"You know, you could build a career out of being great with fashion and great connecting with people."

Sure that he was being sarcastic, Holly rolled her eyes. "Now you sound like my oldest sister. Sequoia."

"Why's that?"

"She's convinced I'll be a diner waitress forever. That if my only skills are taking orders and keeping coffee mugs full, I am going nowhere."

"Has she said that?"

"Not exactly," Holly said. "But I know that's what she thinks."

"Or, is that what *you* think?" Tristan said.

He allowed a long moment for Holly to respond, and when she didn't, he said, "This is where that honesty comes in. If your sister hasn't actually said she believes you're going nowhere, then maybe you've created that story in your mind. Have you considered that? Maybe you believe you're going nowhere."

"Maybe I do."

Had Sequoia really said anything to that effect? Not really, no. She'd asked questions, and in her way, she'd encouraged Holly to do more with her life. And all this only after Holly worried aloud that she wasn't going anywhere.

Interesting.

"I want you to think about some careers that could combine your strengths."

Holly scoffed. "Like what? Shopping?"

Tristan raised an eyebrow. "What if you became a personal shopper?" he said. "You know, where you meet with a client and then do her shopping for her? And she pays you. People who are too busy to shop for themselves, or who don't like shopping, hire other people to do it for them. And from what you've said, you'd be great at getting a handle on what someone likes."

Holly could feel the wheels turning inside her mind. "Actually," she said. "That's a great idea."

"It's not the only possibility," Tristan said. "We could definitely brainstorm together. But I had one other client who started her own business as a personal shopper, and she loved it."

"I'll have to think on that. Maybe I could experiment on my sisters."

"Great idea," Tristan said. "Next time we meet, I'd love to hear a few more ideas, and I'd love for you to come up with a few action steps you can take to dig in and begin exploring whether this is a viable idea for you. I love the idea about personal shopping for the sisters."

He sounded genuinely enthusiastic, and Holly felt enthusiastic, too. Now, she just hoped he didn't ask about her romantic life. She'd hate to disappoint him.

She nodded. "Sounds great."

"Now, let's talk about how you've been spending your time."

Of course, her mind immediately jumped to the scene that had occurred just moments ago in her living room ... and then to the scene that had occurred ten minutes before that behind the bowling alley. She'd love to be spending more of her time that way. But she couldn't admit it to Tristan.

"Are you okay?" Tristan said. "You just broke out in a sweat."

"I'm fine," Holly said. "Just a little warm from all this coffee I'm drinking."

On her computer screen, she saw his eyes dart down to a spot somewhere near her elbow, where she knew there was no coffee. Fortunately, he didn't question her about it, and Holly decided to take control of the conversation.

"I did some hiking earlier today. And then I went bowling."

"Hiking is a great hobby. How did you feel after you were done?"

She thought about the way her skin had tingled after she'd stood atop that bluff with Mack. She thought about the way she'd wanted to kiss him before they hiked back down to the car. And, inevitably, she thought about the way her body had reacted when his was on top of it here in her living room.

"I felt … refreshed."

"Great!" Tristan's enthusiasm was misplaced, but he didn't need to know that. "So do you think hiking is something you'd like to do more of?"

"Absolutely," Holly said.

"Let's talk about what you liked about hiking."

Holly nodded. What had she liked about hiking, aside from being there with Mack?

"I liked seeing something new," she said. "And the scenery was really nice, really pretty. Oh! And the puppy. Quimby. A friend is giving me a puppy and he let me take it hiking."

"Great," Tristan said. "I'd like you to explore a few more hobbies before our next meeting, okay? Make it two or three. I want to really dial down on the elements you enjoy about each one. And remember: action steps for the personal shopping, okay?"

"Okay," Holly said. "I can do that."

Their time was almost up. She was prepared to click out of Skype to ensure they didn't come across the topics of boyfriends or honesty, but no such luck.

"Before we go," Tristan said, "I want to bring up honesty again. I know we have only a few minutes left. But next week we're really going to dig deep. As you know, my coaching isn't about looking to the past for answers. It's about starting from where you are and creating the future you want. But that requires honesty, Holly. Honesty with yourself, with the people in your life, and with me. I want you to be honest with yourself about why you've continued to work at the Broken Egg. Why you seek out your sisters' approval. Why you don't like being alone. Again, we're not going to wallow, here. I just want to identify the emotions that are keeping you stuck, keeping you from moving forward. Okay?"

When Holly nodded, Tristan continued, "I want to share one of my favorite quotes with you. It's from James Faust. He said, 'Honesty is more than not lying. It is truth telling, truth speaking, truth living, and truth loving.' Isn't that great? 'Truth living, and truth loving.' I just love that. And that's what I want for you Holly, and it's what I believe you want for yourself. You want to live your own truth. Am I right?"

He was right. Again, Holly nodded. She felt frozen. She needed to live her own truth, and part of her own truth was that she wanted to be with Mack. In order to do that, she needed to close the curtain on the Alejo act. First, though, she needed to smooth out her sex hair.

Thirty minutes later, hair combed into submission and her stomach in knots, Holly knocked on Mack's door. When he answered, his expression held a mixture of apprehension and something that looked like anger, but maybe he was just guarded.

"Holly," he said. "I'm surprised to see you here."

"I know," Holly said. "Can I come in for a minute?"

He stepped back and held the door open. This was not the warm greeting for which she'd hoped, and before she made a hasty retreat, she had to remind herself that he still thought she had a boyfriend and that, not even an hour ago, she had interrupted what promised to be a very steamy sex session on that premise.

"Do you think I could have something to drink?" she said, thinking she could really use one before she launched into this conversation.

"Sure," he said. "I wasn't sure whether offering would be too presumptuous."

She sighed. He was right. While he retrieved a glass of water, she prepared to forge ahead with whatever traces of confidence she'd developed during her chat with Tristan.

"Mack," she said.

"Holly."

"Can we sit?"

He inhaled but didn't exhale, probably deciding that heaving a big sigh wasn't conducive to getting Holly to say her piece and then get the heck out.

"Sure."

He sat down on the couch. She sat down next to him. If they turned the right way, their knees would touch. But he didn't turn the right way, so she didn't, either.

"I need to tell you something," she said. "Something I should have told you a long time ago."

Strangely, he didn't look surprised, or even that curious. He just looked expectant. This was weird. Maybe she should tell him something else. Something about hiking or the puppy or bowling or Italian food. She could say she didn't like spaghetti or meatballs.

Honesty. Truth telling, truth speaking, truth living, and truth loving.

At that moment, the back door slammed open and the sound of paws on hardwood floor announced a puppy's arrival. Quimby dashed in, feet scrambling as he came around the corner. He ran straight to Holly and jumped onto the couch to bathe her face in puppy kisses. Mack picked him up and set him on the floor, but of course, he couldn't resist putting his front paws on Holly's knees.

As he tried, in vain, to continue licking her face, she took the opportunity to blurt out the one thing she'd come to say: "Mack, I don't have a boyfriend."

He didn't answer, just continued to stare at her. Quimby gave up on her face and started chewing on the toe of her shoe, instead. Never having been one for silence, she plowed on.

"Alejo is a fake. The man at my sister's wedding was a male escort. Alex. Alex the Adventurous." She gave him a chagrined smile and then went on. "He was very nice, very sweet. The perfect gentleman. But I paid him to be there with me. That's why our good-bye was so chaste. More importantly, that's why I've been so … well, so open to spending time with you. Because I don't actually have a boyfriend. But I told you I did because—well, for two reasons, really. First of all, I was afraid that since you pulled me over for drunk driving, you'd never be able to like me. And second, I wanted to focus on myself, to figure out what I'm doing with my life. If I could think of us as friends, maybe even friends with benefits, I could give myself the space to do that. And I wouldn't be disappointed when you broke things off with the woman you pulled over for drunk driving."

There. She'd said it. She'd said it all in a rush, running the words together, but she'd said it. Now she waited, forcing herself to sit in the silence, however uncomfortable it was. From the kitchen came the sound of a clock ticking. Outside, a rooster crowed. The other puppies barked. Quimby stopped chewing her shoe and raised his head. And Holly waited. Finally, Mack spoke.

"I know you don't have a boyfriend, Holly."

"What?"

"I said, I know you don't have a boyfriend."

"I heard you," she said. "But, what do you mean? How do you know? Have you always known?"

"I mean," he said, "that I knew, all along, that you were single. I knew because your sister told me. And yes, I've always known."

"But she told you at the beginning. Before I told her I had a boyfriend. So how did you know? And why didn't you call me out on it?"

Mack sighed again. "I asked your sister right after our first … encounter."

"You mean, the one where you pulled me over?"

Although one corner of his mouth ticked up in what would have been a smile under normal circumstances, he didn't look amused.

"Yes, that's the encounter to which I'm referring. I asked Sequoia if you were seeing anyone, and she said that to her knowledge, you weren't."

"But then I told both of you that I had a boyfriend."

"Holly. I've been a cop for twenty years. That's two decades. I can read people. I knew you were lying. Every time you talked about Alejo, I knew you were lying. So did your sister."

"Wait," Holly said. "So you and Sequoia talked about this?"

"She told me about it after she investigated that Alex the Adventurous yahoo. Was it Male Escorts for Discerning Women? Is that right?"

"You didn't answer my second question."

"You asked so many questions I didn't get a chance," Mack said, and Holly realized she'd said the exact same thing to Sequoia more than once. Mack said, "What was your second question?"

"It was, why didn't you call me out on it?"

"Oh," Mack said. Now he did heave a big sigh. Elbows on the table, he rubbed his forehead hard, relieving tension. "I didn't call you out on it, Holly, because I knew you were on this journey of self-discovery or whatever. I figured that if I pushed you on that topic, I'd push you away. I thought I'd give you time. I thought that if we were meant to be together, things would work out between us. You'd fake dump your fake boyfriend and we could give things a go. Sequoia said it was only a matter of time before you couldn't handle the lie anymore, at which point you'd be single again."

"You guys continued to talk about this?" Holly said.

Now he looked embarrassed. The focus he put on the top of the coffee table was so intense Holly thought he might light it on fire.

"We did," Mack said. "But only because I wanted, you know, to be with you."

Holly nodded. Humiliation was growing inside her body now, swelling like an ocean wave about to break on the shore. And on its tail: anger.

"I see," she said.

"Wait," Mack said. "Are you angry about this?"

"Yes," Holly said. "I'm humiliated and angry. I can't believe the two of you were talking about me, gossiping like that."

His mouth dropped open and he brought his gaze up to level with hers. She could tell that now he was angry, too.

"I can't believe you were living that lie," he said. "Sequoia and I both thought we were doing the right thing by giving you time and space, but obviously that wasn't the case."

"Obviously not," Holly said. "I feel like you played me."

"You feel like *I* played *you*?" Mack said. "Ridiculous. You treated me like we were dating, all the while keeping me at a distance so I couldn't get too close."

That's exactly what she'd been doing, Holly realized. She had been letting him court her, but guarding her heart the whole time. Even though she was supposed to be figuring herself out, getting to know herself, she wasn't. Not only was she holding Mack at arm's length, but she was holding herself at arm's length, too.

At a loss, she didn't respond.

"I think we're done here," Mack said. "I was willing to be patient, to give you time, but now it feels like you're blaming me for that. It looks like you need more space than I realized."

"Giving me space is not what was happening just an hour ago on my couch," Holly said, and she immediately regretted it.

Mack stood up. "You're right. I wasn't giving you space. I thought maybe we could finally move on, be together. I thought that if you felt that passionately about me, that maybe 'Alejo' would disappear."

The unspoken end of that sentence—*and now it's time for you to disappear*—hung in the air.

"When you didn't break things off with Alejo," (here he made air quotes) "I figured you just needed him as a safety net. Now, I feel like maybe it's better things are ending this way. You might actually be insane."

Holly stood up. Mack didn't, so Holly let herself out. As she walked to her car, she could hear Quimby barking through the closed door.

In the car, Holly told herself she wouldn't cry, but the tears fell even after she cranked up the volume on the hard rock station and pounded a fist against her leg while she drove.

It was official: Sequoia and Mack had made a fool of her. Not that she should downplay her own role in this fiasco. She'd been stupid. *Stupid.*

But why hadn't Mack and Sequoia told her what they knew?

Now, Holly had to decide how to handle this. Mack said, "things are ending," which meant there was nothing to handle. It was over before it even began. Which meant there was only one place left to direct her frustration, and that was at Sequoia. Holly turned onto the highway onramp and accelerated, pressing her foot down hard. She didn't even see the car she should have merged with, and its driver honked as he swerved his car into the fast lane to avoid being side-swiped by Holly's.

"Get a hold of yourself, Carr," she said.

She pulled up next to the curb at Sequoia's house, not having bothered to think about whether her sister was working today. As she approached the front door, Elijah opened it. He stood in the doorway, in nothing put a pair of flannel pajama pants slung low on his hips.

Holly, who was storming up the walkway, froze when she saw him.

"Elijah," she said. "Were you sleeping?"

She'd completely forgotten he was on graveyard shift.

"Yeah," he said. "I sometimes sleep over. Sequoia's place is quieter during the day. She's at work."

"Sorry to wake you," Holly said.

"It's fine," he said. "What's up? From the look of you, it's probably better she's not here."

"Probably."

"So … what's up?"

"Well, will you please tell my lovely sister that I'd like to speak with her, in person, as soon as possible?"

"I'm not sure," Elijah said. "Will she live through this proposed in-person meeting?"

"No clue," Holly said. "I do plan to wring her neck."

"Is this about the Mack thing?"

When Holly narrowed her eyes at Elijah, he put his arms up in a defensive move. "Whoa! I thought Sequoia was the only one who could burn a person alive with her eyes. It must be a shared Carr sister trait."

"To which *Mack thing* are you referring?" Holly said.

"You know. The one where Sequoia and Mack's combined suspicions that your boyfriend was fake ..."

His voice trailed off.

"Oh, don't stop," Holly said. "Do go on. Please."

"This isn't going anywhere good," Elijah said.

"So everyone believed Alejo was a fake?" Holly said.

"It became evident when you left the wedding with Mack."

"Wait. How did you—"

"Sequoia and Cara were worried when you didn't come back inside after walking Alejo to the car. Cara went outside to check on you and saw you talking to Mack. She saw you get in his car. Obviously she reported back to Sequoia, who then texted Mack asking what was going on. He wrote back that he was feeding you spaghetti. As friends. With a winky-face emoji."

"So how does eating spaghetti together, as friends, translate to my boyfriend being fake?"

"Because," Elijah said, his tone now bordering on exasperated. "You would never go to another guy's house for spaghetti if you really had a boyfriend. That's what Sequoia said, anyway."

Holly hated to admit, even to herself, that Sequoia was right.

"Ugh," Holly said. She should have been sneakier when she left Jasmine's wedding. She should have turned Mack down. She shouldn't have let his charms get to her.

"Well, just let her know—"

"That you'd like to speak with her, in person, as soon as possible," Elijah said. "Got it."

"Sorry for waking you," Holly said. "And sorry for causing this strange situation."

Then she turned around and headed for her car.

Halfway down the walkway, she had a thought. She turned around and said, "What time does Sequoia get off?"

Elijah looked at his wrist, and when he remembered he wasn't wearing a watch, he shrugged. "Any time now."

"Thanks."

Once she was back in her car, she texted Sequoia, her fingers flying across the screen so quickly the little ticks sounded like machine-gun fire. And maybe they were. *I need to speak with you. In person. ASAP. So I can wring your neck.*

There was really no sense in holding back. Mack had probably notified Sequoia as soon as Holly left his house. Elijah was probably doing so now. So before Sequoia responded, Holly added: *It's about Mack. But I'm sure you already know that. Since the two of you communicate about me regularly.*

Holly stared at the screen, willing a response to come in, but it didn't. So she started her car and drove downtown to wait her sister out. Sequoia's patrol car was in the parking lot, which meant she was probably inside, changing into a running outfit. Holly parked outside the police station, facing the exit Sequoia would use, and watched the door. "You're in for a surprise, sister."

Sequoia came out, sure enough, dressed in running tights and a tank top, her long hair hanging in a braid down her back. Holly noticed the vertical line between Sequoia's eyebrows, which made it look like she'd had a tough day. She was undoubtedly tired. This was, undoubtedly, not the best time for a chat. Still, Holly opened her door, pulled herself up as tall as she could, squared her shoulders, and walked toward her older sister with all the confidence she had. Which wasn't very much.

Sequoia spotted her right away. "I feel like I should start running now. You look scary."

"Sequoia," Holly said. "I have a bone to pick with you."

"That was an unnecessary announcement."

"I can't believe you and Mack were talking about me. Gossiping about how I had a fake boyfriend. You lied to me! You said you hadn't told him."

"I didn't tell him," Sequoia said.

"You said, 'If you don't tell him, then I will.'"

"We'd talked about it," Sequoia said.

"Who? You and Mack? Or you and me?"

"Mack and me," Sequoia said.

"So he already knew. And you knew he knew, and you didn't tell me."

"That would be pretty interfering of me," Sequoia said.

"So what you're telling me," Holly said, "is that you and Mack believed Alejo was a fake boyfriend, and the two of you talked about it and hatched some plan for getting me to 'fess up."

Sequoia shrugged and nodded as if this synopsis were pretty close to accurate. Then she said, "Not exactly, though. He wanted to let things between the two of you play out. He thought you'd eventually come around, say you broke up with your fake boyfriend, and then he could, you know, step in as your real boyfriend. Said he'd stick to the friend role for now."

This did match up with Mack's explanation of what had happened. But still. That explanation hadn't included the part where Mack and Sequoia had talked about her and let her make a fool of herself. For weeks.

"You humiliated me," Holly said, but quickly added, before Sequoia could, "and I humiliated myself."

Sequoia nodded. "I agree. Half-heartedly. That is, if anything, you humiliated yourself. You're the one who made up a fake boyfriend and stuck with that stupid story for weeks."

"I did it to protect myself!"

"What is that supposed to mean? Walk with me. I need to do a warm-up. I've got to get my run in and Elijah and I have a date I need to be home for."

"Fine."

They started walking, in step, and Holly said, "It's what I said before. I did it to create some space for myself. Especially because you'd suddenly taken an interest in my love life."

"It's Jasmine who always pesters you about your love life," Sequoia said, her tone casual and relaxed as if this conversation wasn't bothering her at all. "I took an interest only because I thought Mack would be a good match for you."

"Well, you taking an interest feels like pressure. Not only when it comes to my love life, but also when it comes to the rest of my life."

"It's only because I love you."

Holly was starting to sweat. This conversation wasn't going

anywhere. Sequoia was going to keep turning things around so they were Holly's fault. And maybe they were.

"If you hadn't talked to Mack about me, none of this would have happened," Holly said.

"Correction: if you hadn't made up a fake boyfriend, none of this would have happened. Take some responsibility."

Her words were stern, but her tone was still light.

"Why are you so relaxed?" Holly said. "It's infuriating."

"Because I finally found my place in this world," Sequoia said, lifting her arms to shoulder-height, palms up. "I'm enjoying my job, I'm enjoying Elijah, and I'm enjoying my role as your big sister."

"I'll just bet you are," Holly said. "It's fun for you to watch me fail. Always has been."

Sequoia stopped suddenly, grabbing Holly's arm and spinning her body so they faced each other.

"Wait just one minute," Sequoia said. "You're not failing. You've never been failing. It's just that I see so much potential for you. You don't see it for yourself, but I see it for you. You have a knack for knowing what people want, what they need, what they'll like. You are beautiful, smart, and talented. And you're working as a server at a diner with no plans for something that will really fulfill you. Don't tell me, ever again, that I like seeing you fail. Remember the school talent show when you were in third grade? I was in seventh grade. I didn't even go to school there any more, remember? I made Mom and Dad pull me out of wood shop class so I could come watch you. Even though I was sick of being a captive audience when you practiced your stupid routine a million times. With that stupid umbrella."

"The umbrella," Holly said. "*Singin' in the Rain.*" Her throat was already constricting as she remembered what Sequoia had done at that talent show. What she'd done was prevent Holly from failing.

"I saw you get onstage, and you'd forgotten that damn umbrella. Remember that?"

She'd released Holly's arm, and Holly brought her hands up to cover her face. She scrubbed, hoping the motion would stop her from crying.

"I remember," she whispered. Her arms dropped back down to her sides.

"I jumped up at the beginning of your routine, and I ran all the way around the building to go in the back entrance. It was locked. I went to the next entrance. Locked. Remember how the cafeteria was connected to the auditorium?"

Holly nodded.

"I finally found a way in, through the kitchen. The lunch ladies were cursing me."

Holly felt the first tear slide down her face.

"I ran through there, probably knocking down some of those metal trays they put the food on, you know, and then I ran backstage. I looked in the wings, searching for that stupid umbrella. I was sure you would have left it on the floor or on a chair where you were waiting your turn. But it wasn't there."

"It was in the dressing room," Holly said. "I was so nervous I completely forgot it."

Sequoia nodded. "I scoured that place. I finally found it and I ran back to the wings so I could give it to you. I was so determined to help you. I would not have my little sister go without her umbrella. Even though, if you'd asked me the day before, I'd have said I never wanted to see that stupid thing ever again."

Holly was openly crying now. "And then you stood there, at the edge of the stage, waving your arms to get my attention," she said. "And when I saw you there, my heart just expanded. I was so grateful to you. You saved the day. See? I've never been able to do anything without you."

Now Sequoia wiped a tear from her own eye. "I helped you, Holly, because I didn't want to see you fail. Even though I knew you'd improvise, and your routine would never be a failure. I didn't want you to feel like you'd failed. But I didn't save the day. You saved the day. You carried on with that routine. You could have run off the stage, crying. You could have quit right in the middle of that dance. But you didn't. You kept going. You didn't need me. Yes, I helped you. But you were doing just fine on your own. And now, yes, you've messed things up with Mack. But I don't think you've failed. And you know what? I know you feel like you've failed with yourself, but you haven't, Holly. You've kept going. You're still dancing. And maybe you need a little boost, a little backstage help once in a while, but you're amazing. Just like you were in that stupid talent show routine."

"I was so proud of myself," Holly said.

Sequoia nodded. "I was proud of you, too."

"I'm sorry," Holly said. "I really am."

"I know," Sequoia said. "You should be. Now get out there and figure yourself out. I'd let you wipe your nose on my running shirt, but I plan to do that later. I don't have any tissue to offer you. So get back in your car, drive home, and recreate your Direction Board. However dumb that idea is, at least it'll give you a place to start."

"Fine," Holly said. "That's what I'll do, right now."

"And fix things with Mack. You two would be really great together."

"I don't know about that. I think I ruined things before they had a chance to get started."

Sequoia hugged Holly, squeezing her so hard it was almost too tight, but Holly melted into her embrace.

"I love you," Sequoia said.

"I love you, too," Holly said. "Thank you for believing in me."

"You and your umbrella," Sequoia said.

With that, she kissed Holly on the cheek and started to jog, her braid swinging and her feet hitting the sidewalk in an even rhythm. Holly turned around and walked back to her car, her own steps feeling lighter than they had all day. It was time to focus on Holly. Just Holly.

CHAPTER TWENTY-ONE

After several hours and several cups of coffee, Holly completed a brand new Direction Board. This one had cost a small fortune, as she'd gone to the bookstore and bought a dozen magazines from which to pull new pictures, images, and words. She started with a full-page photo of a woman standing at the peak of a mountain, binoculars in hand. Yes, the binoculars reminded her of Mack, but they also represented seeing a goal and a future for herself, even if it seemed far away from where she stood now.

Words like "Strength" and "Journey" and "Self" and "Solitude" in bold fonts and bright colors surrounded that central photo, and Holly added smaller images: a woman running, to represent exercise; fruits and vegetables, to represent health; someone meditating, to represent self-care; shopping bags, to represent her new career.

The next step, Holly knew, was to create a plan for putting these ideas into action in her life. She bought a new scheduler and penciled in time slots for each item: working at the Broken Egg, exercising, cooking, self-care, and launching her new career. It was midnight by the time she'd finished, and she had her entire week laid out. She was exhausted but invigorated. She was inspired.

Week One was ready and waiting. She planned to go for a hike, solo, and get a massage. She also planned to find some potential clients, and she had a few ideas up her sleeve for that. Tomorrow was the start of her new life. But first, she'd celebrate with a glass of wine. And some music.

Although it had been years since she listened to classical anywhere other than in Mack's car, she pulled out a CD Jasmine had bought her: Classical Favorites. With the volume turned up and that glass of wine in her hand, Holly sat on the couch, practicing mindfulness and fulfilled solitude. She enjoyed the scent of the wine, the feel of the glass against her fingertips. She absorbed the sounds of the piano coming from the speakers.

Something made her think of a quote she'd heard once, something about the smartest, most enlightened people talking about ideas instead of other people or even events. So instead of thinking about people—Sequoia, Jasmine, Alex the Adventurous, *Mack*, for goodness' sake—she thought about ideas.

What did fulfillment mean to her? It meant making a real, tangible difference in people's lives. It meant experiencing a sense of joy and peace, most of the time. She wanted to feel that calm, that serenity that came from being filled with joy. How did people get to that point? Maybe meditation was the answer. She'd really have to practice that. She wasn't sure exactly how to do it. The library probably had books about it. Actually, she'd seen a magazine about it at the bookstore.

Fulfillment also meant lack of anxiety, Holly thought. She had to stop worrying—about what she was going to do with her life, about what other people thought she should or shouldn't do with her life, and about why she cared what other people thought about what she was doing with her life. More meditation.

The wine was gone, and Holly carried the glass to the kitchen. She switched off the lights, locked the front door, and began to get ready for bed. She'd decided her self-care regimen should include a nightly routine, and there was no time like the present to begin implementing it. So, after brushing her teeth, she washed her face, put on some fancy lavender-scented night cream Jasmine had bought her, and sprayed her pillow with a relaxing linen spray. Then, on the little stereo system on her nightstand, she put on the special relaxation playlist she'd created, and she laid down.

It wasn't until she began drifting off, in that moment just before she fell asleep, that she thought of Mack again. She thought of what Sequoia had said, and she wondered if there really was still a chance for them to be together. She was so relaxed that she didn't bother to shush herself, and she fell asleep and dreamed of ocean views and soaring birds.

ALTHOUGH HOLLY'S usual routine was to hit snooze when her alarm went off, on Day One, she found herself anxious to get out of bed and embrace her new attitude. Her Direction Board, hanging on the fridge, reminded her of new priorities, and she drank her coffee, enjoying the taste of each sip on her tongue as she mentally prepared for the day.

First, exercise. Deciding what to do on Day One felt a bit intimidating, as it would set the tone for this new life. But last night, Holly had settled on a brisk walk in nature. It would give her fresh air, sunshine and Vitamin D, and the chance to start the day with thought and intention. Something like running would be good in the future, but she wanted to ease into things.

So she pulled on some leggings and a sweatshirt and set out for the beach.

Holly had never walked the beach alone; she always thought people would find that weird (as if, she thought now, they were even thinking about what she was doing). On the contrary, she wasn't the only one going solo this morning, despite the crisp air and the cold spray of the ocean. The other walkers were friendly, giving her a silent wave or a cheery, "good-morning," or a nod as they passed.

"Why did I never do this before?" she asked a seagull that was sitting just at the edge of the dry sand. It cocked its head at her, apparently contemplating the answer. Holly felt delighted to be out in the world, and she felt like the world was delighted to see her, too. As she walked, she practiced mindfulness. She listened to the waves slide along the shore, and noticed their foamy edges as they rolled back out. Gulls called overhead, and a huge pelican dove into the water with a faint splashing sound, returning to the surface with its pouch stuffed full. The scents of kelp and salt filled the air. Holly found herself smiling as she walked back home, her skin and fingertips cool from the kiss of the fall breeze.

Next up: a shower, with music and fancy body wash (again, a gift from Jasmine), and then it was off to work, where she hoped she'd also nail down her first personal shopping client. Instead of rushing through her grooming, Holly took her time, shaving her legs and applying not just mascara, but eyeshadow and lipstick as well.

Jaclyn and Phil Connelly arrived at ten a.m., just as they always did. They sat in their usual booth, and ordered their usual drinks. The entire process set butterflies to fluttering in Holly's stomach. She told herself this was the first step in launching a new career, and when she delivered Jaclyn's iced coffee with a splash of cream and a pinch of sugar, she went for it:

"I have a proposal for you, Jaclyn," she said.

Jaclyn looked at Holly over the tops of her glasses. "As long as it doesn't require me to eat anything with that Hollandaise sauce Phil loves so much."

"No, no, it's nothing like that," Holly said. "It's just that I'm starting a new business and—"

"Don't ask Jaclyn for business advice," Phil said, and Holly could have hit him over the head with a menu. Or a frying pan. She'd just been getting up her nerve. "She bases her wine choices on what the labels look like."

"Well, actually," Holly said. "My proposal runs along those lines. Sort of."

Jaclyn really did whack Phil with a menu, and said, "Let her talk, Phil."

She winked at Holly. "Go ahead, Hon."

Holly took a deep breath and dove in, explaining that she was starting a new personal shopping service and Jaclyn had the opportunity to be her first client. Then, she made the offer: "So I'll take you on at no cost, and I'll select three outfits, including accessories, for you. All I ask is that I can get a testimonial from you and put you down as a reference."

Phil opened his mouth to speak, but Jaclyn cut him off with another whack from the menu. "Oh, I just couldn't do that, Honey," Jaclyn said.

Holly felt deflated.

"I insist on paying you," Jaclyn said. "This all sounds wonderful. Absolutely wonderful. I can't tell you how busy I am, with volunteering at the senior center and the humane society, and taking those art classes at the college. I would love for you to choose some new outfits for me."

"She's always complaining about her wardrobe," Phil said. "I'm always telling her, 'Go shopping, Jackie,' but she says she doesn't have time. 'I don't have time, Phil,' she says. 'I wish I had someone to go for me.'"

"That's true," Jaclyn said. "I really have said that. And he tells me, 'It's because you're so chatty, Jackie. If you weren't so chatty, you'd have a whole heck of a lot more time on your hands.'"

"Which is true," Phil said. "But she says to me, 'I like being chatty, Phil. That's something that brings me joy. Okay?'"

"I do," Jaclyn said. "But you know what else will bring me joy? You shopping for me. There, Phil. How do you like that?"

"I like it," Phil said. "I like it a lot. And if we like what she picks out, maybe she can shop for me, too, eh?"

"Great," Holly said. She extended a hand to shake. "It's a deal."

"When can we get started?" Jaclyn said.

Holly froze. She hadn't really been prepared for someone to accept her offer so quickly, right here on the spot. She'd need a questionnaire. She'd need some sort of photos or other outfit examples for Jaclyn to peruse. Under normal circumstances, Holly would give Jaclyn a vague answer, like the dreaded, "I'll get back to you on that."

But today, she made a quick decision. It was simple: she would just email Jaclyn a questionnaire, along with several outfit samples. "I'll email you some materials tonight, if that's okay. After I get off work. Can I get your email address?"

After work, Holly headed to the massage parlor, one of those places where members pay for a certain number of massages each month. The idea of regular massages seemed equally self-indulgent and appealing. She'd never been one for self-indulgence, but now that she was turning over a new leaf, she thought she could learn to embrace it.

That is, until she saw Mack's ex-girlfriend and current business partner, Jess, sitting in the waiting room. If this was a movie, she thought, the relaxing music would be screeching to a halt right now, at the very moment Jess was narrowing her green eyes at Holly and shutting her celebrity gossip magazine in slow motion. Holly scanned the waiting room for a spot to sit, but realized immediately that none of the open seats would shield her from being visible to Jess. So she chose a chair that was in the same row as Jess's, a few spots down. Hopefully another self-indulgent woman would come along to sit between them.

Jess was like a tiger that had zeroed in on its prey. "Holly, isn't it?"

"Yes." Holly managed a small smile, but she was sure her sisters would say it looked more like a grimace. "Jess, right?"

"Right!" Her tone was too bright. "So, where's Mack? This is, like, his idea of a romantic date. Couples massage. Or did he send you here alone so he could have some time to work on his *gardening* skills?"

Holly was grateful the waiting room was so dark that Jess couldn't see her face as she remembered the cucumber incident.

"Actually," she said, clearing her voice when she found it a bit sticky, "Mack and I aren't—we—I mean, we're not together. I'm here solo. Today." She was babbling, and Jess didn't step in to stop her. "I mean, not just today. Whenever I come here, it will be solo. So."

"Ah, I see," Jess said. "I thought something seemed different about Mack. I didn't realize the two of you had broken up, but that explains why he was so … well, never mind. Let's just say he was a little more friendly than usual."

"We didn't break up," Holly said. "We were never really together."

Jess shook her head. "This doesn't make sense. I thought—"

Holly could have dropped to her knees and thanked the gods of social awkwardness for saving her at that moment. Jess's massage therapist, a burly-looking, long-ponytailed man whose name tag identified him as Ivan stepped into the opening of the hallway and grinned at her.

"See you around," Jess said.

Great. Now Holly would be thinking about Mack being "friendly" to Jess, whatever that meant. Well, it meant he ran to her as soon as any hope of being with Holly was gone. So she was definitely at the top of his list. Another massage therapist came to the entrance of the waiting room and called Holly's name. During the short walk down the dimly-lit hallway, Holly took a moment to refocus, to center her thoughts on self-care and relaxation.

Still, even as the massage therapist—a petite woman named Lyla—kneaded Holly's neck and shoulders with surprising ferocity, Holly pictured Mack and Jess, laying on side by side massage tables. Would he have invited Holly to get a couple's massage if they had stayed together? For some reason, Holly didn't picture him as the massage-liking type.

Oh, well, she told herself as Lyla's elbows dug in to her upper back. This was about Holly. Just Holly. She wouldn't let Mack or Jess or anyone else float into her thoughts right now. With that, she closed her eyes, took a deep breath, and enjoyed her massage.

Afterward, she felt considerably more relaxed; so much so that she went ahead and bought a membership. She considered this a victory, because the Old Holly would have run out of the building screaming the moment she saw Jess in the waiting room. And she definitely would not have even considered buying a membership, knowing Jess was a regular. The New Holly could get past it. Even if she did see Jess every time she came for a massage, that tension would wear off at some point, wouldn't it?

As long as she didn't see Mack there *with* Jess, she'd be able to handle it. Now she'd go home and cook herself a nice meal. Which she'd eat, alone. Just Holly.

Cooking had never been Holly's strong suit, and she typically bought her tofu burritos or veggie pizzas pre-made. She'd thought about buying something frozen to pop in the oven, but the New Holly talked her into going to the grocery store and buying the ingredients for a simple pasta dish.

"You're worth it," she said to herself as she added onions to her cart along with the squash and tomatoes. "You deserve a nice meal. With wine."

"Wine will be wonderful," said an old woman who'd stopped to select potatoes from the bin next to the onions. "Are you cooking for a special someone?"

"Just me," Holly said.

"Well, you *are* special," the woman said. "Enjoy."

"You know," Holly said, "I think I will."

"At least you know nobody will be complaining that you put in too much pepper," the woman said. She winked as she walked away.

The pasta was delicious. And the wine complemented it perfectly. Yes, Holly followed a recipe, but maybe she'd give herself a tiny bit of credit for having a knack for cooking. She told herself it was only natural that her thoughts drifted to Mack while she ate. He'd fed her pasta. His mom owned an Italian restaurant. Where they served pasta. Thinking about Mama Rosa's made her think about the afternoon they'd shared. The hiking, the eating, the bowling. And that made her think about how stupidly she'd acted. Not only when cut their potential love-making session short, but also during the entire time she'd pretended to have a boyfriend.

"That was really stupid, Carr," she said, glad Sequoia wasn't there to agree with her. "You owe several people apologies."

She'd start with her sisters. In fact, there was no time like the present. She texted Sequoia: *Can I join you for your run tomorrow?*

And she texted Jasmine: *Want to get coffee tomorrow?*

There. She could talk to each sister in her element.

And then, maybe she'd finish up with Mack. Or maybe not. Because she felt like he owed her an apology, too, for letting her make a fool of herself.

First, though, she had a new career to launch.

CHAPTER TWENTY-TWO

Holly and Jaclyn met for coffee and a consult after Holly's shift at the Broken Egg. Holly took the time to go home and change, and when she walked into The Grind, Jaclyn jumped up out of her chair. "Oh, Holly, you look wonderful!"

Holly wasn't wearing anything special—just a pair of skinny jeans and a tunic with hunter boots—but she had refreshed her makeup and smoothed her hair into submission. The look was distinctly different from what she wore to work every day. Jaclyn hugged her before sitting back down.

"I'll admit," she said as Holly slid into the booth across from her, "I wasn't sure how this would go, what with you wearing jeans and a t-shirt every time I've seen you. I had no idea what your fashion sense would be like. But Phil told me, 'Just give her a chance, Jackie. She's a cute girl. Even if you hate what she buys you, you can wear it once to the Broken Egg and then never wear it again.' But, Honey! I loved the samples you emailed me last night. And after seeing you today, looking so good, I can't wait to see what you choose for me."

Holly wrote down everything Jaclyn said about the samples, and ended their consult excited to go shopping. Before that, though, she had two other meetings to check off her to-do list: one with each of her sisters. Sequoia had responded to Holly's text yesterday with a wide-eyed emoji, but had said that of course Holly could join her for a run. And Jasmine had said, *Sure! Time/place?*

The time was now and the place was here, Holly thought. She'd decided to start with Jasmine because she was the peacemaker and would probably accept Holly's apology with a shrug before changing the subject. Jasmine walked through the door of the coffee shop as Jaclyn walked out. Holly steeled herself with a deep breath and stood up to greet her sister. As they waited in line at the front counter together, Holly found that she didn't know what to say.

"Nice tan," she said at the same time as Jasmine said, "Nice day."

"Did you spend lots of time at the beach on your honeymoon?" Holly said.

Jasmine nodded. "Yeah. It was nice."

Holly nodded. Why was this so awkward? The two of them ordered drinks and returned to the booth without speaking again.

"So, what's up?" Jasmine said.

"Can't I just have a friendly coffee date with my sister?" Holly said.

Jasmine smiled. "You can, but I don't think that's why we're gathered here today. I can tell from your awkward silence, and also from the fact that you didn't invite Sequoia, that you have something to say. So, spill."

"Fine," Holly said, relieved to cut to the chase. "I wanted to apologize for having a fake boyfriend. And letting the story play out for way longer than it should have. I mean, it shouldn't have played out at all, and I am sorry for being dishonest with you. Especially during this special time in your life, when you were getting married and everything."

Exactly as she'd expected, Jasmine shrugged. "It's okay, Holly. I actually get it. And I take some of the blame, too. I mean, I'm always asking about your love life. As if you need the exact same things I have, in order to be happy. I didn't think about it before this whole Alejo episode, but I'm sure you feel a lot of pressure. You probably just wanted to shut me up."

Holly laughed. "I wouldn't put it like that. But I did want some space. I wanted us all to be able to focus on your special day. But still. I shouldn't have lied to you."

Jasmine waved one dismissive hand. "It's fine, really. I'd imagine you won't do it again. You'll either get a real boyfriend, or you won't. Although, that co-worker of Sequoia's? Mack? He's pretty good-looking, right? And it seems like he has a thing for you."

"Jasmine, stop! You're doing it right now!"

Jasmine had the decency to look chagrined. Holly said, "I'm going to focus on me for a while, okay? I'm starting a new career, I'm taking better care of myself, and I'm a lot happier. No man necessary."

They spent the rest of their time together chatting about Jasmine's honeymoon and Holly's business, and by the time they said good-bye in the parking lot, Holly had almost forgotten how much she was dreading her apology to Sequoia.

"Sequoia's next, isn't she?" Jasmine said as she opened the driver's door of her car.

"How'd you know?"

"You went all quiet," Jasmine said. "I could just feel the nerves."

"You can read me like a book, sister," Holly said.

"It'll be fine," Jasmine said. "Just get it over with. Just blurt it out. Fast, like waxing eyebrows."

With that, she got into her car and drove away. Holly went home to change into exercise clothes, and then she drove to the police station to meet Sequoia.

Just channel your inner Sequoia, Holly told herself as her oldest sister walked towards her, looking as confident and in control as ever. Sequoia had probably never pretended to be something she wasn't. She had probably never worried about what other people thought. In fact, that was actually one of her character flaws: she often spoke without regard for anyone else's feelings.

"This isn't about Sequoia," Holly whispered to herself. "This is about you."

"Talking to yourself?" Sequoia said.

"Yep," Holly said. "Just a pep talk."

"I know. You hate running. I'll take it easy on you."

She was swinging her arms, now, which Holly assumed was part of her warm-up.

"That's not it," Holly said. "And I don't actually hate running, you know."

Sequoia jogged in place. "Then what do you need a pep talk for?"

"Sequoia, just hold still," Holly said. She was surprised at the commanding tone in her voice, and apparently, so was Sequoia, who froze, looking wary.

"Sorry," she said. "Just warming up. You said you wanted to run so ..."

"I lied," Holly said. "I don't want to run. I just want to talk to you."

"Okay," Sequoia said, drawing the word out. "What's up?"

Just like waxing eyebrows.

"I'm sorry for lying about Alejo."

"Ah," Sequoia said. Holly expected her to begin a lecture, so she was surprised when Sequoia said. "It's okay. It's mostly Jasmine's fault." When Holly opened her mouth to defend Jasmine, Sequoia said, "I'm kidding. I know I'm at fault, too. And I know you'll find your way, in your own time. I'm sorry for pressuring you all the time, too. About your entire life, not just your love life."

Well. That had gone better than expected. Holly felt like they should shake hands or something. But then Sequoia pulled her in for a hug, which was also unexpected.

"You know," Sequoia said. "You should stop worrying so much about what everyone else thinks. You should just do what you're going to do, when you're going to do it."

Holly nodded. "That's what I'm working on. But thanks for the permission."

"Okay," Sequoia said. "You're welcome. And now that you've gotten that off your chest, get outta here so I can run."

As Holly walked back to her car, Sequoia hollered, "Love you, Holly."

Grinning, Holly turned around and shouted back, "Love you too, Sis."

Having made both apologies, Holly felt a sense of closure on the

Alejo debacle. But she knew it wouldn't be complete until she apologized to Mack, too. Maybe she didn't need complete closure. Maybe she could just forget it had ever happened.

Of course, living in a town as small as Seabreeze, forgetting something like that was next to impossible.

CHAPTER TWENTY-THREE

EVEN THOUGH HOLLY KNEW IT WAS ONLY A MATTER OF TIME BEFORE SHE ran into Mack, she didn't expect it to happen so quickly after he ended the thing that had never started between them. She was shopping at Ruffles Downtown, and was probably distracted because she was working on her first project for a client. She had slung a gray cowl neck sweater over her arm, for Jaclyn, and a bright blue tunic over her shoulder, for herself. Now, she was flicking through the pants on the back rack, searching for a pair of dark jeans Jaclyn could pair with the sweater.

"That gray is really too bland for you."

The voice came from behind her, and Holly's body responded immediately, chills running down her neck to her torso. Then it remembered that she and Mack weren't on speaking terms, and her stomach swirled with anxiety. What would she say to him? Maybe if she didn't turn around, didn't make eye contact, he'd walk away and they'd never have to talk again. Even though this seemed like a perfectly reasonable idea, she rotated to face him, feeling like a little ballerina inside of a music box.

"It's not for me," she said, positive that her face, frozen except for her mouth, looked plastic. "It's for a client."

Mack looked as nervous as she felt. His fingers drummed out a rhythm on his legs, and when he saw Holly notice, he balled his hands into fists at his sides. "A client?"

"Yeah," Holly said. "Remember Jaclyn and Phil, the older couple who always eat at the Broken Egg?"

Mack nodded. "Yeah. She always orders the French toast and he always orders the meat platter."

"Yes!" Holly said. "That's them. I'm using Jaclyn as a guinea pig for my new business. Personal shopping."

Mack nodded again. This was awkward.

"What are you doing here?" Holly said. What she really meant was, *Who are you shopping for?* Ruffles Downtown did not sell men's clothing.

"It's my mom's birthday," Mack said. He rolled his eyes. "I never know what to buy her. The woman has everything. But she's offended if I get her a gift card or something. She says that's impersonal. I say it's practical, but you know women…"

Holly headed for the center of the store, where a long table held a glittering display of jewelry. Mama Rosa's had been decorated in deep reds, and the pair of earrings Holly lifted off the table would complement the restaurant perfectly. She handed them to Mack, and he grinned at her.

"Well, that was easy."

She grinned back at him.

They stood there, grinning at each other, for at least a half-minute, during which Holly felt herself falling for Mack all over again. If her life were a movie, she'd be seeing him in soft focus with quiet romantic music playing. Then the scene would cut to a montage of the things they had done together: it would start with him pulling her over, and someone would edit in hearts floating between them as he asked for her driver's license.

And, cut.

This would never do.

"I've got to finish up, here," Holly said.

"Of course," Mack said.

He walked to the front of the store to pay for the earrings, his strides fast and his posture stiff. Holly took her time selecting another sweater and a scarf for Jaclyn, allowing herself to mourn for just one more moment before focusing on her future rather than her past—on what could be rather than what could have been. For once, she avoided small talk with the cashier, and told herself she'd walk straight to the car, drive straight home, and immerse herself in planning her new life. She wouldn't let one bad experience ruin everything good that she could create. In fact, she could learn from this. There had to be a lesson in here, somewhere.

"It's time to rethink this."

Was that the voice of the divine, revealing the lesson to her? It had to be. Rethink what, exactly? Holly was so involved in her own thoughts that she didn't realize Mack was leaning against the driver's door of her car until she practically bumped into him.

"Oh," she said. "It's you."

"It's me," he said. "Did you hear what I said?"

"About what?"

"That it's time to rethink this."

"Oh," Holly said again. Why was she repeating herself? Why did being around Mack make her say and do stupid things? "What are we rethinking?" She had backed away from him, and they stood facing each other, a foot apart.

"This," he said. He took her face in his hands and kissed her. It was gentle at first, but when her body relaxed, he wrapped his arms around her waist. The intensity increased, and Holly felt herself surrendering. When he finally ended the kiss, she stepped back again, putting enough space between them so that she could breathe without inhaling his scent.

"Mack, I—I owe you an apology. I'm really sorry I lied to you. I'm sorry I made up a fake boyfriend. And I'm sorry I didn't give us an honest try."

"You don't owe me an apology," he said. "If anything, I owe you one. I should have pursued you on my own. Without asking your sister for help. I was just afraid you wouldn't be interested in the guy who pulled you over. Wait. Why do you look so incredulous?"

"Because I was afraid you wouldn't be interested in the woman you pulled over. I was afraid you'd always think of me as a drunk driver."

"Yeah, a totally sexy drunk driver who I couldn't wait to get my hands on."

Holly shook her head. "Seriously?"

"Seriously," Mack said. "Of course, when I first saw you, I figured I'd never have a chance with you. You know, since it would be totally unprofessional of me to ask you out while I was hauling you to jail. And even if that wasn't the case, I'd always be that guy who pulled you over. But then I thought that since you were Carr's —I mean Sequoia's—sister, maybe I could make it happen. With a little help. I thought maybe she could convince you I'm actually a decent guy."

"Huh," Holly said. "And to think that this whole time, I've been convinced that you'd never think I was a decent girl."

"Oh, you're more than decent," Mack said, drawing her close again. "You're incredible."

"Only, I lied to you for weeks."

"I knew you were lying," Mack said.

"Then why didn't you call me on it?"

"I was afraid that if I did, you'd book it and never talk to me again."

"What a mess," Holly said.

"Definitely," Mack said. "Definitely a mess. What do you say we clean it up?"

"Clean it up, like, start over?"

"Yeah," Mack said. "Clean slate. Fresh start."

"I think I'd like that," Holly said.

He kissed her again, and this time, she dropped her shopping bag, wrapped her arms around him, and kissed him back.

That night, Holly gathered with her sisters and Cara to look at Jasmine's honeymoon photos. Cara—the only one Holly hadn't updated on her personal life—had asked for an update on what she was now calling The Mack Situation.

Holly had given her the quick version, and she was just finishing up.

"And so," Holly said, "we're starting over."

"Just don't start like you did before," Sequoia said. "I don't want to bail you out of jail."

Holly elbowed her. "Okay. Roger that. And I just want to remind you that neither of your relationships started out picture-perfectly. Let us not forget that Jasmine was dating two guys at once when she fell for Hudson."

Jasmine nodded. "This is true. And let me remind you both that Sequoia wasn't even dating Elijah when she fell for him. I mean, are you guys even dating now? Or are you just two people who are practically co-habitating and also having regular sex?"

"Regular *hot* sex, thanks to that Kama Sutra book," Sequoia said.

"I don't know why you didn't get me a copy of that book," Holly said.

"She didn't think you needed one," Cara said. "Alejo seemed like such a—professional."

The girls snickered.

"You can borrow mine," Sequoia said. "I've got a few good ones memorized."

"Try page seventy-two," Jasmine said.

"You guys kill me," Holly said. "This is embarrassing. Show us the rest of the honeymoon pictures so I can get out of here, you perverts."

Jasmine had already created a huge photo album, and she flipped through it, narrating the trip photo by photo, her face radiant with newly-wedded bliss. There were pictures of the beach at sunset, the forest in the bright afternoon light, and Jasmine and Hudson grinning from the deck of a whale-watching boat. Holly left an hour later, armed with the Kama Sutra book and a bottle of wine.

CHAPTER TWENTY-FOUR

Mack opened his door and Holly nearly swooned. He was wearing a towel around his waist and his hair was still wet from the shower.

"You look nice," she managed.

"You're early," he said, leaning forward to kiss her before stepping back to let her in. "Let me open that so you can have a glass while I get dressed."

"Oh, don't bother," Holly said.

Mack raised an eyebrow. "I mean, open the wine." She handed it to him. "But don't bother getting dressed. There's something I want to show you."

"Well," he said. "I like the sound of this."

While he opened and poured the wine, she took the Kama Sutra book out of her purse and set it on the table. "Check out page forty-five. And page seventy-two. I mean, check out the whole book. Pick a page, any page."

They were standing on opposite sides of the bar. Mack looked at the book's cover, then at Holly, and then at the cover again. He opened the book to page forty-five, and then gave a long, low whistle. "This is what you wanted to show me?"

"Yeah," she said. She cleared her throat and took a gulp of wine. "I thought it might be a nice place to, um, start."

Was it a coincidence that his six-pack was forming the backdrop for his hands holding the book on the counter? Holly didn't think so. Mack came around the end of the bar and ran his hands from Holly's shoulders to her wrists.

"I think it will be," he said. "But first, this."

He took her wine and set it down. Then he pulled her shirt over her head and unhooked her bra. He draped them both across the back of a barstool and then peeled off her leggings.

Mack picked up both glasses of wine and handed one of them to her, then grabbed the book off the counter. "After you."

As they walked down the hallway, he said, "Great view. Better than the hiking trail."

Holly felt her body heating up with anticipation, and even more so when she walked into his bedroom and saw his bed. It was massive and tall, and she could only imagine what he'd be able to do with those four posts and a few pairs of handcuffs. The wine must be kicking in.

"We should probably get warmed up before we try out what we saw on page forty-five," Mack said, setting their glasses on the night-stand. "Maybe do some stretches. Lay down, woman."

Holly obeyed. Instead of stretches, though, Mack ran his finger-tips lightly over Holly's skin, starting at her neck, roaming down to her hips, and circling her breasts. His tongue followed the same trail, lingering on her nipples and just above her lady parts. She was shiv-ering, aching for him to be inside of her, and she gasped when he rolled on top and entered her.

He gave her two long strokes, just enough to bring her to the edge, and their eyes met. Holly was surprised to see tenderness in his expression. She wanted to say something, to tell him how she felt about him, but she didn't know how to put it into words. Then the moment was gone. Mack flipped her onto her stomach and began kissing her neck, her shoulder blades, and her spine. Again, his fingers trailed gently over her skin until she was arching against him.

Now, he rolled her onto her side and laid down next to her so they were face to face. He was smiling, and she groaned.

"I think you're good and warmed up now," he said.

"But are *you*?" she said.

She reached down between them, and now he sighed when she stroked him, slowly.

"I'm pretty warm," he said. He reached down to stop her hand from moving. "Maybe we should try page forty-five now."

"Do you remember what to do?" Holly said.

"I think so," Mack said. "Let's give it a try."

They shifted to sitting, and Holly felt her entire body throbbing as Mack positioned himself behind her. As soon as she brought her body down onto his, he cried out, then rocked his hips, plunging into her again and again until she thought she'd break apart. Within seconds, she felt her own release, an explosion that left her body shattered.

Mack had one arm wrapped around her waist, and his face buried in her neck. "Well, I'd say that was effective."

Holly hadn't meant to fall asleep, but waking up naked, in Mack's arms, was so pleasant she thought she'd have to do it more often. He was running his fingertips from her shoulder to her elbow, sending thrills all over her body.

"So," he said, "I probably should have mentioned this earlier, but it's my mom's birthday and I have to go to her party."

"You did mention it was her birthday," Holly said. "Remember? When I saw you at Ruffles?"

"No, I don't remember that. I was in distress."

"Because you had to buy her a present?"

"No, because I ran into you and didn't know what to say," he said.

"Hmm. Well, you should have brought me home and showed me that Kama Sutra book," Holly said.

"If only I'd known."

"How long do we have?" Holly said.

"Thirty minutes," Mack said.

She turned so they were facing each other. "So, enough time for a quickie?"

"I'd like that," Mack said, "but I was thinking you might want to, you know, join me."

"At your mom's birthday party?"

"Yeah. I think she'd like that."

"Wait. First the restaurant and now her birthday party. Do you think she's going to think we're serious?"

Mack took Holly's hand and brought it down between them. He was hard again, and she gripped him as he said, "I don't know about you, but I'm very serious."

"Okay. I'll go. But none of this funny business. I have to look presentable, which means I have to shower."

"Care for company?"

"AH! I KNEW IT!" Annamaria greeted Mack and Holly at the door, her expression triumphant. "I knew I saw the light in your eyes, Mack."

"Aw, Ma," Mack said, but Annamaria was already pulling Holly into a hug. "Come in, come in, Sweetheart. I knew you were special the moment I saw you at Mama Rosa's. Mack never brings women to Mama Rosa's."

Holly sneaked a glance at Mack, who looked guilty. He held up his hands. "What? I don't want my mother to interrogate them."

"Would I ever interrogate a lady as lovely as this?" Annamaria said. Then she answered herself: "Yes, yes I would."

The fact that this statement made Holly nervous must have showed on her face, because Annamaria laughed. "Don't worry, sweetheart, I like you already. Any woman who can finish Mama Rosa's meatballs earns my automatic respect."

When Annamaria opened her earrings, though, she looked from Mack to Holly and back to Mack, a smile spreading slowly across her face.

"I knew she was special, Mack," she said again. "I knew it."

"WELL, IT'S OFFICIAL," Mack said that night. He'd driven her back to his house, and they were standing in the driveway. "My mom loves you."

"Of course she does," Holly said. "I ate her meatballs and I'm an excellent shopper."

She leaned against the driver's side of her car, and he stood in front of her, holding both of her hands.

"And you know what?" He'd stepped closer to her, and he brought his forehead down to touch hers.

"What?" she said.

"*I* love you, too."

In that moment, Holly thought, everything felt right. They were standing there, at the center of the earth, and the world was turning around them. It was perfect. And then Mack kissed her, and she said, "Well, that's just perfect, because I love *you*, too."

EPILOGUE

Quimby wouldn't stop chewing up ornaments. The Christmas tree stood in Holly's living room, its colored lights reflecting off the shiny wood floor and dancing over the remnants of a chewed-up Santa Claus.

The front door opened and Mack came in. Quimby barked and abandoned the dog bone Holly had convinced him to chew.

"The tree looks awesome through the front window," Mack said. "Even minus all the ornaments."

"You deserve all the credit, for talking me into getting my first Christmas tree."

"I can't believe you've never had your own tree," Mack said, not for the first time.

"I never thought it was worth it, before," Holly said. "Since it's always been just me."

Mack set his grocery bags on the dining table and came back to wrap his arms around Holly. "It's more than worth it."

"I can't believe you talked me into hosting Christmas dinner."

Now Mack nuzzled her neck. "I can't, either. I should have convinced you to spend the entire evening alone, with me."

Holly laughed, and Quimby barked again, this time to announce a new round of visitors. The front door opened again, and Jasmine, Hudson, Sequoia, and Elijah walked in.

"Best Christmas ever," Holly said.

Mack said, "Damn straight."

THE END

Turn the page for a sneak peak of *The Dating Intervention*, the first book in the Intervention Series.

PREVIEW: THE DATING INTERVENTION

BOOK 1 IN THE INTERVENTION SERIES

CHAPTER ONE

Eight years ago

It was time for Delaney Collins, doctor of veterinary medicine, to rethink her life.

She was just getting started, really. She was one year into her career as a veterinarian and the job—which she'd considered a calling for years—had seemed perfect. Until now.

The phone call she'd just received confirmed what she'd suspected all along: she was a fraud. She couldn't handle a serious situation, wasn't cut out for it. Pressing her lips together as hard as she could, in an effort not to cry, she placed the phone's handset in the receiver. Then, she took off her doctor's coat—the one she'd had embroidered with her name one year ago to the day. She crumpled it up, threw it in the trash, and walked out of the building.

Yes, she had patient appointments lined up. One of the other vets was on vacation and Delaney was covering for her. But this was a defining moment, one where Delaney realized that despite a four-year postgraduate degree, she wasn't cut out to work in a field that put someone's life in her hands.

As she got into her car, the tears flowing freely from her eyes and streaming down her face now, she replayed the events leading up to this epiphany. It started three days ago, when the Desert Veterinary Clinic's receptionist, Barb Dennis, paged Delaney over the intercom, her smoke-infused voice carrying a touch of humor.

"Doctor Collins, your favorite patient is in exam room five."

Delaney saved the chart she was working on and picked up the phone, dialing the front desk.

When Barb picked up, Delaney said, "Howie and Max?"

"I gave them to you—"

"Again."

"Again," Barb confirmed, "because you're the only one who's nice enough to give Max a full exam, every single time Howie brings him in."

"He's sweet."

"He spent the past five minutes talking to me about the new crosswalk signal at Central and Third," Barb said.

"There's a new crosswalk signal?"

"Apparently. One that begins the countdown before an old man and his old dog can make it halfway across the street."

"Huh," Delaney said. "What'd he bring Max in for, today?"

"Depression."

"All right," Delaney said. "I'll go in now."

"Hey, didn't you double major in psychology?" Barb said before Delaney hung up.

"Yeah," Delaney said. "But not dog psychology."

Human psychology told Delaney Howie was lonely. An eighty-four-year-old retired high school teacher, he'd spent most of his life surrounded by people. But he was slowing down, and couldn't get out as often as he used to. Max was an English Bulldog whose age in dog years most definitely exceeded Howie's. The pair of them were in at least once a week, and because she was the newbie, the other vets at the clinic let her handle Howie's increasingly frequent appointments. Delaney didn't mind. Probably because she was the newbie, she found them charming. She enjoyed hearing Howie's stories about his days teaching English, how he'd made his students sing jingles at the start of every period, and how he'd put on weekly competitions to encourage them to learn Latin roots.

And because she was the newbie, she completely missed the fact that there really *was* something wrong with Max this time. That's when Dr. Collins made a terrible mistake, one from which she could never recover, professionally or personally. If that mistake had affected Max, and Max alone, she could have gotten past it.

But, two days after that appointment, it spread. Three days after that appointment—significantly, on the anniversary of her signing hiring papers at Desert Veterinary Clinic—she received the phone call that proved she wasn't capable of something this serious. And she quit.

She went back to the cozy safety of her small hometown, promising herself she'd never get a life-and-death job again, and furthermore, that she'd never tell anyone—not even her best friends —what she'd done.

CHAPTER TWO

Present day

The moments where life seems perfect (or at least, perfectly medi-ocre) usually signify things are about to go awry. Maybe even Very Awry. Like an opalescent bubble, the illusion can burst in an instant.

Delaney Collins had just arrived at that realization for the second time. At thirty-four, just when her life should be taking shape, it had instead come to an abrupt halt.

"Fail-proof! It was supposed to be fail-proof!"

Delaney shook the last few drops of her Guinness into her mouth. She set the empty bottle down with more force than she meant to and flinched, although she figured no one else in Rowdy's Saloon noticed. The laughter, the cheering and the twinkling colored lights directly contrasted and probably amplified Delaney's sour mood, and they served as decent camouflage for her outburst.

"Nothing's fail-proof," said her best friends Summer Gray and Josie Garcia.

Summer shrugged one shoulder and added, "Except abstinence."

"Which Summer has obviously not been practicing," Josie said.

Summer elbowed Josie, amusement making her nose crinkle. "Funny. Four kids is a nice, even number."

The girls, assembled at Rowdy's for their weekly Happy Hour meeting, sat around their usual high-top table. Josie traced the rim of her glass with a fingertip and narrowed her eyes at Delaney. "Seriously, though. Nothing's fail-proof. Especially when it comes to dating. Did you really think *any* dating system could be fail-proof?"

"I need another beer."

Delaney looked around Rowdy's for the server but he was busy passing out flaming shots to a group of sales sharks in loose ties. She put her head on the table and sighed.

"How could this have happened?"

She didn't realize she'd spoken out loud until Josie answered. "We've known you for twenty years, Dee," she said. "And I have to say, since you ditched veterinary medicine and moved back to Juniper, things just haven't been the same."

Delaney sat up, and Josie covered Delaney's hand with her own. "I mean, I never would have said this nine years ago when you were at the University of Arizona kicking ass with that crazy class load, or when you graduated and were kicking ass as a veterinarian, but today, my sister, it's no real surprise you've just been dumped by three—count 'em: *uno, dos, tres*—guys in two days."

Oh, that.

Not that Summer and Josie even knew why she'd stopped working as a veterinarian and come back to Juniper. But still. If her life was so obviously on the wrong track, why hadn't they said something before now?

With growing embarrassment, Delaney looked first at Summer, then at Josie.

"Wait. Are you saying it's me?" She didn't wait for a response. "You are, aren't you?"

Summer and Josie exchanged a look. Summer's attention snapped to the ice cubes floating in her glass. Josie stared at a spot on the table.

The answer rolled through Delaney's awareness like lava.

Finally, Summer spoke. "Delaney Collins," she said in what Delaney always referred to as her Mom voice. "You know it's you."

"You know that as your honorary sisters, we're bound to be honest with you. And you're the common denominator," Josie said. Her voice sounded cheerful, but her smile was sad.

Delaney was half-joking when she asked, "What does that mean again, Mrs. Garcia?" but Josie's answer stung.

"It means you're the one thing all three of your boyfriends have in common," Josie said.

"They're not my boyfriends," Delaney said.

"They're just guys I'm dating," Summer and Josie said in unison, their tone mocking.

Delaney flinched. She could hear herself saying these same words over and over during the past several months. Years, maybe.

"It's semantics," Josie said. "You know what we mean. It's not that there's anything wrong with *you*, exactly, it's—"

"Can we talk about something else?" Delaney said. She hated the defensiveness in her own voice and tried to soften it. "Summer? Any good yoga classes lately? Josie? Have you been shoe shopping?"

"You're not getting out of this conversation," Summer said. "What Josie's trying to say is that you always choose the wrong guys. To be honest, I'm not even sure I know what your system is. Was. Whatever. What is it?"

"It's an informal system."

"Are you talking to us or the table?" Josie asked.

"The table. You guys are bitches."

The girls laughed, which broke the tension enough that Delaney responded.

"It's a system that allows me to select between three and five men, each of whom fulfill a different need. I.E. a sex god, a philosopher and an adventure hound."

Summer rolled her eyes and Delaney continued. "This system ensures I have a constant flow of social engagements and, more importantly, at least two backup men if something, you know, fails to work out with one of the men."

Summer nodded. "So tell us what happened, exactly. How'd you end up single for the first time in years?"

"Hasn't she always been single?" Josie said.

"Josie! Seriously!" Delaney felt herself spluttering.

Is it true? Delaney dug into her memory. Yes, she was always dating someone … but no, she was never truly *with* a man. A tiny voice piped up inside her head: *Maybe you do have issues!* She silenced it. Who were Summer and Josie to have such strong opinions on her dating life? They'd both been off the dating scene for years.

"Well, you have," Josie said. "When is the last time you were in a committed relationship you actually cared about?"

"And speaking of that," Summer said, "have you ever really thought about the future? I mean, do you plan to just keep dating several men at once, perpetually? And working at a bar?"

She looked around Rowdy's, and then locked her eyes on Delaney's. "It's about time you put that big brain to use again. You didn't do a double major for nothing."

"Yeah," Josie said. "Who gets degrees in psychology and veterinary medicine? At the same time? You have a gift, sister." She tapped the side of her head with her pointer finger."

"You do," Summer said. "And the pets of Juniper need you. Surely, there's an open veterinary position somewhere in town."

Instead of answering, Delaney picked up her Guinness bottle again. Still empty. Her last real relationship had been a long time ago. At the time, she thought they were committed to each other and she thought of nothing other than their future. That turned out to be a complete waste of energy. Not to mention the heartache involved. And veterinary medicine? She couldn't do it. Ever again. Forget about the big brain and the expensive degree. She wasn't cut out for it. Her stomach swirled at the thought.

"Yep, your beer's still empty," Josie said. "Hey, you work here. Go get another one so we can finish this conversation. You can't even remember your last actual relationship, can you?"

"Josie," Summer said. "Of course she can remember. It was that guy, what was his name? The one who always wore his hat slightly off-kilter and didn't tie his shoes. Tom? Travis? Tyler?"

"Oh yeah," Josie said. "But does that even count? He totally cheated on her."

"Of course it counts," Summer said. "I mean, he put a ring on her finger, didn't he?"

Yes. Tucker (not Tom, Travis or Tyler) had cheated on Delaney. Heart in a scramble, mortified beyond belief, Delaney had decided then that she'd never again put all her dating eggs into one faulty man basket. Even a man basket who somehow managed to swing a two-carat diamond ring. Because he bought one for his other fiancée, too, even while Delaney was selecting tiger lilies and oysters for their upcoming wedding. And he ended up marrying that Other Girl, while Delaney spent what should have been her own wedding day in mourning. Now, five years later, she still felt the sting. And while her friends meant well, their dismissal of her heartbreak as insignificant hurt her feelings.

"Which, may I remind you ladies," she said, holding up her pointer finger, "is exactly why I created this fail-proof system."

"Right," Josie said, relentless. "But it failed. Why don't you tell us about that?"

Delaney propped her chin on her hand, hoping the casual pose did something to conceal the depression that had started to sneak in. "Mark—"

"Steamy Mark Cortez?"

"Yes. Steamy Mark Cortez. He's totally changed. Which I don't want to talk about. Obviously."

"Obviously," her friends said.

"Changed, like, swore off sex? Or changed, like, morphed into The Beast or something?"

"Summer. He changed, like, he wants to get married."

For the briefest of moments, Delaney's best friends sat in stunned silence.

"Whoa, crickets," Delaney said. "Did you not think anyone would ever want to marry me?"

"It's not that." Summer said. "You're better than a strawberry shake."

Delaney grinned, remembering the moment they'd come up with

the little compliment. It happened in seventh grade, when Delaney gave her crush, an eighth-grader named Joe Jansen, a note asking if he wanted to go out with her. A week passed, and Joe Jansen had yet to respond. To be fair, Joe, the all-star athlete with a razor-edge crew cut, and Delaney, with her frizzy hair and forty-pound backpack, didn't quite fit into the same category. Dejected, Delaney pouted all day Friday. To cheer her up, Summer suggested the three of them go out for milkshakes. While they sat around the table at the ice cream shop, Delaney wondered aloud what was wrong with her, and Summer responded, "Nothing's wrong with you. You're better than a strawberry shake."

The three of them had used that phrase as a pick-me-up hundreds of times since.

"It's not that," Summer said again. "It's just that we can't believe you let him believe that was possible."

What is wrong with my friends? Delaney plowed on. "Zachary is philosophically superior. Which you probably already knew. He's always spouting off about some stupid paper or another and–"

"—and Xander?" Summer said.

Delaney put her forehead down on the table. "Sexually unsatisfied. And I need to be more honest with myself."

"Are you *kidding*?" Josie threw her hands up in mock exasperation, but her eyes twinkled with mischief and something else. "*Dios mío*! He said you need to be *honest* with yourself?!"

"I can't tell if you're joking or not," Delaney said, pouting into her empty bottle.

Joe Jansen had finally answered Delaney's note the following Monday, telling their entire pre-algebra class she was a dumb dumb dork for writing it in the first place. He'd written *NO WAY* in response to her, *Would you like to go to the movies with me?* and waved the note around for the whole class to see.

More than ready to think about something else, Delaney pointed to a black and white photo on the wall. In it, a cowboy, arm stretched above his head, rode a bull whose feet hung high above the ground in a twisting jump.

"That's Mark," she said. Then, pointing to a placid donkey

standing in the background, she said, "That's Xander. It's no wonder we broke up."

She looked up just in time to see Josie nod at Summer, who nodded back and took a deep breath.

"Delaney," she said. "We have a … proposal for you to consider."

"Well, it's not up for consideration, exactly," Josie said. "It's more like a requirement for your love life."

"You've *talked* about this!" Delaney said. "You guys have been discussing my love life!"

"Of course we have," Summer said, placing a hand over Delaney's on the table.

"And not just your love life," Josie said. "Your whole life."

Summer added, "We've been discussing each other's lives, love or otherwise, since we were what? Fourteen?"

"That's true," Josie said. "Since we started calling ourselves the Milkshake Sisters. Remember when you guys made me that little quiz to help me decide whether I should kiss Elijah Parker behind our seventh grade homeroom?"

"Minus one point for the pimple on his nose. Add one for his cute smile," Josie said.

"He sealed the deal when he offered to carry your lunch to the cafeteria," Summer said.

"Three points," Delaney said. "Pushed him right into the 'definitely should kiss him' category."

"Ah, those were the days," Josie said.

"Anyway, Delaney," Summer said, anxious to return to the subject at hand, "your love life is like our love life."

Delaney looked at Summer and raised her eyebrows. Both Summer and Josie were married and Summer had a handful of kids. More than a handful. Their love lives were as much like Delaney's as a Fairmont is like a Motel 6.

"Well, okay," Summer said. "It's not. Not exactly. But that's what we want to talk about."

Josie cleared her throat. "We want to try an experiment."

"An experiment?" Delaney repeated.

"Yes," Summer said, drawing out the word.

Josie inhaled deeply.

"Um, okay," Delaney said. Was she actually feeling nervous? After the conversation they'd just had, it was no surprise. "What is it?"

"For the next six weeks," Josie said, her dark eyes boring into Delaney's, "you relinquish control of your dating life. Summer and I make all the decisions. You make none."

"Wait. What? I make none of the decisions?"

"Well, you can decide what to eat for breakfast."

ACKNOWLEDGMENTS

So many friends and family members have supported me in the writing of "Just Holly" … too many to list. You know who you are.

Big thanks to my Advance Review Team (especially the eagle-eyed people who caught a few errors!), copyeditor Donna Rich (who caught more than a few errors!), and my talented, visionary cover designers, Rebecca and Andrew at Design for Writers.

ABOUT THE AUTHOR

Hilary Dartt loves great adventures, whether she's writing, reading, or living them. The author of nine women's fiction novels, Hilary lives in Arizona's high desert with her husband, their three children, her Weimaraner and running partner, Leia, a failed barn cat, and a flock of chickens. She loves camping, exploring in the Jeep, and dance parties with her kids. Learn more at www.hilarydartt.com.

www.ingramcontent.com/pod-product-compliance
Lightning Source LLC
Chambersburg PA
CBHW050336190726
48284CB00007BB/2036